A Simpler Life

A Pine Valley Novel

Vanessa E. Kelman

WORD COLLAGE PUBLISHING

Copyright © 2025 by Vanessa E. Kelman

All rights reserved. No portion of this book may be reproduced in any form without written permission from the publisher or author, except as permitted by U.S. copyright law.

This book is a work of fiction. Any similarity to real persons, living or dead, is purely coincidental and not intended by the author.

ISBN 978-1-961761-22-3 (print edition)

ISBN 978-1-961761-23-0 (ebook edition)

To my children, Avery and Emily, who make life challenging but are so worth it.
I love you more than I could possibly say.

Chapter 1

April

"Jeremy! Emma!" Lindsay Powell called up the stairs. "Time to get up! The bus will be here soon!" Then she returned to the kitchen to stuff sandwiches into lunch bags, fill water bottles, and gather homework papers into folders.

Hearing nothing but silence coming from upstairs, she yelled up one more time before reluctantly making the climb to get her kids moving. Her fourteen-year-old son Jeremy was sitting on his bed, earbuds stuck in his ears as he listened to what was probably a gaming podcast on his cell phone. He, at least, was dressed. Lindsay pulled one of his earbuds out and told him to head downstairs to grab breakfast.

Emma, Lindsay's twelve-year-old daughter, still had her head buried under the covers.

Lindsay sighed. "Come on, Em," she said, pulling the covers off her daughter. "You need to get ready for school."

Emma groaned and tried to take the covers back.

"I want you downstairs in five minutes. No excuses. Or no phone."

Emma groaned again but sat up. Lindsay patted her knee.

"Five minutes," she said again. Then she went back down the stairs to finish getting herself ready.

Jeremy was sitting at the kitchen table eating a bowl of cereal. Lindsay kissed him on the top of his head, then poured herself a second cup of coffee to sip as she packed her own lunch.

By the time Emma came downstairs, the kids had two minutes to race out the door to catch their bus. Following the flurry of activity, Lindsay took a deep breath and collapsed onto a chair. She had about fifteen minutes before she needed to leave, and they were the most peaceful fifteen minutes of her day.

Lindsay closed her eyes as she finished her coffee. There had to be a better way. She felt like she was running on fumes these days, with barely enough energy to make it through. Something had to give.

It was nine o'clock that night before Lindsay felt she could breathe again. The kids were upstairs – quiet, at least, if not asleep – and she curled up in an overstuffed chair with her laptop. She had bills to pay and paperwork to fill out for Jeremy.

Two months and school would be out for the summer. She should really figure out camps before they all filled up. Would she be able to swing it this year, though? She had just had that huge car repair, and she was still paying off the roof repair from last fall. But how could she afford not to? It wasn't as if she could leave them home alone all summer. And any kind of childcare would be just as expensive as camp.

Lindsay took a deep breath and closed her eyes. She was going around in circles. Her life had become one big spiral, and she felt like she was sinking deeper and deeper into some dark, bottomless pit.

As Lindsay sat staring at her computer screen, zoning out to the blinking cursor waiting for her to type in a website address, her mind drifted. When had life gotten so complicated? Actually, it wasn't even that it was complicated. It was just...cluttered, full of to do lists and errands and running to one commitment after another. How had that happened?

Lindsay thought back, to before the kids, before her disaster of a marriage, before college and responsibilities took over. She remembered her own school years, full but happy, not running from one thing to another but spending time with friends, following her actual interests and passions rather than spending every spare minute occupied with some activity or staring at a screen. That was what she wanted for her kids: actual connections, with others and themselves. And that was what she wanted for herself: to feel alive, not a zombie struggling to survive.

She closed her eyes and rubbed her hands down her face. Thinking back also made her think about her parents. They had been close, but when Lindsay had wanted to move away for college, then a job, then marriage, they had supported her. They had wanted her to be happy. And she had been, for a while. Before life interfered. She wondered how they were doing. She hadn't talked to them in ages.

With a quick glance at the wall clock, Lindsay debated if it was too late to call them. Maybe she could call the motel number. That way they could let the machine pick up if they were settled for the night. Lindsay pulled out her cell phone and found the number, took another deep breath, and made the call.

"Pine Valley Motel," a woman's voice answered. "Sylvie speaking."

"Mom," Lindsay replied. "It's me."

"Lindsay!" her mother exclaimed. "It's after nine! Are you okay? Did something happen?"

Lindsay heard the alarm in her mother's voice, but she was just so grateful to be talking to her mom. Tears began welling in her eyes. She swallowed them down before responding. "Sorry. Everything's fine."

A pause lingered before Lindsay's mom spoke. "I'll believe that there's no emergency, but I don't believe everything's fine. What's going on?"

The love and concern she heard were Lindsay's undoing. "Oh, Mom. I don't even know where to start."

"Well, let's start at the beginning. It's been a while, but I won't ask how you've been. That much is obvious. So tell me: did something happen, or is life just getting you down?"

"Just life, I guess." Lindsay sniffed. "Did you feel like this when I was younger? Like you were barely treading water?"

Sylvie sighed. "Sometimes. Being a mom is tough, and I was working what seemed like all the time when we took over the motel. But things were different then, and Pine Valley was smaller, less busy than where you are. I could give you and your brother a bit of freedom."

"I feel like I can't breathe sometimes, like my life is just an endless stream of responsibilities and I'm failing at everything."

Silence fell for a moment. "I think a lot of people feel that way, especially now with all the technology vying for our attention."

Lindsay heard a ringing in the background.

"Oh, honey, hold on a second. One of my guests needs something. Be right back."

Sylvie's voice was replaced by gentle hold music, and as Lindsay waited for her mother to return, she processed what her mother had said. Yes, life was hectic, but where they lived could be part of the problem. Maybe they all needed a change of scenery. Not just a vacation, but a real change.

"Sorry about that, Lindsay. When duty calls..." Sylvie's voice faded. "Anyway, what was I saying?"

"Just that what I'm going through is common. But what you said before, about where we live, I think you may be right. There are so many distractions, so many things fighting for our attention. Maybe we need a break from all this busy-ness."

"Okay. What are you thinking?"

"Not sure yet. But I think it involves a trip to Pine Valley."

Sylvie Cooper slid into bed beside her husband Ed and rubbed his shoulder. "Are you awake?"

Ed grumbled a bit before rolling over to face her. "I am now."

Sylvie felt bad for disturbing him. They usually alternated nights covering the desk, and it had been his turn to get to bed early. "Sorry. But you'll never believe who called tonight."

"VIP?" Ed guessed, his eyes still closed.

"One of the most important people. Lindsay."

"Lindsay?" Ed opened one eye. "Is everything okay?"

Sylvie sighed. "Yes and no. But they're coming to visit."

"Aren't the kids in school?"

"She's thinking the summer. All summer. She asked me to help find a house to rent."

"They can't stay here?"

"They need more than a room, Ed. Especially for two months."

Ed sighed. "Okay. Well, it'll be good to see them. It's been a while."

"Yes, it has. I hope the visit helps."

"With what?"

"She just needs a break. You remember what life with kids was like."

Ed grunted.

"And maybe..." Sylvie's voice faded.

"Maybe what?" Ed asked when she didn't continue.

"Maybe she can help us, too?" It came out a question. She knew Ed hated asking for help.

"We don't need help, Sylv," Ed said gruffly.

Sylvie didn't respond. They did need help, even if Ed didn't want to admit it. She didn't know how much longer the motel could survive. But she wouldn't push the issue. She would just spend the next couple of months laying the foundation. By the time Lindsay arrived, they would be ready.

Chapter 2

June

"Three more days of school!" Emma exclaimed as she came bouncing into the kitchen. For once Lindsay hadn't had to drag her out of bed. Jeremy wasn't far behind.

As the kids gathered their lunches and backpacks, Lindsay pondered when she should discuss the summer with them. So far she had taken the easy way out by not saying anything. They hadn't asked, so she had kept quiet. But time was running out.

Jeremy opened the door to head to the bus stop, and as he and Emma stepped outside, Lindsay called, "family meeting after dinner tonight!" She didn't know if they had heard her, but she would find out soon enough. Clubs were over for the year. Homework was pretty much non-existant. They could find a few minutes for her to break the news. She only hoped it would go smoothly.

Lindsay worried all day at work, while prepping dinner, and while they ate. She didn't even fight it when the kids begged to use their phones during dinner. While that was usually a hard "no," today she figured she would pick her battles. And she suspected she had a rough one ahead.

By the time Lindsay had finished loading the dishwasher, the kids had retreated to their bedrooms. She called up to them, and a couple of minutes later they came back down, grumbling all the way. Well, they were off to a great start.

When they were all seated in the living room, Lindsay began. "I wanted to discuss the plan for the summer," she said. The kids visibly relaxed.

Emma shrugged. "I figured we were doing camps like last year," she said. Then she perked up. "Are we taking a vacation this year?" she asked, grinning.

Jeremy grinned, too. "Yeah! Let's go somewhere. I read about this tech museum that's all hands-on."

"You are such a nerd," Emma responded, rolling her eyes.

Lindsay put up a hand before the bickering could commence. "That's enough." Taking a deep breath, she then said, "summer will look different this year, but we won't be going to a tech museum. Sorry, Jeremy."

The kids shared a look, like they knew they wouldn't like what was coming next.

"We're going to visit Gran and Pops."

Jeremy groaned. "In Pine Valley? It's so boring there."

"Seriously, Mom. How long do we have to go for?" Emma added.

"We...will be spending the summer there."

The complaints started in earnest then, the kids' voices becoming a jumbled-up buzz of annoyance. Lindsay held up a hand again and waited for them to settle down.

"I know it's a lot quieter there than what you're used to, but that's actually one of the reasons we're going." Jeremy let out a disgruntled sigh, and Emma crossed her arms, leaned back in her seat, and huffed. "I think we could use this time to slow down a bit, reconnect, maybe breathe a little."

"So, in other words, get bored out of our minds." Jeremy crossed his arms, too, and leaned back with a scowl. Then he leaned forward again. "Wait, don't you have to go to work? Are you staying here while we get banished?"

"Nobody's getting banished. And, yes, I have to work. But I have some vacation time, and I've gotten permission to work remotely for a bit." Work had been her biggest concern. Lindsay hadn't been sure how she would make it work. But she knew – and her boss knew – that she was a vital part of the staff. She had just had to make it sound like she could either work remotely or not at all. That discussion had been more nerve-wracking than confronting her kids.

Silence fell. Finally, Emma looked at her mother and grumbled, "when do we leave?"

Lindsay took a deep breath. "Well, school ends on Wednesday, and I figure we'll need a couple days to pack and whatnot, so we'll plan to leave on Saturday."

Silence fell again.

"Can we go upstairs now?" Jeremy asked after a minute, still scowling.

"Sure." The kids scrambled back upstairs, and Lindsay sighed. They weren't happy, but she figured it could have gone worse. Hopefully they would survive the summer.

Jake Figueroa slammed the door of his patrol car and strolled up to the car parked in front of it. He had seen a rise in speeding lately, and that did not make him happy.

Life as a police officer in Pine Valley was usually pretty low key. The occasional theft, traffic accident, or missing dog kept them busy enough. The previous year, an apartment building had collapsed, due in large part to the owner's negligence when it came to safety and repairs. That fiasco had thrown him — and the entire department — for a loop. But that, thankfully, seemed to be behind them.

Jake hadn't grown up in Pine Valley, but he had lived nearby. When he decided to become a police officer, he figured a small town would be a good way to get his feet wet. After a while, he had longed for more excitement, so he moved to the city of Waterbury and done a stint at a station there, but that had gotten old fast. He was usually a laidback guy who saw the best in everyone, and witnessing how horrible people could be to each other had been depressing. He had felt himself growing cynical, hardened. And he didn't like how that had felt. So he had moved back, grateful for the petty crime that was the Pine Valley department's bread and butter. There was probably a middle ground to be had somewhere, but for now he was happy where he was.

Jake handed the teen his ticket, wrote up the report, and went on his way. Half an hour and he could grab some dinner. He was glad the diner was back up and running. He could really go for a burger. Just as he was about to hand things off, though, another car sped past him. What was going on?

By the time Jake had clocked out, he had written more tickets in one day than he usually did in a month. Though a far cry from what he experienced for crime in the city, it was definitely a concerning uptick for Pine Valley. He suspected it was time to open an investigation.

When he opened the front door of the diner, Maggie greeted him. The smile on her face was nearly as bright as the light glinting off her new wedding band. She and Richard had gotten married just last month. The party that had followed after the ceremony had filled the diner and spilled into the street. He had been on duty that day, unexpectedly summoned to help with crowd control. The entire town loved Maggie, and he had felt more like a guest than an on-duty cop. The atmosphere had been festive, joyous, and Jake didn't think he had smiled so much before that day or since. It looked like marriage was still agreeing with Maggie.

"Officer Jake!" she greeted. "How nice to see you. Eating in?"

Jake usually ordered takeout, especially when still in his uniform. But it had been a strange, trying day. He could use the upbeat atmosphere of the diner tonight. He nodded. "Sounds good. The counter's fine."

"You got it." Maggie gestured to an empty seat, then headed behind the counter to get him a menu and pour him a glass of water.

After glancing at the menu, Jake ordered the burger he'd been craving and impulsively added a vanilla milkshake to go with it.

"A milkshake kind of day, huh? Need to talk about it?"

Jake chuckled. "Nah, I'm good. Just need a little something sweet, I suppose."

Maggie patted his hand. "I completely understand. Coming right up."

As he sipped his water and waited for his meal, Jake looked around the diner. It had gotten a facelift after the kitchen fire last fall and still looked fresh and new. It was hard to believe this diner had been standing for well over fifty years.

His mind was wandering now. He spent way too much time alone with his thoughts. While he didn't mind the solitude, he had found himself feeling fidgety lately, looking for an outlet for — what? What did he need to let out? He supposed he just wanted to be seen, not just as a symbol of the law he was hired to uphold, but as a person. Even Maggie, so friendly and welcoming to all, had greeted him as Officer Jake. But he was more than that. And being alone ensured that no one ever saw that. It was just him and his thoughts. Always and forever. Before he had moved away, he had friends in town. They would get together, have a few drinks, play cards or video games. But life moved on, and his buddies had families of their own now, with little spare time to hang out with him. Maybe he should try to make some new friends. But how the hell did grown men make friends?

Maggie set down his platter and milkshake, startling him from his reverie. She saw him jump and smiled.

"Sorry about that. Didn't mean to scare you."

He returned the smile. "No worries. Just off in my own little world."

"Happens to the best of us. Enjoy your shake." She smiled again and left him to eat. And ponder his fate.

Chapter 3

"I know it's not perfect," Sylvie said as she opened the door to the rental house. "But the pickings were slim for short-term rentals, especially with furniture. We're not exactly a vacation hot spot. We're lucky Richard got married when he did."

"Richard?" Lindsay asked, stepping over the threshold. Jeremy and Emma shuffled in behind her, silent except for occasional dramatic sighs. They had barely spoken five words to her since she had broken the news. She was grateful they had at least greeted their grandparents with affection.

"This was his place, but he moved into his new wife's house, so it opened up. His daughter and son-in-law own the house. The in-law apartment is just one bedroom, but the sofa in the living room is a pull-out. I thought we could pick up a cheap bed to add to the bedroom, maybe a room divider or something."

"We'll make it work. I brought an air mattress, too. I appreciate you handling the arrangements." Lindsay placed her suitcase in the living room and took a look around. She could see a galley kitchen toward the back, with a small table just outside it, between the kitchen and living room. She could only guess the stairs in front of her led to the bedroom. What was the bathroom situation? Could they handle sharing a bathroom for two months? Could the kids handle sharing a bedroom? Should she and Emma share the bedroom instead? Or would the pullout be for her? So long, privacy. But they would get through this. It would be good for them, learning to make do with less. People did this all the time.

Lindsay took a deep breath. The kids seemed frozen in front of her. They had been on their phones, but now they stood looking around them with nearly identical expressions of disbelief and mild disgust. Obviously, they hadn't yet seen the brilliance of her plan. She had to admit she was struggling, too.

"I know it isn't much," she began, as much for her own benefit as that of the kids. "But this will be great. It'll bring us closer."

Their eyes shifted to her. "We'll be closer, all right," Jeremy muttered. "Where's my room?"

"You guys will be staying upstairs," Lindsay replied, and they all trekked up the stairs, the only sound their shoes clattering against the wood.

The bedroom was a good size, and the bathroom was just across the hall.

"We have to share a bed?" Emma screeched as she assessed the situation.

"No, " Lindsay assured her. "We have the air mattress for tonight, and tomorrow we'll go pick something up. Gran knows of a place not far from here. You'll each have your own bed."

"But we have to share a room," Jeremy said.

"You guys used to love sleepovers."

"Yeah, like five years ago."

Lindsay sighed. "It's either that or you sleep on the pullout sofa, Jeremy, and Emma and I share the bedroom. It's just for a couple months."

"Whatever." Jeremy tossed his duffel bag on the floor by the door and flopped onto the bed. A minute later the earbuds were out, and Jeremy was in his own little world.

A desk stood by the window, with a cushy chair tucked under it. Emma claimed the chair and pulled it out. It wasn't long before her phone was out again and her thumbs were typing furiously, no doubt complaining to one of her friends.

Lindsay closed her eyes and took another deep breath. Sylvie patted her shoulder, and the two of them went back downstairs.

"You knew it would be an adjustment," Sylvie said when they were back in the living room.

"I know. I just didn't expect... I don't know what I expected. Magic?"

Sylvie gave her an empathetic smile. "It'll be okay," she said. "Give it time." After a moment's pause, Sylvie clapped her hands together. "Okay," she said. "I'm going to leave you to it. I picked up a few things at the store, so you've got coffee and milk and cereal and stuff. Basics. I got a rotisserie chicken, pasta, in case you didn't feel like going out again tonight. But if you're up to it, we'd love to have you over for dinner. Give it some thought, see how the kids do, and let me know."

"You're an angel, Mom."

"I do what I can." She gave Lindsay a hug.

Lindsay didn't want to let go. Could she stay curled up in her mother's arms forever? Life was so much easier here. She sniffled.

"It'll be okay," Silvie repeated softly. "It takes time, but you are strong. And you're doing what you need to do. They may not see it, but someday they'll appreciate it."

Lindsay pulled back and wiped her damp eyes. "I hope so."

Sylvie squeezed Lindsay's hands. "Settle in, and we'll talk later."

"Thanks, Mom."

Sylvie handed Lindsay the key and bid her farewell. Lindsay watched her leave, swallowed down her tears, and took yet another deep breath. She could do this.

Sylvie drove back to the motel, processing the interaction with Lindsay. The situation was worse than she had thought, but surely nothing a little time at home couldn't cure. Her own problems could wait. She hoped. Right now, she would focus on getting the kids settled and not lashing out at their mother. She would offer to take the kids sometimes, to give Lindsay a break. While Lindsay had taken the first and last weeks of summer off as vacation time, she would need to get work done in between, and that would be difficult with kids underfoot. She would look into offerings at the library and the community center, too. There were bound to be at least a few activities the kids would be interested in. If she could get them off their phones.

As she pushed open the door to the motel office, Ed lifted his eyes from the computer and greeted her with an up-bob of his head.

"Lindsay and the kids get settled in?" he asked.

Sylvie sighed. "I guess. It's going to be a tough adjustment. The kids sure are mad at Lindsay for bringing them here."

"Wish I knew how to help," Ed said after a moment.

"Me, too. For now, I'm going to see if I can find some things to keep them occupied and out of trouble. And bake cupcakes."

"Cupcakes?" Ed flashed Sylvie a grin.

"In case the kids come over later."

"And for me, right?"

Sylvie chuckled. "You might get one or two. If the kids don't eat them all first."

Ed grunted. Sylvie made her way to the door at the back of the office that led to their living quarters. She wished they had been able to offer Lindsay and the kids space here, but things would have been even tighter than at the rental. While they had had extra bedrooms when their kids had been younger, those rooms had long since been converted to be part of the motel. They had reasoned that if the kids ever came to visit, they could stay at the motel. The rest of the time, the income potential would help make ends meet. They never expected to need more space long-term.

Sylvie sighed again. She had been doing that a lot lately, and not just because of Lindsay's situation. The converted rooms were just two of the many that sat empty more often than not. They were fortunate the renovation costs were long since paid off; she truly didn't know how they would survive if they still had those payments. As it was, they were barely keeping the lights on.

Her hope was that Lindsay, who had a head for marketing and the degree to back it up, would be able to give them some direction, ideas to help them turn things around. While Ed was resistant to change, she was sure Lindsay could convince him. If she was able to ease her own stress, first. They could help each other.

And it would start with cupcakes. She hoped they would come to dinner.

Chapter 4

Jake sat in his patrol car, watching the cars go by as he listened to his scanner. The speeding issue had abated, as suddenly as it had begun, but something wasn't sitting well with him. Had it just been a fluke? Some newcomers or visitors who didn't want to follow the rules of the road? Or was something else going on? His gut told him to remain vigilant, that the sudden quiet was only a reprieve, not an end. But he would take the reprieve, however long it lasted.

He sipped his coffee as his mind processed the speeding incidents, seeking out patterns or clues. Different neighborhoods, different times of day. The only thing the incidents had in common was the age of the offenders: all teens between sixteen and eighteen. Maybe the local driving school wasn't emphasizing the importance of following speed limits. Or maybe there just wasn't enough in town to keep kids occupied and they had to find their thrills somewhere. Which led him to wonder what the next attempts would bring, if that was the case. If he was honest, Jake could understand the appeal in causing mischief when one was bored. Anything to liven up the day. And the kids probably didn't see any harm, didn't think it was really affecting anyone else. The problem arose when those "harmless" bits of mischief began to escalate. That's what his gut was telling him to look out for. Was there a way to prevent it from happening? If the cause really was a lack of things to do, maybe the town could do something to encourage safe, lawful fun. But what? He would have to give it some thought.

By the time he got home that night, he wasn't any closer to figuring things out, but he was grateful for a slow day. In his line of work, a slow day was a good day. He had discussed the situation with some of his colleagues, and they had drawn the same conclusions he had. The overall decision had been to wait and see, but to make special note of any possible similarities with any new crimes that happened to occur. Jake supposed he could accept that, though he was usually less inclined to sit on his laurels and wait.

Jake changed out of his uniform, then, after grabbing a beer from the fridge, opened his laptop and sat at the breakfast bar in his kitchen. He had missed a baseball game earlier in the day and wanted to check stats, but once that was done, he found himself at loose ends. Usually he was content reading, turning on his Xbox, or watching a movie to pass the time, but he found himself getting fidgety more and more lately. Maybe it was the increasing alienation he had been feeling, or maybe the situation at work just had his mind working overtime, and his body was struggling to keep up. Regardless of the reason, Jake found himself getting up and grabbing his keys. He had to *move*.

He picked up his cell phone, fished around in a drawer for a set of earbuds, and headed out the door. Maybe listening to a podcast while taking a walk would satisfy him. He was pretty sure there was a new episode of a sci-fi show he liked. And, if nothing else, the exercise was a good idea after a day of sitting in a patrol car. He really should get back into an exercise routine. The more sedentary lifestyle he had acquired with his move back to Pine Valley had started becoming apparent around his midsection. Maybe he should join a gym. That would get him out of the house, interacting with other people as he attempted to get back in shape. It was worth consideration. But in the meantime, he would go for a walk. Or maybe a jog. He really was feeling antsy.

The summer had started off relatively cool, and Jake was grateful the oppressive humidity he was sure was on its way hadn't arrived yet. While he loved having seasons in Connecticut, he did not love the humid summers. Give him fall any day. But today wasn't too bad, with a light breeze that kept the climbing temperatures at bay.

School was out for the summer, and Jake had started seeing more kids and teens out and about, playing outside, hanging out in town, picking up summer jobs. It got him thinking about the potential crime uptick he saw coming, but he pushed the thought down and pushed "play" on his phone instead. He had to turn his brain off; he was off the clock.

Jake lived in an apartment building near the outskirts of town. Thankfully, he hadn't been involved in the building collapse of the previous year. He had a good, honest landlord who didn't skimp on safety. But he could see the demolition site from his building. With the owner in prison, he wasn't sure what would happen to the land, and he sometimes walked by to see if any progress had been made on the clean-up. Today, however, he headed in the opposite direction. If his intention was to get his mind off work, jogging past a former crime scene likely wasn't the best way to go about it.

The opposite direction led toward a road that eventually split, to move either further into the surrounding forest or loop around and head back to town. With the sun still up for hours and his goal of settling his mind and body down, Jake opted to head toward the forest. Even if he couldn't hear the birds chirping and critters scurrying with his earbuds in, the sights and overall serenity would soothe him. He hoped.

As he jogged, Jake passed a few fellow residents, and he nodded or gave a brief wave as they passed. Those he didn't immediately recognize from around town got his mind working, trying to place them or connect them to families he did know. With a low growl of frustration, Jake tried to bring his attention back to his podcast. He needed to get out of work mode.

He jogged further into the forest, acknowledging with a glance at his phone that he should probably head back soon. He had left without eating dinner, and his stomach was starting to let him know that hadn't been a good idea. He slowed his jog to a walk to give his body a rest, walked around a small clearing, then turned to head back on the trail.

Sunlight filtered through the treetops, making lacy shadows on the ground. One patch of sunlight, however, angled toward a large, flat rock and glinted off something tucked at its base. Jake squatted to try and make it out. It wasn't unusual for hikers to lose something in the woods. He would dig it out and bring it back to the station.

What he dug out, however, had obviously been left there intentionally. It was a plastic bag filled with what appeared to be a thief's stash. A few wallets, a watch, a couple of pieces of jewelry. Jake held the bag, turning it over in his hands, unsure how best to proceed. If the thief had wanted to dispose of the items, he could have stuck them in the trash. Why leave them in a bag in the woods, unless he planned to come back for them — or add to them? Was this his trophy case? Proof to show others? How many people were involved?

He could bring the bag back to the station, attempt to find the owners of the lost items. Or he could try and catch the thief when they came back to claim the bag. Who knew when that would be, though. He would have to discuss the situation with a detective back at the station. In the meantime, though, he needed to make a decision.

Jake looked around to see if anyone else was in the area. What was the best way to do this? He didn't want to tamper with evidence, but it wasn't like he carried a pair of gloves in his back pocket. Maybe he had a tissue or something in his wallet. He believed in being prepared.

He found a crumpled tissue in one of the pockets of his wallet and dug it out. Thank heaven for small favors. Then he opened the bag, removed each item carefully using the tissue, took pictures of it, and placed it back in the bag. He wasn't opposed to a stakeout; it certainly wouldn't be his first. But he also didn't want to waste his time if the thief never came back. The wallets had been stripped of cash, but credit cards and identification were still present. The jewelry appeared to be low-end, possibly just costume jewelry, though he wasn't an expert in the area. If he had to guess, he would say the thief or thieves were amateurs, looking for a quick thrill rather than a big score. Would they notice if he at least removed the IDs and credit cards? Better not. Not only could the thieves notice, but he would be tampering with evidence. Should he just leave everything here?

Jake placed everything else back in the bag, adjusting it to look like it had before. Then he tucked the bag back under the rock and stood up, brushing his hands off on his jeans. He had pictures of the IDs, so he could check to see if any reports had been filed for stolen items. He would discuss the situation with a detective to get their take. And he would come back in a couple of days to see if anything had changed. Was this the next step up they had expected? Or did they have another group of troublemakers on their hands?

Chapter 5

Lindsay had done her best to unpack and acclimate to her summer home, but time had ticked steadily by, and she was getting hungry. The kids had been worryingly quiet. She didn't know if they had accepted reality or were still sulking. Either way, they had to figure out dinner, so Lindsay reluctantly made the climb to their room.

The kids lounged in much the same positions as she had left them in. They barely looked up when she entered the room.

Lindsay knocked on the doorframe, waited for their eyes to meet her gaze, and attempted a smile. "Hey, guys. We have to figure out dinner. Gran invited us to dinner, but if you would rather stay here, I could make chicken and pasta."

Jeremy and Emma shared a look, then they both shrugged. If she wasn't feeling so discouraged, Lindsay would have laughed. The kids hadn't been so in sync in years. At least misery was bringing them closer.

Lindsay took a deep breath. If they wouldn't decide, she would. And she needed to get out of this house that was quickly feeling like a prison.

"Okay, then, Gran's it is. Get your shoes back on and meet me downstairs in five minutes."

She turned and headed back downstairs, pushing down the tears that were threatening to flow again. She knew it would take time to turn things around, but she hadn't expected such blatant misery and hostility. It wasn't as if she was forcing them to do hard manual labor. Though, now that she thought about it, maybe that wouldn't be such a bad idea. She could ask her dad if he had any projects they could help with. Maybe it would teach them responsibility. Goodness knew they could use it.

They piled back into the car in silence, kids still with their faces glued to their phones. She never let them have this much screen time. She should probably say something, but she just didn't feel equipped to handle another argument right now. As they pulled into the motel parking lot, though, she had to at least set some ground rules.

"Okay, guys," she began. Then she waited until they both put their phones down and looked at her. She met their gazes in the rearview mirror. "You can be mad at me all you want, but Gran and Pops haven't done anything wrong. So I expect you to be respectful, and civil, and polite. There will be no screens at dinner. Afterward is up for discussion *if* you behave during dinner." They both scowled but didn't argue. Lindsay took a deep breath and closed her eyes. "Okay. Let's go in."

They may have resented being stuck in Pine Valley, but the kids loved their grandparents and greeted them with hugs and small smiles. Lindsay felt at least a little tension release from her shoulders. She greeted her parents, and they all made their way to the apartment at the back. The office was equipped with a bell, and Sylvie brought the cordless phone to the apartment in case anyone needed them, but Lindsay hadn't seen many cars in the parking lot, so she suspected it would be a quiet evening.

Though the space had been updated when it had been renovated, the decor hadn't changed much, and Lindsay felt transported back to her childhood. Her visits home in recent years had been few and far between, and, especially with her recent stress and anxiety, she craved the familiar comforts of home. Her parents had bought the motel when she was in elementary school and her brother was in middle school. Sylvie had wanted a way to be home with the kids, and this provided them with the means for both parents to be home and on hand for whatever the kids needed. She was sure it hadn't been perfect or easy on her parents, but Lindsay and her brother had never had reason to question their love, support, or the security they longed to provide, so they made it work. It was the same feeling she wanted for her kids. She just wasn't sure how to go about it, since all her efforts thus far seemed to have failed. Maybe her parents would be able to help.

On the table were all the kids' favorites: homemade macaroni and cheese, fried chicken, and her mother's famous buttermilk biscuits. Comfort food all the way, with a salad on the side as a nod to a balanced meal. Her kids actually seemed enthusiastic as they put their phones away and took a seat at the table. Lindsay felt like crying again. What would she do without her parents?

Sylvie watched the kids dig into their meals with gusto. She was glad she had gone through the trouble of making their favorites. Though she and Ed would have certainly enjoyed the meal if it had been just them, having the kids appreciate her food made everything much better. She was glad Lindsay had taken her up on the offer.

Conversation consisted mostly of small talk while they ate, catching up on bits of news while tiptoeing around the elephant in the room that was the plan for the summer. She could see Lindsay relax somewhat during the meal, but until the kids were settled, Sylvie suspected Lindsay wouldn't really unwind. She wondered if sharing her own concerns about the motel would offer a good distraction. Maybe after dinner she would broach the subject.

Once the dinner dishes were cleared, the kids turned to Lindsay, and she gave a curt nod. Apparently there was some kind of understood agreement, as the kids then scurried to the living room and took their phones out. Sylvie watched them a moment, sighed, and turned to Lindsay. "Still not talking to you?"

Lindsay shook her head and looked down at the table. "Not really. I'm lucky if I get acknowledgement. Once we get back to the house, we'll have to figure out the sleeping arrangements, and I'm expecting eye rolls and complaints. I'm letting things slide for today, but I'll need to start setting ground rules tomorrow if I don't want it to be like this all summer." Her lower lip trembled. "I knew they would be unhappy, but I didn't expect it to be this bad."

"They're kids. They rebel. While not ideal, I think it probably feels worse than it is because you're feeling so fragile yourself. It will get better."

"I hope so." Lindsay took a deep breath then turned to her father. "Dad, I was actually hoping to ask you a favor."

"Of course," Ed answered. "What do you need?"

"Well, I was thinking the kids will need something to keep them busy, burn off some energy so they're not on their phones all day. I want to find some activities in town, but in the meantime, I was wondering if you had any projects or anything that you could use their help with. Fixing stuff, even cleaning rooms. Show them the value of hard work and all that."

Ed chuckled. "Then they'll really have something to complain about, huh?" He grinned. "I'll see what I can come up with."

"Thanks, Dad."

"Of course." He patted her hand. "What are grandpas for, if not to put their grandkids to work?"

Lindsay gave a small smile. It didn't quite reach her eyes, but it was better than nothing. Sylvie cleared her throat, took a glance at Ed, then turned back to Lindsay.

"Actually, Lindsay, I was wondering if you might be able to do us a favor, too. I thought it might get your mind off things."

Lindsay raised her eyebrows in surprise. "Not sure what I could do, but I'd be happy to help if I can."

Sylvie paused. It had seemed so simple, so straightforward, but now that the time had come to actually discuss it, she found she was reluctant. Talking about one's troubles made them all seem that much more real.

"Mom?" Lindsay reached out a hand for her mother's. "Is something wrong?" She sighed. "Here I've been going on and on about my problems. What is it?"

"Well, the thing is..." Her voice faded. She cleared her throat again and met Lindsay's gaze. "The motel is having trouble staying afloat." There. She had said it.

Lindsay's eyebrows perked upward again. "Business is down?"

Sylvie nodded. "Business is down. Costs are up. I said it earlier: Pine Valley isn't exactly a tourist hot spot. We did pretty well when you and Joey were growing up, but the past few years, with the new bed and breakfasts taking all the customers looking for quaint weekends or walks through nature, and the schools switching to regional so we can't even count on the sports teams coming through at the championships...it's been tough."

Lindsay turned to face her dad, then back to Sylvie. "I'm so sorry to hear that. But how can I possibly help?"

"Well," Sylvie began again, glancing at Ed before continuing, "I...we...thought that maybe you would have some ideas for us. From a marketing perspective. Maybe see things we could do to bring in more customers."

Understanding dawned on Lindsay's face. "Got it."

"And, well, I thought it might be a good distraction, get your mind off the issues with the kids. We'll swap problems for a bit." Sylvie flashed a small smile. "If you're open to it, of course."

Lindsay squeezed Sylvie's hand. "Of course I'll help," she said. "It's the least I can do. I'll try to do some brainstorming tonight."

Sylvie squeezed back. She felt better already.

Chapter 6

By the time they made it back to the rental house, Jeremy and Emma were glued to their screens again and ignoring Lindsay. But, despite the fact that nothing had really changed, something about the conversation with her parents had given her a bit more of a backbone. Maybe it was knowing she had their support. Maybe it had been the reminder that she was more than a disgruntled mother, that she had more to offer than two grouchy kids. Whatever the reason, when she closed the front door behind them, Lindsay stood up straight and clapped her hands twice, as loudly as she could. The kids' faces jumped up from their screens.

"Okay, listen up. I know you're mad at me. I know you hate the idea of spending the summer here. But that's what's happening, and the sooner you get used to the idea, the easier it will be on all of us. This summer can go one of two ways: you can continue to moan and groan and complain about anything and everything and stay stuck in your miserable state; or you can suck it up and deal. You cannot stay fused to your phones all summer. If you attempt to, they will be taken away. Tomorrow you will be spending the day with Gran and Pops, and I will be doing some exploring and research and looking for things the two of you might be interested in. I'm sure the library has some things going on, and probably the community center. Maybe it's not too late to get you into camps or something. I'll have to see what I can find. That will help us decide how the coming weeks will go. I also need to get another bed or something. But for now, put the phones away. We need to figure out the sleeping situation."

While the kids didn't mind sharing a room in the light of day, they insisted they did not want to share a room to sleep. So Lindsay would share with Emma, and Jeremy would have the pull-out sofa. She supposed it was the best scenario. Anything to limit the bickering.

With suitcases in their appropriate destinations and air mattress inflated, Lindsay told the kids to get ready for bed. She had discovered a half bathroom on the first floor, so they could have their own space if they preferred. While they got changed and brushed their teeth, Lindsay got the beds made up, set up her computer on the desk upstairs, and began to unpack her own clothes. The bravado of the past half hour was starting to fade. She suspected once the kids were settled that she would be locking herself in one of the bathrooms and having a good, long cry. It was going to be a long summer.

"So what are you going to have the kids do tomorrow?" Sylvie asked Ed as he changed for bed. It was her turn to watch the desk this evening, at least until ten or so when the office was only open to emergencies. But she was curious as to his plan.

He chuckled. "Haven't quite decided yet. Not sure if they need a wake-up call to the real world or something to ease them into the summer. I could put them to work cleaning the rooms after our guests leave."

Sylvie shot Ed a look. "Sure, if our goal is to ensure they stay miserable."

"Hey, maybe they would cut their mother some slack, then. Realize they don't have it so bad with her."

"Yes, the kids were grumpy, and they've taken it out on Lindsay, but that's just because they don't want to be here. From what she's said, they're not usually that irritable."

"Then what's the problem? I thought they were here so we could get them in line."

Sylvie shook her head and chuckled. "Oh, Ed. It's a good thing I still love you. Because you sure don't listen."

Ed harrumphed. "I listened with my eyes. And as far as I'm concerned, those kids spent way too much time staring at little screens."

"Then give them a reason to do something else." Sylvia kissed Ed's cheek. "Get some rest. We'll talk more in the morning."

She closed the door to the bedroom and returned to the office. She anticipated a quiet night, as usual, and she had a book tucked in a drawer under the counter to help pass the time. But her mind wasn't interested in fiction tonight. It kept drifting toward the events of the day, and the conversation after dinner. So much to worry about: Lindsay, the kids, the motel. She hoped the summer would help them all. But that didn't relieve her stress in the meantime.

They had two overnight guests, and each was only there for one night. They had a single reservation scheduled to arrive the next day, but at least that would be for the entire week. The previous fall, when the apartment building in town had collapsed, they had taken in many of the suddenly homeless for a time, but she hadn't felt right charging them much if anything. Certainly not full price. If insurance companies hadn't helped cover the cost, they would have been at a loss that month. But it had been nice to have regular guests, people to greet in the morning and see moving about the property. She had missed that.

When her kids had been younger, and they had bought the motel, she and Ed had been excited to make improvements to not only the building, but the land around it. Pine Valley wasn't known for its entertainment options, or its tourist appeal, but they wanted the motel to be welcoming, a place that guests would appreciate and want to return to. To encourage families to stay, they had decided to install a small playground set, a basketball hoop, and a horseshoe pit. They put together maps with the local nature trails, and Sylvie had set up a corner of the front office with a bookcase filled with books and board games guests could borrow, along with a couple of armchairs and a coffee maker. They received compliments on their offerings, and guests visiting friends and family or looking for a break from reality would come and stay for a bit, enjoy the amenities, and make Sylvie feel like they had gotten it right.

In the years since, two bed and breakfasts had opened up in town, capitalizing on the natural beauty of the area. One had since closed, but the other was thriving, and both had taken a portion of their business. It seemed the rest sought more high-tech, fun-filled locations, far from the likes of Pine Valley. The playground had rusted out and been discarded, and some of the furniture in the office and in some of the rooms had seen better days. They kept as many rooms as possible in tip-top shape and did their best to maintain the rest to at least satisfactory condition, in the event of a sudden rush of business, but, though no one had complained, Sylvie had felt bad about some of the rooms they had rented out in the fall. She knew a few of the beds were starting to creak and some of the bedding was getting shabby. Carpet got worn and towels started to fray. But it was a catch-22. How could they pay to replace things without the business, and how could they attract new business with the current condition?

She wasn't sure what she expected Lindsay to do. Truth be told, part of her wondered if they should just cut their losses and sell the place as is. Then she and Ed could retire, maybe move closer to Lindsay or go someplace warm, travel the world or at least see a little more than they could from the office windows. But the other part of her wasn't quite ready to let go. And that part was winning out. Still, they couldn't let things go as they were. And heaven forbid Ed have a serious discussion about it. No, Sylvie would have to take charge, as she so often did. Give Ed a hammer, and he would do amazing things. But make a plan? That was Sylvie's domain. She just needed a little help this time around. And help had just arrived.

Chapter 7

The air mattress was not the most comfortable bed Lindsay had ever slept on, but she supposed it could have been worse. She would be grateful to have a real mattress to sleep on, though. She hoped she could find something in her meager budget.

Emma was still sound asleep when Lindsay rolled off the mattress as quietly as she could and tiptoed to the bathroom across the hall. She hoped Jeremy was awake downstairs. She would much prefer not having to be silent as she made coffee and had some breakfast.

She needn't have worried. Jeremy was already sitting up on his bed, ear buds in. He pulled one out as he heard her come down the stairs.

"This mattress sucks."

"And good morning to you, too."

Jeremy scowled. "Yeah, good morning."

"I'm sorry the mattress wasn't comfortable. I'm heading to the store today to try and find a bed for myself upstairs. Not sure if we could fit another bed in here, though." She didn't think she could stretch her budget to cover it, either. "You could use the air mattress if that would be more comfortable."

He shrugged. "Whatever." Then he stuck the ear bud back in.

Lindsay sighed. At least he was talking to her today, even if it was just to complain. She hoped he didn't give her parents much trouble.

She started the coffee maker and took a look around to peruse her breakfast options. Her mother had picked up a dozen eggs, so she would probably fry up a couple for herself. The kids usually settled on cereal. She would have to go grocery shopping, though, too. What they had wouldn't last long.

Lindsay rubbed one palm down her face as she waited for her coffee to brew. She didn't know why she had thought spending the summer away from home would be easy. Sure, she remembered the rough layout of Pine Valley well enough, though many changes had taken place since she had spent any real time there. But this small, unfamiliar house, starting from scratch with kitchen essentials and surrounded by unfamiliar furnishings... she could have used a little familiar comfort right about now.

The coffee pot gurgled, and Lindsay poured herself a cup. As she breathed in the aroma, she closed her eyes and tried to focus. Today would be better. The first day in a new place was always tough. They had a better feel for what to expect now, and she would be getting the supplies and information she needed for them to move forward and have a great summer. Once they settled in, they would find their groove. The kids would get over their grumpiness. They could slow down a bit, reconnect as a family. They would learn to appreciate what they had and figure out what they wanted. They would be able to breathe again. She had to believe that.

Jake was off on Sunday, but he swung by the station to discuss what he had found with one of the officers on duty and deliver the stolen cards. That officer agreed to reach out to the owners, so that part at least was out of Jake's hands now. All he had to decide was where to go from here.

His gut was telling him that this was what he had expected – petty crime a step above the reckless driving. Was it the same group of teens looking for new thrills? When he was back at work the next day, he was going to see what he could learn from the locals who had had their wallets stolen. Maybe that would offer some insight, or, at least, a starting point.

But that was tomorrow. He needed a break today. He deserved a break. Taking a deep breath, he decided to start with something simple and head to the grocery store.

The store was busy, but that was fine with Jake. He wasn't in a hurry. And he had no plans for the rest of the day. He took his time perusing the aisles, trying his best to stay out of others' way. Once he was almost run over by a frazzled-looking woman, but he stepped to the side, and she mumbled an apology as she headed down the snack aisle. What must that be like? he wondered. To be constantly busy, struggling to fit in errands between what he assumed to be a variety of other responsibilities. From a quick glance in her cart, he could guess that she had kids, teens probably. He hoped they weren't involved in the string of crimes. With a quick shake of his head, he scolded himself for thinking about work again. But if she hadn't been so frazzled, he suspected she would have been a good person to interview. Not for the stolen goods, but for what kids were interested in, what the town could offer that would entertain them and encourage them to stay out of trouble.

Now that he thought about it, that wasn't a bad idea. He had the time, he had the willingness, and he had the interest. Maybe he could partner with some community leaders to put together an event or two, or something ongoing. They could start with a survey, or, if he found people already connected to the young population, maybe they would already know where to start. Who could he reach out to?

Excited by the idea, Jake picked up his pace and finished his shopping. He would start with a list of possible partners. While he was familiar with many of the town departments, he had to admit he didn't have many contacts at any of them. And he was sure there were other organizations in town who would be interested in helping, maybe the scouts or the Rotary Club. They likely ran their own events and activities, but they would at least be a start. Maybe some members would be willing to take on one more project, or to direct him to others who would.

The only downside was the timing. With it being Sunday, he wasn't sure how many people he would be able to reach. But he could do research and find names and contact information. Would they even have enough time to put something together for the summer, or was he being overly ambitious? He had never done something like this before.

With a deep breath and a grin, Jake settled down at his breakfast bar and took out a pad of paper. Finally, a worthwhile project that would help him meet other people, connect with his community, and maybe let others see a different side of him. This would be good.

Chapter 8

With the kids safely in her parents' care, Lindsay found the weight on her shoulders easing as the day progressed. She had started with a rushed trip to the grocery store after dropping off the kids, just to stock up on essentials and fill in gaps so she could focus on more meaningful tasks. Then, with relatively full cabinets and fridge, she felt ready to tackle the discount store her mother had told her about.

Scratch and dent items and floor models would be available right away, and she could get something decent for less. She wasn't sure she could fit a bed in her car, never mind a mattress, but the store had contact info for a couple of companies who would deliver, so she could get what she needed. What that was was a different story. Lindsay had originally thought she would get a cheap bed and mattress, but looking at the options made her rethink that idea. What would she do with the thing after the summer? It seemed unnecessarily expensive and wasteful. She ended up choosing a futon that was surprisingly comfortable. And, since it was less than she had anticipated, she was able to get a thick mattress topper to add to the pullout for Jeremy. She hoped it would help.

With a delivery date for the futon set for the following day and the topper tucked in her backseat, Lindsay was already feeling better, and she hadn't even tackled the rest of her to do list. Feeling accomplished always did that to her. If she felt she was moving forward, making progress, she felt a little spark of joy. So far, so good.

The library and parks and recreation office hadn't been open since it was Sunday, but their websites had been comprehensive enough. Both offered a variety of activities, but not enough to fill the kids' days. And camps had been full.

They could take some day trips together, Lindsay mused, but she had to work, too, so she couldn't spend the summer gallivanting. Still, at least she had some ideas now, and she was sure the kids wouldn't mind extra screentime at the house. They would just have to find balance.

When Lindsay pulled up to the motel in the middle of the afternoon, she saw the kids doing yardwork, with her dad supervising. Lindsay smiled to herself. She was sure they weren't happy about it, but it looked like they were at least tolerating it without too many complaints.

"Looking good, guys," Lindsay said as she approached. Jeremy shot her a look. Emma blew hair out of her face and shifted a bunch of weeds from one hand to the other. She looked at her grandfather.

"Can we be done now?" she asked.

Ed nodded. "You can be done. You did a great job. Thanks for the help."

The kids added the weeds they were holding to a brown lawn waste bag and wiped their hands on their shorts.

"Why don't you guys grab your stuff?" Lindsay said. She watched them scurry inside, then turned to Ed. "So you put them to work, huh?"

Ed grinned. "Not the whole day. We went for a walk, played some board games, watched a movie. Actually just came out here about a half hour ago."

"I hope they didn't give you too much grief."

"Nothing I couldn't handle, though Jeremy has a bit of a mouth on him."

Lindsay winced. "I know. I'm afraid he got some of his dad's temper."

"Well, I nipped that in the bud. If he starts up again, you send him to me."

Lindsay gave her dad a smile. "You got it."

Jeremy and Emma stepped out of the office then, with Sylvie on their heels.

"You guys can get in the car," Lindsay said. "I just want to talk to Gran for a minute."

Lindsay and Sylvie watched the kids get into the car, then Sylvie turned to her daughter.

"Any luck?" she said.

"Some. I have a futon being delivered tomorrow, and I found some activities the kids might like. I'll have to go through the list with them."

"I forgot to mention – there's an art store in town that does classes and such. Emma especially might be interested."

"Thanks. I'll look into it."

"Of course. And you know we can have them here sometimes, too. We'd love to spend time with them, and it will give you a break, too."

"I don't want to impose more than I have to. I know they're a handful."

"Nonsense. They're just being kids. We can handle it. And they'll help keep us on our toes, keep our minds sharp." Sylvie smiled.

"Thanks, Mom."

"You bet."

They said their good-byes, and Lindsay and the kids headed back to the rental house. As they pulled in, Lindsay saw a woman holding a baby near the front door of the main house. The woman turned to watch them and smiled.

Lindsay met the woman's gaze and returned the smile. She could only assume this was the owner of the house. Her suspicions were confirmed when the woman approached and held out the hand that wasn't holding a baby.

"Hello!" she greeted. "I'm Alyson. You must be Sylvie's daughter."

Lindsay shook the woman's hand. "Hi. Yes, I'm Lindsay." She gestured to Emma and Jeremy. "These are my kids."

Jeremy's eyes were glued to his phone, but Emma looked up at the introduction. Her eyes lit up when she saw the baby.

"What a cute baby!" she said with a grin.

Alyson matched Emma's grin. "Thanks. This is Nicholas. We call him Nicky."

Nicky looked young, maybe a couple of months old, not yet able to hold himself up, though he was trying.

Alyson looked back to Lindsay. "I intended to stop over yesterday, but Nicky was being particularly fussy. I hope you were able to settle in okay."

Lindsay nodded. "Just fine, thanks."

"Good. Well, if you run into any trouble or have any questions, just let us know. My husband Jonathan works from home, and my daughter Katie is often around, too."

"Sounds good. Thanks."

They waved good-bye, and Lindsay and the kids went inside.

"Okay," Lindsay said as she put her purse on an end table by the sofa. "I know you guys had a busy day with Gran and Pops, so I'll let you relax for a bit, but then I want to discuss what I learned today. We need to come up with a game plan for the next few weeks."

After grumbling acknowledgements, Emma went upstairs to the bedroom and Jeremy threw himself onto the sofa bed, still pulled out from the morning. Lindsay had spread out the mattress topper she bought, but if Jeremy noticed, he didn't comment. Oh, well. She tried. And at least he was willing to be in the same room as her today. That was progress.

Sylvie felt ready to collapse after the kids left. It had been a long time since she had had kids to worry about, and, while they didn't require much care per se, the effort it took to keep them engaged and off their phones was exhausting. And frustrating. There had to be a way to get them to care about something else. Surely they had other interests. She would have to ask Lindsay. But in the meantime, she would have to do some brainstorming of her own.

Ed joined her as she was searching the internet for inspiration.

"What are you doing?" he asked.

"Trying to figure out how to get the kids off their screens."

Ed chuckled. "Good luck. I'm about out of ideas."

"Me, too. That's why I'm looking online."

"Isn't Lindsay going to find things for them?"

"She's trying, but I'm sure we're going to have them sometimes, too. And I want us to enjoy the time together, not sit in silence or argue about what to do."

"They seemed to like the board games."

"True. Maybe we can pick up some new ones."

Ed patted Sylvie on the shoulder as he walked past. "Let me know if you need me for anything. I'm going to go try and fix that leaky faucet in unit five."

"Okay," Sylvie said distractedly. "Oh! Maybe the kids would like to learn how to do that kind of stuff."

Ed scratched the back of his neck. "They didn't exactly seem interested in learning anything, but I can try."

"They didn't seem interested in anything. I don't know if it's because they're still upset or if they're always like that."

"I guess now we know why Lindsay's been having a hard time."

"Poor Lindsay."

Silence fell before Ed declared he was off to work. Sylvie resumed her searching. She wouldn't give up. Her daughter and her grandkids needed her.

Chapter 9

Jake was pleased with the list of contacts he had compiled. Now he just had to figure out who was willing to help and what he would have to do to get something off the ground. And somehow get it done while also doing his job and solving the thief situation. Maybe he could do both at once – start a conversation about the event with local businesses and casually ask if they've noticed anything missing. While it looked like the thefts were more the work of pickpockets, it wasn't much of a stretch to think that businesses could have been hit, too. And businesses were more likely to catch something on camera. It was a start, at least. And one that killed two birds with one stone.

His route for the day had him primarily on Main Street, which would be perfect to get him started. He could also check out the town green, both for suspicious kids and as a possible location for an event. He was liking this plan. And he loved that it gave him something to focus on that was productive and positive.

Jake walked into the station, greeted his coworkers, and grabbed what he needed for the day. Just as he was about to head out, he was stopped by one of the department's seasoned detectives, Sherry. She beckoned him over to her desk.

"What's up?" Jake greeted, resting one hip on Sherry's desk. He liked and respected Sherry. She had been in this business for a long time, and she knew her stuff. And, while she could be a bit no-nonsense when it came to dealing with people, she truly cared about the town and its residents.

"I hear you've got a bit of a mystery going on."

"Yeah. I found some stolen goods. Not sure yet where they came from, but I've got my suspicions."

"What are you thinking?"

"I think they're the next step up for a group of young troublemakers. We had a speeding spree not long back, and, when that stopped, I suspected the situation would be escalating."

Sherry nodded. "Let's hope we can nip this in the bud so it doesn't get worse. What's your plan?"

"Well, it seems like the items were stolen from individuals, but when I checked reports, I didn't find any leads. I figured when I'm out on patrol today I'll stop into the businesses on Main Street and see if they've seen anything, had anything missing, or maybe have camera footage that could offer any tips."

"What's the status on the stolen goods?"

"I left the thief's stash in the woods. I suspect it's a bit of a trophy case and that they'll be adding to it. I thought I would keep it there and check periodically for any updates."

"Reasoning?"

"I didn't want the thief to know we were onto him. I'm hoping to catch him – or them – in the act. Easier to prove that way. I figured if I left the stash there, they might be less suspicious."

Sherry nodded again, but more thoughtfully. "I get what you're saying, but we may want to check for fingerprints. And, if we don't have any clues to get us started, it might be hard to catch anyone in the act. Next time you check on it, let's see if we can add a discreet tracking device. Based on location, we might not be able to get camera footage very easily, but if we get any movement on the tracker, we'll at least have a starting point."

"Makes sense. I was going to head out there after work today. I'll let you know when I'm heading home."

"Sounds good. And keep me posted on anything you find with the businesses."

"You got it."

Jake headed out and got into his patrol car. Though his route wasn't far from the station, he liked to bring the car and park it right on Main Street. He liked to think it gave the townspeople more confidence that the department was looking out for them. And if it helped deter crime in the meantime, all the better. Now to see what he could find out about the crimes that had already happened.

Lindsay and the kids had agreed on some of the activities she had found, but with such late notice, she wasn't sure if they would be able to join. So her plan, both to get things started and to get the kids taking more of an interest in the town they would be living in for the next couple of months, was to explore the town on Monday. Screens would be put away, they could check out the library and community center, have lunch in town, and get some fresh air as they explored.

Lindsay had wanted to walk into town, but she suspected the kids would already complain about the multiple excursions she had planned, so they drove to Main Street and parked in a public parking lot.

"Okay," Lindsay began, with more enthusiasm than she felt. "This is it, the start of our summer break. We've had a rocky start, but you guys seemed interested in some of the activities I found, and hopefully we'll come across some more during our adventure today."

"Some adventure," Jeremy mumbled.

Lindsay took a deep breath and tried not to let Jeremy's attitude get her down. "This will be a great opportunity for you guys to meet people, get a feel for the place, and ask questions about any of the programs or activities we found. The library and community center are pretty close, so I figured we'd start there, then stop someplace for lunch."

They got out of the car, and Lindsay reminded them to put their phones away as they started walking.

"I want you to look around, see if anything catches your eye."

Jeremy mumbled something under his breath, and Lindsay stopped walking.

She stood in silence until Jeremy met her eye. "I have had enough of your attitude, young man. I know you're not happy about being here. I know you would rather be home, glued to your screen twenty-four seven. But that is a big part of why we *are* here. You and Emma have become so disconnected with the real world, stuck in a world that exists of school and screens. And it has got to stop. When you were little, you used to like to play and explore and try different things. And I know things change as you get older, but it's like you've lost interest in everything. And that makes me sad, and it makes me worry. I want us to feel connected like we used to be. I want to get to know you again, understand what makes your brain tick." Lindsay looked at Emma, then back to Jeremy. "I want both of you to be the people you were meant to be, not these grumpy, irritable shells of people who wander around, lost in a virtual world."

Emma scuffed the sidewalk with the toe of her sneaker. Jeremy crossed his arms and looked away, down the street. Lindsay sighed.

"I know it won't be an easy adjustment. I'm just asking you to try. Give it a chance. You might be surprised."

"Whatever."

Lindsay tried to put an arm around Jeremy, but he shrugged and ducked away. So she tried Emma. Emma accepted the half-hug but didn't reciprocate. Lindsay closed her eyes and took a deep breath. "Okay, let's head to the library. Gran let me borrow her library card, so we can also look for books and stuff while we're there. I'm sure there'll be something you like."

Lindsay could practically hear the eye roll, but she chose to ignore it. She had said her piece, and now she was going to make the most of the situation. At least they were here, following steadily if not enthusiastically. They hadn't fought about putting the phones away. They weren't fighting with each other. They had expressed at least mild interest in a few of the activities. It was a start.

The library was smaller than the one where they lived, but it felt welcoming. The staff member at the front desk greeted them with a smile and welcomed them to the library.

Lindsay returned the smile. "Hello. My name is Lindsay, and this is Jeremy and Emma. We're spending the summer here in Pine Valley, and we were hoping to participate in some of the activities you have going on."

"Of course! Have you seen our program calendar?"

The woman walked them through the summer reading program and the various events they had scheduled. While a couple of them had full registration lists, several still had availability. Neither Jeremy nor Emma seemed particularly interested in the reading requirements for the summer program, but they were both interested in the prizes they could win, so they signed up and each selected a book to get started. They also registered for the events that seemed most appealing. Lindsay made a note of the days and times so could keep everything organized. Though she usually relied on the calendar app on her phone, she suspected she should probably pick up a paper calendar so the kids could keep track of what was on the agenda, too. This summer was going to be very different than what they were used to.

After thanking the library assistant who had helped them, they left the library and headed to the community center that stood next door. The parks and recreation department had a variety of classes available, as well as summer sports clubs. Though neither kid was very athletic, Jeremy had surprisingly expressed interest in joining the basketball club. Lindsay suspected it was because it occupied more time than the other activities, so it would mean less time to deal with her, but she wasn't going to complain. He could use the exercise, and it would hopefully keep him out of trouble.

With an increasingly-full calendar, they left the community center and paused on the front sidewalk. Lindsay was feeling accomplished, and, therefore, quite optimistic. "I think we're off to a great start," she said with a genuine smile. "How about we get some lunch and decide what to do next?"

They decided to stop at the cafe, where they could grab sandwiches and eat at the counter that looked out at the passers-by. Lindsay allowed the kids to take out their phones while they ate, acknowledging the fact that they had both behaved pretty well at their stops thus far. Maybe the summer wouldn't be so bad after all.

Chapter 10

"Oh, good," Sylvie said, looking down at her phone.

"What's good?" Ed asked, glancing over at her from where he was building a shelf.

"Lindsay just texted me an update. She said the kids have signed up for a bunch of activities at the library and community center. They're going to explore a bit more after lunch, but she said, 'so far so good.'"

"Good."

Sylvie turned her gaze from her phone to the computer in front of her. They had a couple of reservations booked for the coming weekend, but during the week after that, they had nothing. And that worried her. Maybe now that the kids had some activities lined up, Lindsay would be able to come up with some ideas for the motel. Sylvie hated to put that kind of pressure on her daughter, but she wasn't sure what else to do.

"Do you think it would be too soon to invite them over for dinner again?" Sylvie asked after a moment.

"Why would it be?"

"Well, I want to give them some space, give them a chance to connect as a family. I don't want to impose."

"They will have spent all day as a family. Lindsay might need the break."

"Hmm. Maybe. I'll give her the option, no pressure. Or see if she wants to do something later in the week."

Sylvie typed out the message, then silence fell except for the occasional banging of a hammer. She would have to ask Lindsay what the schedule was for the activities the kids had. Lindsay might need help with transportation, or filling in the gaps between activities. And, since they didn't have many guests booked, maybe one of them could even go somewhere with the kids. There were lots of museums and amusement parks and whatnot around. There was bound to be something that appealed to them. They could take a day trip or two. And it would keep her mind off the lack of business.

Lindsay accepted the dinner invitation but offered to pick up pizza instead of having Sylvie cook again. Decision made, Sylvie turned her attention to how best to ask Lindsay for help again without sounding too pushy. Should she give it more time? Wait for Lindsay to bring it up? Or should she just ask straight out? Sylvie sighed, then rubbed her eyes. She hadn't been sleeping well. Maybe she should try to get some rest before the kids came over again.

"Ed, do you mind watching the desk? I think I'm going to go lie down for a bit."

Ed turned to look at her. "Of course. You feeling okay?"

"Yeah, I'm just tired. Didn't get much sleep last night."

"Okay."

He didn't look convinced, but he didn't ask any more questions, so Sylvie retreated to their bedroom. Kicking off her shoes, she sat on the edge of the bed, then lay down. Her doctor had already been concerned about her high blood pressure, and she was sure this stress wasn't helping matters. Maybe they *should* just sell and retire. But what would she do all day? Then again, with no customers, what did she really do all day now? Worry and fuss? Read or do crossword puzzles at the front desk? If they retired, they could travel, or even move closer to Lindsay, see them more often. Of course, all that would cost money, and they didn't exactly have much saved. And she suspected a failing business wouldn't exactly fetch them a high price.

Back to stressing.

Sylvie sighed and closed her eyes, then rolled over to one side. Lindsay would fix it. She would come up with a brilliant plan and make everything better.

With dinner plans settled, and the kids not being horrible, Lindsay was feeling – dare she say it? – somewhat happy. Even if the last few days had been filled with tension and stress, she had needed this break from the routine. And, now that things were starting to fall into place, she could start to think more positively again about her plan. Perhaps this had been the right choice. Even if it ended up being only temporary, at least it was giving her a chance to step back and breathe.

Once lunch was complete, they headed to the art supplies store Sylvie had mentioned. The store's website had mentioned classes but didn't have a schedule posted, so they would have to see what was available and if it would fit in with the activities they already had planned.

The moment they stepped into the store, Emma's face lit up. She was the creative one in the family, often covered in paint or working on a sculpture of some kind. She loved trying new types of projects and was always up for a challenge. Lindsay was glad to see her truly enthusiastic about something. Lately it had seemed as if even Emma's art projects had gone digital, with digital illustrations and animations or creating custom avatars for her friends. While those projects were still creative, Lindsay loved to see her working with her hands and really connecting with her art. Even if a class didn't work out, maybe they could pick up some supplies while they were here.

Lindsay let Emma wander a bit while she asked about classes.

"Hello!" a woman greeted from the register. "Welcome to The Art Spot. How can I help you today?"

Lindsay went through introductions, then inquired about classes.

"We have a variety of classes available, especially now that it's summer. How old are the kids?"

"Jeremy is fourteen, but I don't think he would be interested." Lindsay looked to Jeremy for confirmation. He shook his head silently but forcefully.

The woman laughed. "No problem. And your other child, Emma, was it?"

"Yes, Emma. She's twelve. And this is definitely her kind of thing. She's open to just about anything creative." Lindsay peered around to try and find Emma. "Emma? Can you come over to discuss classes?"

Emma joined them after a moment. "This is such a cool shop."

"Thanks! It's nice to meet you, Emma. My name is Addy. I'm the owner here. I run a couple of the classes, but over the summer Jessica and Jordan handle most of them. They're both college kids, so they're out for the summer. And they're both interested in teaching, so it works out really well. Between the three of us, we have quite the assortment of classes. For your age, I think the best fit would be either pottery, acrylic painting, or maybe watercolors. We have a collage class, too, but most of the kids signed up for that one are younger, so I'm not sure if you would enjoy it as much."

"I like it all."

Addy laughed. "A girl after my own heart! I have found I like it all, too. Let's take a look at the schedule and see what works for you."

Classes from a business were definitely pricier than the town activities, but Lindsay tried not to panic. She figured it was still cheaper than if she had needed camps for the entire summer. She would just ignore the voice in her head trying to factor in the cost of the house rental and the futon and everything else that was sure to come up. She had to do what was right for her kids, even if meant a bit more debt. Priorities, right?

The acrylic painting class was set up more like a camp, so it would involve a full morning every day for a week. The others were once a week for several weeks. Lindsay let Emma pick two, then handed over her credit card and added the classes to her calendar. The camp especially had a lot of overlap with Jeremy's basketball sessions, so that would work out well for her to get some actual work done. The others were more sporadic. But they would make it work. They had to. And, once they got into the swing of things, everything would be fine. The summer would fly by, they would hopefully make some memories and get over this hump, and life could resume a bit more peacefully. She hoped.

Emma picked out a few art supplies to take back to the rental house, then they headed out. They stopped in another shop to pick up a calendar and browse, then spent another hour wandering around Pine Valley, enjoying the beautiful day. Lindsay was surprised but grateful that the kids weren't complaining. Maybe they were letting the sun soothe their senses as she was, or maybe they were just accepting the fact that they were stuck here for a couple of months. Whatever the reason, the peaceful break allowed Lindsay's thoughts to wander, and she thought back to what her mother had said on Saturday night.

It had been a long time since Lindsay had really looked at or thought about the motel. She figured it had been going well, since her parents had never talked about selling or retiring or anything. But if it was really struggling, Lindsay would have to give it some serious thought. What had gone wrong? They had been pretty steadily booked when Lindsay was younger. Had something happened, or had the world just changed that much? Maybe she would ask at dinner. Then take a good, hard look at what was going on. She did this for a living; she could certainly do it for her parents. She just hoped she would be able to help them turn things around.

Chapter 11

The bag of stolen goods was right where Jake had left it. Nothing appeared to have been added, and Jake wasn't sure if he should be relieved or disappointed. How often did the thief or thieves strike? Had they given up already, moved on to other things?

His line of questioning at the various Main Street businesses hadn't offered much insight. A couple of them had noticed the odd item missing here and there, but nothing they were alarmed about. No crime spree was taking place as far as the businesses were concerned. At least, not yet. And most cameras they had were focused inside the businesses, not out on the street, so if the crimes weren't happening within the building, it was unlikely he would have any luck reviewing footage.

Jake slid the bag out from under the rock, then took the small tracker Sherry had given him and tucked it within the folds of one of the wallets. He didn't want it visible. Mission accomplished, he sealed the bag and placed it back where it had been. He hoped something would come of it. The lack of other leads frustrated him.

On a positive note, however, everyone he talked to had seemed interested in a big, community event. Some had suggestions; some were just excited about the potential boost to business. The town green was promising as a location. He hadn't had a chance to touch base with community leaders who weren't business owners, but he would try to get to that tomorrow. He had time. He hoped. The one concern most people had was the timing. They seriously doubted his ability to get something put together by the end of summer. Fall, maybe. Holidays were more likely. Some even doubted that.

But now that Jake had had the idea, he was determined. While he wasn't opposed to future events, that didn't help alleviate the concern of giving the kids something to do and look forward to over the summer. Maybe once things got going, he could put out a call for volunteers. The kids and teens could help with menial tasks, setting up and all that. It would be an added bonus, on top of the event. But first he had to plan the thing. Maybe he should get a committee together. These kinds of things usually had committees, didn't they?

Distracted by his thoughts, Jake almost bumped into a couple of teens as he was leaving the clearing. At the last moment, he hopped to the side. They were just as distracted as he was, talking in hushed tones as they walked. Jake took a few more steps before his mind registered that they could be associated with the robberies. Trying not to make unnecessary noise, he stepped behind a tree and peeked around it.

The teens didn't look dangerous, but something about how they were talking gave him cause for concern. It sounded like they were arguing, though he couldn't tell what about. They walked around the clearing, heads close together, gesturing with their hands. They looked young, maybe sixteen, but tall. Nothing noticeable to identify them. Carefully, Jake slid his cell phone out of his pocket and positioned it to take a picture. He could always delete it if he didn't need it. But just as he was about to tap the button, the teens burst into laughter. One patted the other on the shoulder, and they left the clearing to head back down the trail. Jake shuffled around the tree just in time to not be seen.

Jake released a breath. Apparently, they weren't involved. Or just weren't concerned about it at the moment. Was he going to be suspicious of everyone now? And what if they had come just a few minutes earlier? What would they have said about a cop going through and hiding a bag of stolen items? All he needed now was a scandal in the department. He was going to have to be more careful. And keep his head out of the clouds.

By the time he made it back to his apartment, Jake was disgusted with himself. He had to pick one thing to focus on, or both of his projects would suffer. Maybe if he focused on solving the robbery issue, the event would be less pressing, and he would have more time to devote to getting it right. If the kids responsible were dealt with, they wouldn't be causing trouble. And everyone else was already doing their own thing, so they wouldn't miss an event they knew nothing about. Maybe he should work on setting up the event for the following summer. That seemed more manageable.

Of course that didn't resolve his other reason for doing it: giving himself something to work on. He loved his job, but he needed more than that. He wanted to connect with other people, do something meaningful outside of his day job. He had the time and the desire. He just needed to find a way to compartmentalize or something.

Jake ran his fingers through his hair. He was a mess. Maybe he needed a vacation, a real break from everything. Then he could think about who he really was and what he really wanted. Or maybe he should just join that gym like he had been considering. There was nothing like a good workout to get you out of your own way. He glanced at the clock. Dinner. Then the gym. Then he could figure out what the heck he was doing.

"Been a while since I had pizza," Ed said, patting his belly as he leaned back in his chair.

"Sorry it wasn't anything fancier," Lindsay replied. "Next time I'll get a menu and take orders."

Ed waved a hand at her. "Don't be ridiculous. I like pizza. We just don't usually eat out. It was a treat." He smiled at his daughter. "How was the day?"

The kids had retreated to the sofa with their phones, and Lindsay took a deep breath as she leaned back in her own chair. "All things considered, pretty good. We signed up for a whole bunch of activities, and I picked up a calendar to keep track of them all. Kids were actually pretty well-behaved, so no real issues."

"Happy to hear it."

Sylvie collected plates and brought them to the sink while Lindsay fiddled with a napkin, folding it over and over. "I started thinking about what you said about the motel, Mom."

Sylvie took a deep breath, then turned back to the dining table and sat down. Maybe this was it.

"I admit I've been so wrapped up in my own little world that I haven't given it much thought in a while. But as we were pulling in, I took a look around. While everything is neat and clean, I could see the wear and tear, too. I'm guessing you haven't had the funds to really maintain the property."

"Dad does what he can, as do I, but it is hard to find the money to replace things when they could really use it."

"If you really want me to put together some ideas, I'd be happy to do so. But I'll need to see what we're dealing with. I'd like to take a more thorough look around and discuss your current processes and procedures, and anything you've tried in the past."

Sylvie leaned forward and rested her arms on the table. "Of course. When would you like to do that?"

"If it's okay with you, I can take a walk around now, while the kids are occupied. And then maybe tomorrow you can show me the business stuff? The books are helpful, but I also want to take a look at the reservation system you're using, any current advertising you're doing, all that. And we can discuss any ideas you've had, or things you've noticed."

"I'll get things together for you. What time were you thinking?"

"The kids have a program at the library tomorrow afternoon, one of the few things they're doing together. So that might be a good opportunity. It won't be long, maybe an hour or so, but that will get us started."

"Sounds good. I'll get everything ready in the morning so we're all set."

Lindsay smiled, then pushed her chair back and stood up. "Great. I'll go take a look around. Can I peek in some of the rooms, too?"

"Of course. Unit three is currently occupied, but the others should be fine. Keys are behind the desk."

"I'll get them for you," Ed said, standing up to join Lindsay. "And I'll give you a little tour."

Ed and Lindsay went into the office, leaving Sylvie in the apartment with the kids. She smiled to herself. If Ed was taking an interest in Lindsay's efforts, that was a good sign. It meant he was on board, just as she had hoped. Now she just had to hope that the motel wasn't a lost cause all together.

Chapter 12

While Lindsay loved her dad, she didn't often spend time with just him. He wasn't an overly affectionate man, though she knew he would give her the shirt off his back if it would help. Walking with him as he had shown her the situation at the motel, however, her heart had gone out to him. It was obvious he tried to maintain things as best he could. And from a distance, everything looked fine. When she had started paying close attention, though, she could see things that needed replacing, areas that just couldn't be mended anymore. It was quite possible that this was part of the reason for the decline in business. But she suspected it wasn't the only one. And she hoped she was right.

The following day, after a low-key morning at the rental house, Lindsay dropped the kids off at the library, then headed to the motel. Sylvie was waiting in the office, and she greeted Lindsay with a smile.

"I pulled the information you asked about, and I have the online things up on the computer," Sylvie said after Lindsay greeted her with a hug. "It's a pretty sad state of affairs."

Lindsay flipped through the financial records, noted times when business seemed to improve, particularly around the holidays. She could only assume demand was high due to the time of year. And, of course, the time when the motel was at full capacity thanks to the apartment building collapse the previous fall.

"It looks like things didn't get really bad until maybe six or seven years ago."

"That's when the new B and Bs opened up. There were two that opened in quick succession, though one closed down a few years later."

"They took a lot of the business?"

Sylvie nodded. "That's my best guess. Nothing really changed on our end."

Lindsay paused. "Not to sound insensitive, but had things started to look...worn?...before then?"

Sylvie thought for a moment. "Perhaps a little bit. But we were able to replace things more frequently back then, since we had more customers. So some areas may have looked a little shabby, but nothing too bad."

"What kind of customers were you getting before then?"

"What do you mean?"

"Well, you said things changed when the B and Bs opened, but I always think of B and Bs as a couples thing. Were you getting a lot of couples before then?"

"Hmm. I hadn't really thought about it, to tell you the truth. We had some couples, sure, but a lot of families, too. I think the B and B that's still up and running – Nate and Joanna's place – they have some larger rooms to accommodate families. That might be why they've been able to stick it out. I think the other place was smaller."

"Okay." Lindsay made some notes on a legal pad she had brought with her. She was getting into business mode now, shifting her way of thinking into how to help the client. "I remember when I was a kid, you had a play area set up outside, but I don't remember seeing it when I walked around yesterday. What happened to that?"

"Oh, it started falling apart, so we had to get rid of it. At that point, business had started to decline, so we couldn't afford to replace it."

"What about the other stuff? I see you still have a shelf with books and games. Didn't you used to have maps or something?"

"Yes. I make sure to keep the shelves stocked, though I'm sure it could use some updating. We have the maps, but no one's asked for one in a long time."

Lindsay made a few more notes, then turned her attention to the computer. "Okay. Now let's take a look at how you get the word out. How do people know you exist?"

"We have a website, with a reservation system, but, to be honest, it hasn't been worth the expense lately. Most of our business comes from repeat customers, or local people telling their families and friends to stay with us."

Lindsay perused the website, which she could tell right off the bat needed updating. It looked outdated, ran slowly, and didn't consist of much more than a picture of the outside and a "book now" link.

"Oh, Mom. This needs a major overhaul."

Sylvie sighed. "I'm sure it does. But, while I can surf the web as well as the next gal, I don't know anything about that stuff. A friend in town put together that website years ago, when the internet really started taking off. And I wouldn't even know how to update it if I wanted to."

"Okay." Lindsay sighed. Website overhaul, updated amenities, more publicity. Did the town have a website they could piggyback onto? What else could they do that would be cheap but have a big impact? Her thoughts floated back to the activities of the previous day. Paid events, maybe? They didn't have an indoor space, but they had the space for outdoor stuff. "Hey, Mom, where do people hold big parties and events? The person we're renting the house from, the guy got married, right? Where did the wedding take place?"

"Well, the ceremony was at the church in town, but the reception took place at their diner. They have a party room there, and it made the most sense for them."

"But where do other people get married? I met someone yesterday who looked like she was engaged, judging by the ring on her finger. Where would she be able to have a reception? I wouldn't think the party room at a diner would be big enough for most wedding receptions or really big parties."

"I hadn't heard about anyone else in town getting married! Who was it?"

"The woman at the art place, Addy or something."

"Oh! Addy's getting married! That's wonderful news."

"Yes, I'm sure it is, Mom, but where would she do it?"

"Well, I don't know how religious she and Mike are, but the reception would probably take place out of town, or maybe outside. Unless they used the diner, too. I know she and Maggie are close, and I don't think either she or Mike has a big family."

"There aren't any other event facilities in town?"

"No, I don't think so. Maybe the community center, but that's more like a gymnasium. But if you're thinking of us doing something like that here, that seems very expensive."

Lindsay thought for a moment. "Hmm. Maybe not as expensive as you think, since you wouldn't have many costs ahead of time. You have the land. Even if you just offered outdoor events, with those big tents you can rent. You would get the money from the event and use it to pay for the associated costs."

"I suppose. I think we'd better start with something smaller, though."

Lindsay sighed. "You're probably right. I think we really need to start with the website. Everyone goes online now, and you can't rely on local people sending you business. I'm guessing you don't have any of the login information, do you? For the domain or hosting sites?"

"I have no idea what you're talking about. But anything related to the website should be in a folder in that filing cabinet behind you."

Lindsay pulled out a drawer of the cabinet and shuffled through folders until she found the one about the website. A quick glance told her it had the information she needed. Thank goodness for small favors. "Perfect. I have to go pick up the kids now, but is it okay to take this with me? I'll take a look at things tonight and see what I can come up with."

"Of course. I appreciate it."

"Great. I'll give you a call in the morning, once we've come up with a game plan for the day, okay?"

"Sounds good."

They hugged each other farewell, and Lindsay left to get the kids. Her head was swimming with ideas, but she had to keep reminding herself that this wasn't one of her big, wealthy clients. This was her parents, and they did not have the money for a big renovation project or grandiose ideas. She had to keep things simple. It would be like when she was first starting out. No team to crunch numbers or run data reports. No huge budget to run experiments with. But, when she thought about it, she preferred keeping it simple. Not only did she thrive on challenge, but she loved thinking of creative ways to solve problems. Emma got her creativity from Lindsay, after all. And Lindsay was confident that if she couldn't find a way to save this motel, no one could.

There was nothing like a good workout to clear the cobwebs from your head, Jake decided.

The night before, he had driven to the next town over and joined a twenty-four-hour gym there. His schedule could fluctuate, and he never knew when he would be available, so he figured that was his best shot. And, though he hadn't wanted to start with anything too intense, he had put in a decent starter workout that same night. Today he was heading back to meet with one of the gym's trainers, to see if they could put together a workout schedule for him. While he didn't consider himself horribly out of shape, he knew he wasn't as strong as he used to be. He had simply gotten into the habit of sitting too much, exercising too little, and snacking a bit too often.

In addition to getting healthy, Jake also looked forward to clearing the mental clutter and being able to focus more than he had lately. He needed routine, goals, and a plan. And this was a good one to get him going.

The trainer worked with him to put together a routine to ease him back into shape, and by the time Jake finished the first set, he was already feeling the effort in muscles he had forgotten he had. But with every repetition, he felt more like his old self: the confident, secure, and content Jake he was before all this uncertainty and his identity crisis set in. He was still strong, mentally and physically. This would make him stronger. Then he could face whatever came his way.

As Jake drove home that night, he was glad he had taken this step, relieved to be making positive progress in his life. While he still acknowledged the importance of both the robbery case and the community event, he also acknowledged that he had been getting a little too obsessed with them. Just like with his workout routine, he needed balance in his life. So he would come up with a plan.

First, he needed to evaluate his priorities. Catching the thief or thieves was definitely a priority, but that was his job. Letting it trickle into his personal life at all hours of the day needed to stop. And he had other responsibilities at work, too. While he could definitely assist with a case like this, it was really the work for the detectives. And, since Sherry had seemed to be on top of things, he would get her more involved. He would let her take the lead and see where he could assist, instead.

Second, he needed to acknowledge that while the community event had become one of his priorities, there was no way he could do it on his own. Other people seemed interested in helping him. He needed to let them. Even if he ended up being in charge of the thing, he needed to bring others on board, get their expertise, and make a solid course of action.

Third, he needed to get out of his head. He was getting involved in new activities; that was good. He was finding ways to interact with more people and spend less time alone in his apartment, also good. He was more than a badge, and he wasn't alone in the world. He needed to embrace who he was and let things play out.

So, plan: prioritize, bring in other people, do stuff. Easy. No problem. He could do this.

Chapter 13

ylvie sat in the motel office, waiting for the phone to ring and staring at the computer screen. After Lindsay had left, she had taken a good look at the website, trying to see it as a stranger would. The result made her cringe. It had been so long since she had even looked at the website. Usually, she just logged into the reservation system to see if any bookings had come through. The website itself sat unattended, forgotten. But now, well, she had seen enough websites to know that theirs was just pathetic.

She had asked Lindsay to help them, she knew that. And she was grateful for the help. But now that things had started, she couldn't help but wonder if it was going to be worth all the effort. Even if they got the website whipped into shape, and even if people started making reservations in droves, what would they think when they actually got here? Sylvie suspected they would see it as a bait-and-switch scheme. A spiffy website could draw them in, but the state of the motel could just as easily push them away. The motel itself needed a major overhaul, not just the website. But what were their options? They didn't have the cash on hand. And Sylvie hated the thought of taking out a loan or some other such thing and hoping that it would pay off.

The whole process seemed like a set of dominoes, all lined up, ready to topple. The more she thought about it, the more that needed doing. Website, replacing things in the rooms, replacing things on the grounds. Where would it end? What would they need to not only get people here, but keep them coming back? Keep them spreading the word so business continued? Was it worth it? And what if, after everything was said and done, the business couldn't be saved? Would they end up broke, in debt, with nothing but wasted time behind them? And, even if the business did survive, did she want to keep running it? She and Ed weren't getting any younger. All this time and work, just to bring in more business that would give them more work to do. Did she want that?

Sylvie knew she should talk to Ed about it, get his two cents. But he was not one to give up. He would insist that of course it was worth it, that they couldn't just abandon the motel and everything they had put in over the years. He would want to keep going until it was no longer an option. While she often appreciated his tenacity, he also had a tendency to live with his head in the sand, ignoring the problems.

She supposed they could always sell the motel if it started improving. It would be worth something then. But how would it feel to walk away after putting in all that effort? It would be like one of those TV shows, where they renovate dilapidated houses just to turn around and sell them. Would she feel differently if the motel was in tip-top shape, bringing in people and money and looking like it did years ago? Would an invigorated motel invigorate her, too?

Sylvie rubbed her chest. All of this overthinking was giving her heartburn. Maybe she just needed a vacation, a break from all this pressure. Maybe they should just close the motel for a bit while they evaluated their options. Would she be able to breathe more easily then? It wasn't as if they would lose much business if they closed. They wouldn't be in any worse shape than they were now.

Now that she thought about it, that wasn't a bad idea. If they decided to really tackle the issues with the motel, then they could reopen with a refreshed look. And if they didn't, well, it could fade into oblivion. They should be able to get at least some money for the land, if nothing else. As Lindsay had pointed out, they did have a decent amount of land. And if they closed, she and Ed would have more time to spend with the kids. They would have the flexibility to leave the premises for more than a couple of hours at a time.

The thought made her feel as if a weight had been lifted from her shoulders. To be without the pressure of the motel, even for a short while, was incredibly appealing.

Sylvie took a look at their reservation calendar. They had a couple over the weekend, nothing the following week, and just one the weekend after. After that, the calendar was clear. While that knowledge usually brought panic and depression, it now filled her with peace. After a moment's hesitation, she adjusted the settings on the reservation system to indicate reservations would not be available after their last scheduled booking. She could always turn them back on later. But in the meantime, she had to have a serious conversation with her husband.

Lindsay went through the folder about the website, shaking her head all the while. Not only was the website outdated, but they were spending too much for what they were getting. They were probably better off starting from scratch and then figuring out how to incorporate the reservation system into the new site. She strongly suspected there wouldn't be funds to hire someone to build a website, but they could probably go with one of the simple build-your-own-website companies. They didn't need anything fancy. They could take pictures themselves, share information about local attractions and businesses, and then have the link to make a reservation. Pretty much anything would be better than what they currently had. They just needed a way to highlight the natural beauty of the area, make a trip to Pine Valley sound appealing, and make the motel attractive. From the right angle, anything could look good.

Lindsay rocked her head back and forth to stretch her neck. She did worry about *actually* making the motel look good, though. Getting people here was one thing, but getting them to stay and want to come back was a whole other ball game. She remembered when she was a kid the motel had been a friendly, inviting place. The recreational amenities her parents had put into place had drawn families to stay and kept them coming back. Of course they hadn't had much competition at the time, but surely they could compete with one bed and breakfast. Was there a way to recreate the outdoor space without spending tons of money? And what could they do to refresh the rooms? New bedding? Artwork? She would have to see what the budget actually was to make improvements, if there even was one. Then she could see what would give them the biggest bang for their buck.

When the kids were in bed, she would see what she could find for website building platforms. If she could save money on that end, she would at least have that money to play with. But in the meantime, she had to figure out dinner.

By the time the kids were in bed, Lindsay had gone through various scenarios in her head, but she was also exhausted. Much too tired to tackle research right now. While the kids were behaving with less hostility – and had seemed to enjoy the program at the library that afternoon – she still felt stressed about their situation. And now, adding her parents' situation to her own, the stress had just multiplied. Why was she here?

As crazy as it seemed now, part of Lindsay had actually thought that leaving the stale, busy lives that had left them unfulfilled and replacing it with a slower, more relaxed pace would improve matters. But so far life had been just as busy and even less settled. She didn't know what she was doing, what she *should* be doing, or where to go from here. In an attempt to keep the kids busy and out of trouble, she had been looking for as many activities as possible to fill the days. But how was that any better than what they had been doing before? Moving from one task to another, one activity to another, until she was little more than an overworked chauffeur? And any down time was still filled with the kids on screens and her working. The only thing that had changed was an increased feeling of instability and anxiety.

Lindsay grabbed her phone and stepped outside onto the small deck at the back of the house. Though the day had been on the hotter side, the evening was cool, and Lindsay closed her eyes and breathed in deeply. The deck was big enough for a small table and a chair, and Lindsay sat down and looked around her. She could see a row of houses stretching out to either side, but behind the houses was part of the many woods that made up the surrounding area. Lindsay shivered. She wasn't used to being around so much nature anymore.

When she was a kid, she and her brother and their friends would run and play in the woods, making forts and pretending they were explorers or off on some quest. It was part of life. But now, she was used to the hustle and bustle of life in the suburbs and work in the city, with more cement and pavement than greenery. Manicured lawns and local parks were the extent of the nature in her life these days.

Lindsay leaned back and closed her eyes again. The air was fresher here, the scents of all that nature tickling her nose. She could feel the knots in her stomach loosen, the pressure in her temples ease. She was so used to being always on the go, she had lost sight of the reason for being here.

The kids needed activities, yes. She couldn't expect them to just lie around all day, satisfied by the natural beauty around them as they meditated or whatever. And she would need them occupied so she didn't have to worry while she was working. But they needed to work on finding balance. They needed to actually embrace the slower pace, rather than try to fill it with what they were used to.

She suspected it would revive the hostility. It would involve limiting screen time, encouraging play, and at their ages, she was sure they would resent that. She could already hear the arguments about their not being kids anymore, and Lindsay chuckled softly to herself. But maybe they would meet other kids in some of their activities. They could make friends. And, while she was sure even kids in Pine Valley had cell phones and video games, she had to believe that they had other ways of spending their time, too. Didn't they?

Chapter 14

The quest to form a committee for the community event had been successful, and Jake could now add three local businesspeople, the children's librarian, two members each of the local Lions Club and Rotary Club, and a fellow member of the police force to the group. Their first meeting would take place that Thursday, and Jake was feeling quite proud of himself for the effort.

Unfortunately, the situation with the robberies hadn't progressed quite as well. There had been no movement on the tracker, and Jake hadn't seen or heard anything suspicious around town. His gut told him the thief or thieves weren't done yet, but without any leads or action, he was getting antsy.

But, he reminded himself, that was work, and he had to try to step back from it, for at least a little while. The trainer at the gym had recommended working out only three times a week to start, so he didn't overexert himself, but he still had the event to focus on. So he spent Tuesday night pacing his apartment and brainstorming ideas for the event.

As the one who had come up with the idea, he planned on being in charge of at least the first committee meeting, so he needed to put together an agenda. And, if they decided to try and organize something for the summer, they would need to act quickly. A few of the members had wanted to push the first meeting to the following week, but Jake knew the longer they waited, the less likely they would meet the deadline he had imposed on himself. He would ask for opinions and suggestions when they met, but he hoped at least part of the committee was on the same page as he was.

He had never considered himself an impatient or demanding man, but the more he thought about it, the more those words seemed to fit his personality lately, and he didn't like it. Even if he had understandable reasons for wanting the event to take place before summer was out, was he being unreasonable with that goal? In a perfect world, the event would already be planned and scheduled, ready to take place that week or the next. He wished he had had the idea months ago. But he had to work with what he had. And he had to acknowledge that might mean he had to give a little, push the event to the fall or beyond. They could always hold another event next summer.

That won't help with the crime this summer, though. He couldn't keep the thought from his mind. Why was he so convinced that the teens causing the trouble were doing so out of boredom? And why was he so convinced that a single event would keep them from acting out the rest of the time? It wasn't as if a single event would take up much of their time. Unless the teens volunteered to help plan and set up the event, it would really just take up a few hours of their lives. And, of course, there was no guarantee the troublemakers would even participate in the event. He could be putting all this stress and pressure on himself for nothing.

Jake paused his pacing and ran a hand down his face, then through his hair. He was stressing himself out. He needed to breathe. Grabbing his phone and keys, Jake left the apartment and went outside.

The moment Jake stepped outside, he took a deep breath. It was nearly midnight, and the air was still. He could hear crickets and the occasional owl, the soft rustle of branches in the wind, and the scurrying of animals in nearby brush. This was his favorite part of living in Pine Valley: the peace and serenity of being surrounded by nature without being isolated and alone. He knew this was a good community, filled with good people. And even if the occasional bad apple made an appearance, they didn't ruin the barrel. The others more than made up for it.

But, Jake thought as he sat on the stoop in front of his building, knowing what he did so far about the recent trouble, he didn't believe the troublemakers were really bad apples. He suspected they were just kids looking for a thrill. Nothing thus far indicated they wanted to really cause harm. The residents who had had their wallets stolen hadn't even encountered fraudulent charges on their credit cards, at least not yet. Maybe that was why Jake was letting this affect him so much. He didn't want the kids to keep escalating their efforts. He didn't want them to ruin their lives or the lives of others just because they took things too far. He had seen too much of that in Waterbury. He wanted to nip things in the bud.

Jake leaned back on his hands and sighed. He should probably head to bed. He was working a late shift the following day, but he wanted to go to the gym in the morning and stop by the hiding place in the woods to see if anything had changed. If they didn't get action on the stash soon, he would have to take it to the station and see if they could get fingerprints or any other evidence. Sherry wouldn't let the trail grow cold just because he wanted to catch them in the act.

Maybe what they really needed was a series of events, or something ongoing that kids could get involved with. That was bound to have a greater impact than a single event on a single day. But what would fit the bill? It wasn't like there weren't other activities in town, just nothing, apparently, to keep these kids out of trouble. No, not kids. *Teens*. That was the problem. In his experience, there came an age when activities suddenly seemed too babyish. How would his event be any different? Teens who thought they were too cool for the other stuff going on wouldn't be drawn to a typical small-town fair or festival. He needed to find a way to make his event – or whatever they decided to put together – appealing to the right demographic. He would have to add that to the agenda. Maybe some of the other members of the committee would have some ideas. He was apparently tapped out.

The forecast for Wednesday looked hot and humid, but Lindsay wasn't willing to give up on her thoughts from the night before just yet. She figured if they got an early-enough start, they could get in a great nature walk before the day heated up.

Getting the kids on board, however, was easier said than done. Despite getting to bed at a reasonable hour, neither liked to get to sleep very promptly. That meant groggy mornings if she didn't let them sleep in. So she had to decide if it made more sense to ease them into her plan or wake them up and risk reviving the hostility.

Maybe she should work on getting herself situated before dragging them into it. If she could make the case that it had helped her to slow down and step back from a hectic life and constant screens, then perhaps they would be more willing to try themselves.

Decision made, Lindsay scribbled a quick note, left it on the dining table, and put her sneakers on. She would take a peaceful walk herself, soothe her senses, and see how she felt. Her kids didn't even think anything was wrong. Why would they want to work on her timetable? Besides, she could use the time to herself.

She stepped out into the sunshine. It was already getting a bit sticky, but if she took it slowly, it shouldn't be too bad. And once she got out of the sun and into the shade of the woods, she was sure it would feel cooler.

With no obligations until she had to take the kids to the community center after lunch, Lindsay opted to take her time. She closed her eyes periodically and breathed deeply, letting the fresh air fill her lungs. A light breeze made tree branches sway ever so slightly. Leaves and pine needles rustled as squirrels and chipmunks scurried through the underbrush. Birds chirped above her, and her feet crunched the ground below her. She could feel her shoulders ease. This was exactly what she needed.

With time on her side, and the tranquility of the woods around her, it took Lindsay a while to realize she was hopelessly lost. She hadn't explored these woods in quite some time, and she had forgotten how they continued to meander around the town. She supposed if she continued in one direction she was bound to hit a road, but, considering how easy it was to get turned around in the forest, she couldn't count on herself to not walk in circles instead. Or, if she did encounter a road, it would likely be one far from her starting point.

Lindsay sighed. So much for relaxing. Now she had to worry about how to get back, especially since, according to her watch, she had been out here longer than she had expected.

She came across a clearing and decided to rest a bit and figure out what to do. Finding a large rock to sit on, she pulled out her cell phone. What were the odds she would get a signal in here? After holding the phone up in several locations, she had to abandon that idea. She would just have to follow one of the trails as best she could and hope for the best.

As she stood back up, Lindsay heard footsteps moving through the brush. They were coming from a different path than the one she had been travelling, and she panicked for a moment as she debated what to do. Friend or foe? Would this person be able to help her get back to where she needed to be, or should she be alarmed and hide instead? Knowing her luck, she would probably end up hiding in a patch of poison ivy. Surrendering to her fate, Lindsay straightened her shoulders and waited.

Chapter 15

Jake hadn't expected to find anyone in the clearing. It was still early, and he figured the suspected thieves would still be in bed. The trails usually got busier later in the day.

The woman looked vaguely familiar, but he couldn't exactly place her. She was likely someone he had just met in passing. While he had an eye for faces, he didn't always know where he remembered them from. Still, she looked friendly enough, if somewhat wary.

"Good morning," he greeted with a smile. Having someone there put a monkey wrench in his plans to check the stash, but no reason he couldn't be friendly. He could always check it later, or after she had moved on.

"Hello," the woman replied. She seemed rooted to the spot, and he wondered if she was waiting for him to leave or make the first move. The thought occurred to him that perhaps she was involved in the burglaries, but his gut told him that was way off base.

"I didn't expect to see anyone out and about this early. I'm Jake." He held out his hand after introducing himself, and after a moment's hesitation, the woman took it.

"Lindsay."

"Nice to meet you, Lindsay. I don't think I've seen you around. Are you new to town?"

The woman hesitated again. "I'm here for the summer. Visiting my parents."

"Ah. Well, welcome. I'll let you get back to your hike. See you around." He put up a hand in farewell and turned to head back in the direction he had come from. He had moved just a few feet when the woman's voice interrupted him.

"Uh, actually..." Her voice faded, and he turned back to face her.

"Something wrong?"

She rubbed one arm with her other hand and looked away from him. "I seem to have gotten myself turned around. Any chance you can point me in the right direction?"

Jake grinned. "Sure. Where you heading?"

"Uh. Wildwood Drive?"

Jake gave a low whistle. "You must have been out here a while. That's clear on the other side of the woods."

Lindsay sighed. "I was afraid of that. I was enjoying the peace and quiet and lost track of time."

"No problem. It just might be tough to give you directions. But I have some time. I can either walk you back that way, or I can take you down my usual path and give you street directions from there." He gestured with his thumb.

"I don't want to put you out."

"It's no trouble. Always happy to help. I'm a police officer, so it's kind of in the job description." He grinned again. The woman visibly relaxed, though she tried not to show it.

"We can go down your usual path. It'll probably be quicker."

Jake nodded once. "You got it. This way." He waved her along to follow him. After a few moments he figured he might as well strike up a conversation. Silence could be awkward between strangers, and you never knew what you could learn by simply chatting with people. "So you been in town long?"

Lindsay shook her head. "Just a few days. I grew up here, but it's been a long time since I've been back. And I haven't been in these woods since I was a kid. I forgot how big and confusing they could be."

"Even seasoned hikers can get turned around. There's been talk about marking some of the paths, but there's always a handful of townspeople who insist on leaving nature alone. It's not like a few signs would destroy habitats, but somehow they always end up winning."

"I guess that happens everywhere."

"Yup." Silence fell. "So who are your parents? I know just about everyone in town."

Lindsay paused, as if gauging if she could trust him. "Um, Ed and Sylvie Cooper? They run the motel?"

"Ah, of course. Maybe that's why you looked kind of familiar. You're the spitting image of Sylvie."

Lindsay gave a small smile.

"You said you're spending the summer here?"

Lindsay nodded. "Yeah, me and my kids."

Jake stopped walking, causing Lindsay to almost bump into him. He snapped his fingers. "*That's* where I know you from. I saw you in the grocery store. This past weekend. I happened to see your grocery cart, and it looked like you had kids."

Lindsay's eyes widened in alarm. He must sound like a madman. Or a stalker or something. He attempted a laugh.

"Sorry, that must sound really weird. Let me explain. I'm trying to organize this community event thing, a way to bring people together, give the kids and teens something to do to stay out of trouble, that kind of thing. But, not having kids myself, I've been looking for inspiration, and insight from people who have or work with them. It's kind of been taking over my thought process lately, so when I saw a grocery cart filled with things that seemed indicative of what kids and teens would likely enjoy, it stuck with me." He paused. Her shoulders had eased back down slightly, but not completely. "And that reaction is why I didn't approach you in the store." He laughed again. "Guess I should have kept my mouth shut. I'm not actually crazy; I promise."

She didn't seem sure, but they resumed their walk. After a couple of minutes of awkward silence, Jake tried again.

"Since I have now thoroughly embarrassed myself, maybe I should go all in. I would love some insight into what makes kids tick. I'm trying to figure out the best way to get them engaged and interested in the event I'm planning."

Lindsay barked out a laugh. "I'm not sure I'm the best person to ask."

Jake looked at her quizzically. "Why not?"

She sighed. "Truth is, we're not just here to visit my parents. We're here so I can figure out where the heck I've gone wrong and try to get our lives back on track. All my kids seem to want to do is complain and stare at their phones."

"How old are they?"

"Twelve and fourteen."

Jake nodded. "From what I've seen, that sounds pretty typical."

"I'm hoping to reconnect with them, find ways to get them interested in other things, but it looks like it's going to take a while. They hardly talked to me for three days after finding out we were spending the summer here."

"That's tough."

Lindsay closed her eyes and sighed. "Yeah. But I'm not giving up. I just figure I'll work on getting myself straightened out, then I'll work on them. That's why I decided to take a walk this morning. Guess that didn't turn out too well."

"I wouldn't say that. You said you were enjoying it before you got lost."

"I suppose."

Silence fell again, but it didn't feel quite as awkward now. After several minutes, Jake saw the edge of the road that marked the beginning of the trail.

"We're almost there," he said. He gestured toward the road. When they reached it, he turned to face Lindsay and held out his hand again. "Well, Lindsay, it was a pleasure meeting you." He gave her directions to get back home, then pulled out his wallet. Taking out a business card, he said, "if you need anything while you're in town, don't hesitate to call. Or if you suddenly gain amazing insight into the teenage mind." He grinned.

Lindsay returned the smile, took the card, and tucked it into her pocket. "Thanks. And thanks for getting me unlost."

"Any time."

She gave him a small wave and headed off in the direction Jake had mentioned. He watched her go, then released a breath. That had been unexpected, but not entirely unpleasant. She seemed nice. And attractive. Not that he was looking. But he wasn't *not* looking. Too bad she was only here for the summer. And with kids, there was little chance of a summer fling.

Shaking his head to clear the thoughts, he looked back down the path through the woods. Should he head back to the clearing now? Glancing at his watch, he shook his head again. Better not. If he wanted to have time for the gym, he should get going. He turned to look at Lindsay's retreating back. At least it hadn't been a completely wasted excursion.

Chapter 16

By the time Lindsay got back to the rental house, the kids were awake and eating breakfast.

"Where were you, Mom?" Emma asked, spoon paused halfway to her mouth.

"I just went for a walk."

"You were gone forever," Jeremy said, not even bothering to look up from his phone.

"Nice to know I was missed." Lindsay took off her sneakers and went into the kitchen to make herself a cup of coffee. "You guys have the gaming thing at the community center this afternoon, but nothing until then. What did you want to do?"

The kids both shrugged, and Lindsay sighed. Nothing new.

"After you guys eat breakfast, I want you to get dressed and ready for the day."

"I thought you said we didn't have anything to do until later," Jeremy said, eyes still glued to his screen.

"Just because we don't have a scheduled activity doesn't mean there's nothing we can do. We could go for a walk."

"You just went for a walk," Emma replied.

"True. But it was nice. Peaceful. It's nice to be able to relax and enjoy the calm. I thought you might like to go, too."

Jeremy scowled into his phone. Emma gave a doubtful look.

Lindsay sighed again. They'd get there eventually. "Doesn't have to be a walk. We could just do something together. Gran and Pops said you seemed to like playing board games with them the other day."

Jeremy shrugged. "I guess. But we don't have any board games here."

"True. But we could go out and get some. There's bound to be someplace in town that sells them, or we could take a drive."

The suggestion was met with silence. Lindsay closed her eyes, took a deep breath, and took a sip of coffee.

"I'm open to suggestions, too. Part of the reason for coming here this summer was to spend time together, slow down a bit. Maybe spend time away from devices." She gave the kids a pointed look, but neither noticed. Oh well. They had all summer. But they were definitely taking more screen breaks. Starting today. "We could head to the town green with our books. I know you guys wanted to earn some tickets to try and win prizes at the library. You have to read for that." More silence.

The kids finished their bowls of cereal but remained seated at the table, still absorbed in whatever they were doing on their devices. When Lindsay noticed, she clapped her hands loudly. Twice. The kids jumped.

"Okay, this is what's happening. Screens are getting turned off. You are getting dressed and brushing your teeth. We are leaving this house. Your phones are staying here. We are spending two hours without screens. I can decide what we're doing, or you can. Either way, it's happening."

The kids erupted into protests, but Lindsay ignored it. She walked to the table, grabbed their phones, turned them off, and stuck one in each front pocket of her jeans.

"Move."

Emma stomped loudly up the stairs. Jeremy grabbed clothes out of his suitcase and went into the downstairs bathroom, slamming the door behind him. Good. At least she had gotten some kind of response out of them. She was tired of wandering around, sad and depressed because her kids were mad at her for coming here. She was fed up with letting them walk all over her. She was fed up with being stressed and anxious. She missed the family they used to be when the kids were little. It was time to get that family back.

Lindsay had texted Sylvie to update her on what she had seen in the website folder and promised to be in touch when the kids were occupied with their activity later that day. That left Sylvie with a free morning. Not that that was anything new. These days Sylvie's time was mostly filled with books, puzzles, crosswords, and movies. She tried to get outside and walk to town every once in a while, to try and stay active. But the days blended together, and it was depressing. It was like she was retired already, but without the freedom. Maybe she should talk to Ed about her idea from the day before. She had originally planned on bringing it up after dinner but had chickened out.

Sylvie wasn't sure exactly how Ed filled his days, just that he was often puttering about outside or working in one of the rooms. He had a tool shed at the back of the building, and she knew he did a bit of woodworking in there, but otherwise he just seemed to look for little projects here and there to keep himself occupied. She had to admit the motel would look a lot worse if he didn't. Despite the wear and tear, nothing was broken or falling apart. Any issues that arose were dealt with quickly.

Not knowing exactly where he would be, Sylvie took the cordless phone off the base, stuck it in her pocket, and left the office to go looking. She found him weeding the flower patch that surrounded the motel's sign near the street.

"It's getting hot," she said as she approached.

"Yup. Humid, too." He stood up and wiped his brow with the top of one arm. "I'll probably head inside soon. I just noticed some things getting out of hand here yesterday and figured I would take care of them."

"I'll pour you some lemonade. Then I wanted to discuss something with you."

Ed stared at her a moment. "Am I going to like what you want to discuss?"

Sylvie sighed. "I honestly don't know."

Silence fell until Ed sighed, too, and said, "okay."

Sylvie went back into the office, walked through to the apartment, and poured two glasses of lemonade. Ed joined her a few minutes later. After taking a big gulp of lemonade, he put the glass down on the kitchen table and pulled out a chair.

Sylvie wasn't sure how to begin, so she took a sip of her own lemonade and sat down across from Ed. He came to her rescue when he began instead.

"Now, before you start on whatever you wanted to discuss, I wanted to let you know I've been doing some thinking, too. I know things have been tough around here, and I know you've been unhappy. You wander around here, not knowing what to do with yourself, when you used to be so excited, greeting people and getting them what they needed, making sure they knew where to go and what to see. Heck, even doing the books seemed to make you happy. But I haven't seen a real smile from you in ages." He reached across the table to take one of her hands. "I know I don't say it much, but I love you, Sylvie, and I hate seeing you like this. I just don't know what to do about it."

Sylvie felt tears coming to her eyes, and she swallowed before responding. "I used to love running the motel. I used to love seeing all our guests, the families with the kids and the older folks coming to get away from it all. I thought Lindsay could help us make it like it used to be."

"And maybe she can. It seemed like she had ideas to get business up."

"Maybe. But I look around at how bad things have gotten, and I can't help but think that will just make more problems."

"Why would that make more problems? More business, more money, we can fix things up and make them nice again."

"But the people we're trying to get in here will see it how it is now. They'll see the shabby comforters and the worn-out towels, the faded paint and chipping trim. Even if we sell out every room from now until the end of the year, how many of those people will want to come back? And how many would even want to stay once they see it in person? They might think they got tricked and give us bad reviews, which would make things even worse."

Ed sighed and leaned back. "So what do you want to do? Pack up and give up?"

"I don't know." Sylvie closed her eyes and rested her head on her hands. After a moment she looked up. "I think it's something we need to really think about. Even if...even if we get a lot of people, and those people stay and don't mind the shabbiness, are we prepared for the business to take off again?"

"I'm not following."

Sylvie took a deep breath. "We're not exactly young, Ed. When we were younger, we could tackle projects with energy and excitement. We could handle groups of people. We could take on challenges and figure things out, and do it all with smiles on our faces. What if business picks up, and we just don't have the energy to keep up with it anymore?"

"I've been hearing a lot of hypotheticals here, Sylvie. Fact of the matter is, we don't know what's going to happen. We don't know if business will take off, or if people will be happy or upset, or how we'll feel. But it sounds to me like you're trying to come up with reasons to stop, to give up the motel, whatever. Is that what you want?"

Sylvie felt a tear trickle down her face. She didn't know what she wanted; that was the problem. "I don't know, Ed."

"Okay... It seems to me that that's what we should really be discussing here, not some hypothetical 'what if' stuff."

"I thought maybe we could take a break. I know we haven't been getting a lot of reservations, but maybe pause them altogether for a while and take some time to figure it all out."

"If that's what you want to do, that's fine. I want you to be happy, and it's not much of a loss if we miss out on a few reservations. How long were you thinking? A week? Two? A month?"

"Maybe start with a couple of weeks and see how it goes?"

"Okay." Ed sighed. "When do you want to start?"

"We have a reservation the weekend after this one, so I was thinking after that."

"Fine." He stood up. "I wanted to go touch up the trim in a couple of the bathrooms. I've got my cell on if you need me."

Sylvie watched him go. She couldn't tell if he was truly on board, but at least he was giving her time to figure things out. She would make a list, go through their options, see what seemed the best choice. She should talk to Lindsay, too, get her take on things. Then they could decide if the Pine Valley Motel was worth trying to save.

Chapter 17

"Jake, we need to talk about those robberies." Sherry's voice attacked him as soon as he entered the office. He had known it was coming.

"Yeah, I know. I figure I'll get the stash from its hiding place tomorrow, and we can dust for prints."

Sherry nodded. "That's a start. We need something. We've been having people call to check on the progress, see if other items have been recovered."

"Got it. I assume no movement on the tracker?"

"Nothing yet. I'll let you know if I get any hits."

Jake prepped for the day and went out to his assignment. He really wished he had gotten to check on the stash, but it probably didn't matter anyway. No movement on the tracker meant it hadn't gone anywhere. But the tracker probably wouldn't pick up on minor movements, like if someone picked up the bag and added to it. He wanted to know if the thieves were still at it.

He was on traffic duty that day, which left him way too much time to mull over the robberies and his inability to do anything about them. Directing traffic through a construction zone took up part of the day, but it didn't require much mental effort. And trying to catch speeders wasn't much better. That just reminded him that if, as he suspected, the same group of teens was responsible for the robberies as the speeding spree, there was a chance they would escalate again.

By the time he got home that night, he was kicking himself for not going back to check on the stash that morning. The gym could have waited. This was more important. Whatever happened to getting his priorities straight? First thing the following morning, he was going to head out and grab it.

He wondered if Lindsay would be there again, though he figured it was pretty unlikely. And, even if she was, she would probably steer well clear of him. After that stalkerish conversation about the grocery store, he was ready to kick himself. What had he been thinking? The problem was: his mind was stuck on obsession mode, going over everything on a loop. Until he made progress on something, he suspected he would continue to feel uneasy. But he had a plan: grab the stash in the morning, meet with the event committee in the evening. Tomorrow would be a productive day. Now he just needed to get some sleep so he was ready for it.

"We've decided to take a break."

Lindsay adjusted the phone against her ear and furrowed her brow. "A break from what?" She was on the phone with her mother, trying to catch up with what was going on. She had called while the kids were in their rec program, but Sylvie hadn't answered.

"From the motel."

"You want to take a break *now*? When we're trying to get more people to stay?"

Lindsay could hear Sylvie sigh. "I know it seems out of the blue, but hear me out. You know this motel has been our life for years now. And I'm not saying I regret that. But if we bring in more people, they're going to see how shabby things have gotten, so they may not want to stay, or come back. But if we take on the time and expense of fixing things up before they come, and business picks up, then we'll be super busy, and we're not getting any younger, and that's a lot of work. But if we don't fix things up, and the people come but don't stay, then trying to get them there will have been a waste of time."

Lindsay pinched the bridge of her nose. "You're not making much sense, Mom, but I get it. I was having some of the same concerns as I was figuring out the website. Bringing in more people when the motel is looking less than its best might cause problems. But why take a break?"

"Because your father and I need to figure out what we actually want to do. And that will take time. We may not want to revive the motel. But we don't want to rush into any decisions, one way or the other."

"So, should I pause the marketing efforts?"

"Just for now. We both have to do some thinking and discuss the situation more. Plus, this will give us more time with Jeremy and Emma."

"If that's really what you want, Mom."

"It's what feels right just now."

"Okay."

Lindsay had stepped outside onto the back deck while they spoke. The kids were inside on their screens, but she wasn't too worried. They actually hadn't had that much time on them today. They had gone for a drive, picked up a few board games and other things to keep themselves occupied, had some lunch, then gone to the community center. Afterward they had learned there was a public pool in the next town over that they could use for just a few bucks, so they had decided to go swimming. After the initial resentment over having their phones taken away, they had actually been pretty relaxed, receptive to ideas, and engaged in conversation. It had been a refreshing change. Lindsay wasn't sure how long it would last, but she would take it for as long as she could.

They said their good-byes, and Lindsay sat down. It was still sticky out, but not as hot, so she figured if she didn't move too much it should be fairly comfortable. She had found herself craving the fresh air lately, wanting to be outside as much as possible. Back at home, there simply wasn't time to sit around, and, even if there had been, the background noises of traffic and lawn mowers detracted from the tranquility she felt here. Not that she hadn't heard cars or lawn mowers in Pine Valley, but it was less frequent, and seemed less intrusive somehow. It wasn't constant, just a part of life that popped up once in a while.

Lindsay closed her eyes and breathed deeply. She hadn't expected the announcement from her mother, but, considering she had been thinking along the same lines, she wasn't surprised. It was a big decision, with lots of moving pieces. Her parents were getting to the age when they should be slowing down, not building a business back up. But they had spent the last few years slowing down, almost to a stop. Were they ready for action again, or did they need freedom from the worries of the business so they could actually enjoy their free time? What would happen to the motel, though, if they decided to walk away? Would they be able to sell it in its current state, or would it fade into oblivion, getting more and more dilapidated until it became a ruin, a blight on the town?

What should she do in the meantime? Obviously, she had the kids and work to worry about, but if her parents decided to revive the motel after all, should she have a list of ideas ready to go? Or should she wait for more direction from them? If she was honest, she had been enjoying the opportunity to think creatively and problem solve. So much of her job now was interpreting data, figuring out conversion rates and which ads would perform better. They had copywriters and designers for most of the fun stuff. When had her job become drudgery?

No, she rationalized. It wasn't drudgery, just different. And she had made the conscious decision to shift into the analytical side of things. When the kids were young, so much of her mental energy was taken up with making sure their needs were met, that they were playing and learning and exploring and having the opportunities kids should have. Her husband hadn't been much of a partner, working long hours and then spending most of his time at home complaining or locking himself into his office to do who knew what. Everything had fallen to her, and the burden of being creative day in and day out while also handling everything else had just been too much. But numbers? Numbers she could handle. She had been good with numbers and figuring things out. And without the need to come up with new ideas on a regular basis, she had been able to breathe a bit more. It could still be creative, just in a different way.

The kids were older now, more self-sufficient, and the husband had been kicked to the curb five years prior. But she had stuck with the analytics, working behind the scenes to make sure the other departments had what they needed for successful campaigns. Having the opportunity to tackle all sides of the situation for her parents had been a refreshing change of pace. Her fingers practically itched to design a new website, play with copy and photo placement, figure out all the links and info the motel could offer to draw in families. She thought of potential business partnerships and curb appeal and refreshing rooms and just all the things that could make the motel even better than it had been when she was a kid.

So, should she take a break, too? Or should she keep going with the ideas and lists and figuring things out? Would it hurt if she kept going? The website didn't have to go live. The sketches and lists could be for her eyes only. She was reluctant to give up that part of her now that she had found it again.

Lindsay sighed. It had been a long day. Not a bad one, but she was tired. She needed time to figure everything out, too. And she had it. That was what this summer was supposed to be about: stepping back from life and reconnecting with her family. She had two months to figure out life. No problem.

Chapter 18

Sylvie lay staring at her bedroom ceiling. She was overthinking again, and, as a result, was having trouble sleeping. Ed lay sleeping soundly beside her, but she just couldn't get her mind to settle down. With a sigh, she decided to get up. No sense getting frustrated and possibly disturbing Ed.

She made herself a cup of tea and brought it into the motel office, where she sat in one of the armchairs by the bookshelf and looked out the front windows. With the lights off, she could see the entire front yard before her, and she sighed again. When had her life become so dull? She used to have a full social life and an interesting job. She loved meeting new people and trying new things, looking for new ways to spruce up the motel or new ideas to share with their guests. What had happened?

Business had slowed, yes, but they had still had guests. But with the reduced business came the money woes, and feeling stressed discouraged her from thinking creatively or putting in more effort than was necessary. She supposed she was just as much to blame for the business failing as the B and Bs were. She had lost the passion. Her life had become checking boxes and watching the time tick slowly by.

She was glad Ed had agreed to taking a break, but she wasn't sure how she would figure out how to proceed. She missed the fun, spirited woman she had been. But she also craved freedom. The motel had become an albatross, and part of her wanted to throw it off and spread her arms wide and fly. Would she be any happier, though? Without purpose, without tasks? What would she do? She supposed she could do anything. She could become involved in the community again. Take up some hobbies that didn't involve staying in one place.

Back when the motel was popular and bringing in a good living, they had had staff – someone to help in the office and someone to help clean the rooms. It had been enough that she and Ed could go out to eat once in a while or enjoy a movie out. When the kids had been younger, they could take a short vacation in the off season or go on day trips to museums or amusement parks. When business crashed, they had had to let go of their staff, which meant she and Ed had to stay on the property. She supposed they could have found a way. But they didn't have the disposable income to go out and have fun, so what was the point?

That had been four years ago. Four years of feeling chained to the motel. Four years of getting more and more listless, until she had to wonder why even bother. Maybe if they had brought Lindsay in earlier, they could have revived things before they got so bad. But Lindsay had been going through her own troubles. Their conversations had been filled with tears and worries. Sylvie was the mother. She couldn't add more burdens to her struggling daughter's load. So she had waited, hoping things would get better.

Sylvie's eyes filled with tears. She was sick and tired of feeling like this. If they closed the motel, maybe they could try to sell the land if not the building. Maybe someone would be willing to pay enough that they could retire at least semi-comfortably. They could have a fresh start near Lindsay, help with the kids, find some joy again. Would that be enough?

Sylvie looked around the office. She knew every corner: every peeling corner of the wallpaper, every chipped corner of the trim, every scuffed corner of the desk. Part of her wanted to revive it to its former glory, with fresh paint and flowers and beautiful lighting fixtures and new chairs. And part of her wanted to kick and scream and tear everything out.

The part that wanted to destroy it all was winning now. But this was her home, had been her home for the past thirty years. She couldn't just give up on it, could she? They had happy memories here, full of laughter and hope.

Sylvie stood up and put her teacup on a side table. Then, opening the door carefully so as not to wake Ed, she stepped out into the night.

The air was heavy, sticky and warm. She suspected they would get thunderstorms the following day. But it suited her mood as it was, and she walked from one end of the building to the next, taking in the dark windows and faded siding. One of the outside lights was starting to flicker. She would have to remember to tell Ed to replace the bulb. The parking lot was cracking; the poles that held up the main sign were starting to rust.

She could remember how it used to be. She remembered the fresh pavement, the newly painted siding. She remembered their excitement when they had replaced the sign after taking over the motel. It had been a long time since she had thought of those first days. They had bought the motel, eager to provide a good life for their kids. Ed had been getting burned out at his day job, and with the kids getting a little older, she had wanted to do something more than the part-time grocery cashier work she had been doing. They had been saving what they could, trying to figure out what to do when the motel was listed. It had seen better days, but they weren't afraid of a little elbow grease. They could sell their house and get a mortgage for the motel, instead. They could use their savings to fix things up and get people to visit their little town.

Those had been the days of family road trips, when families looked for quiet, inexpensive vacations. Sylvie could see the potential, and it was just a question of taking out little ads in hotel guides or on restaurant placemats. They brought people in and made it a lovely place for families to connect, enjoy nature, and spend time together.

Would people even want that kind of thing again? If they decided to spruce everything up, start over, push to get people here, would it even pay off? Nate and Joanna seemed to be doing fine with their bed and breakfast, but the other one had closed in just a few short years. Maybe there just wasn't enough business.

Maybe too many people wanted the big, flashy vacations now. Maybe they would be stuck with the people visiting family members or escaping the hustle and bustle, in which case, what difference did it make? Why go through all the trouble for a tiny bump in business, if any?

Sylvie closed her eyes and breathed in the sticky air. She wasn't getting anywhere. She wasn't solving anything by rehashing the past or overthinking the future. They had to make a decision and stick with it.

But, she thought as she made her way back inside to try and sleep, she couldn't help but wonder about the people who had sold them the motel. Had they been in the same position she was?

Chapter 19

The trail was quiet Thursday morning. Jake was able to check on the stash without issue. He was, however, both saddened and invigorated by the fact that new items had been added to the bag. New info, new leads. And he didn't think the thieves would have added new items if they suspected they had been caught.

The new items didn't have any identifying marks that he could tell. More jewelry, a couple of trading cards. It was an odd assortment of items, with little rhyme or reason. But if anyone reported them missing, he could ask for any information they might have. And, in the meantime, they could dust for prints and see what else they could find out.

Knowing he would be taking the stolen goods, Jake had brought a backpack with him, and he placed the bag inside it now. He wondered what would happen when the thieves realized the bag was gone. Would they panic? Turn themselves in? Think some wild creature had wandered off with it? He could only hope that they had just added the new items and wouldn't be back to check on it for a while. That would give him time to pursue any leads.

Sherry was glad to have the stolen goods in their possession, and she took the bag from him to process any fingerprints that might be on the bag. When the results came back, however, there were no hits on the fingerprints they found. That meant a dead end, but one that Jake wasn't convinced didn't mean anything.

If the thieves were teens, as he suspected, they wouldn't have fingerprints in the system yet. They may never have had a job, or at least not one that did background checks. And if they had never been suspected of a crime before, there would have been no reason for the police to get them. Sherry was going to investigate what other leads the items may provide, and see if anything matched to reported crimes.

In the meantime, Jake felt at loose ends. With the case out of his hands, he wasn't sure how best to proceed. Should he wipe his hands clean, or should he pursue other avenues of investigation? He was working the center of town beat again, so he could talk to business owners again. Or he could just bring it up at the committee meeting that night. Or, he thought as he processed the situation, he could talk to people who might have heard something, even if they weren't themselves involved. In a small town, that meant two places: the local bar, and the local diner. Since he suspected teens, it wasn't likely the bar would be productive, unless they were adding fake IDs to the list of crimes. But with the bar, Andy's Tavern, not being open until later that afternoon, anyway, Jake decided that lunch at the diner just might offer some insight. Until then, he would hit the pavement.

The weather was hot and sticky again, so the sidewalks weren't very crowded. He wondered if the weather would affect the event he was planning. If they opted to have it outside, and it was unpleasant like this – or worse, raining – he suspected turnout would be lower. It was something to consider when they decided on location. But holding it indoors also meant less visibility, less chance of passers-by checking things out. Maybe they could have an inclement weather date.

Jake had just gotten back into his patrol car when a call came through about a fender bender on a street off Main. He replied that he would respond to the call, and off he went. The accident was straightforward, with no injuries. He took down the report information, entered it into the computer in his patrol car, and moved along.

The morning was passing slowly. He should be grateful for the low number of incidents. But he was feeling antsy again. Maybe he would have an early lunch.

He was greeted and seated by one of the college kids who worked at the diner, which wasn't ideal. He was really hoping to get Maggie or Richard, someone who would be in a better position to answer his questions. But he saw Richard manning the flat-top grill in the kitchen, so perhaps he would get his chance.

Jake sat at the counter, and, catching Richard's eye through the window into the kitchen, greeted him with a wave. Richard smiled and returned the wave. After finishing up with his current order, Richard came into the dining area, wiping his hands on a dishcloth as he walked.

"Hello, Jake. How have you been?" He reached out to shake Jake's hand, and Jake reciprocated.

"Can't complain. How are you? How's married life?"

"Life is good." Richard smiled. He looked like someone very content with his lot in life, and Jake couldn't blame him. Recently married to a woman he loved dearly, with a successful business and new grandchild. He hoped when he was Richard's age that he could be just as content.

"Glad to hear it."

"What can I get started for you?"

Jake ordered the daily special, but, just as Richard was turning to fill the order, Jake stopped him. "I was also hoping to chat for a bit."

"Sure thing. Let me turn your order into the kitchen, and I'll be right out."

Richard returned a few moments later with Jake's soda. "So, what's up?"

"Seems we have a thief in town. Nothing big, little stuff, but a repeat offender. I thought you might have seen or heard something that could point me in the right direction."

"Hmm." Richard rubbed his chin as he thought. "Can't say that I have, but I'll definitely keep my eyes and ears open. Maggie might have heard something. She tends to get more of the gossip. She hasn't said anything to me, but she'll be in in about a half hour. I can ask her."

"I appreciate it. Or maybe I'll be able to catch her before I leave."

They chatted for a few more minutes, until Jake's food was ready. Then, Richard handed him the plate and left Jake to eat and think.

Cocky teens could easily be running their mouths about their activities, but they could also be doing so elsewhere, in their group of friends. He wondered if there was a way to get someone closer, to be a kind of informant. But without knowing who, or where, or even how old, he wasn't sure how that would work. And it wasn't exactly like they had teens on the force. He would have to keep brainstorming. Maybe Maggie would have some leads for him.

With the success of the previous day, Lindsay was feeling optimistic about the day ahead. Emma started one of her weekly art classes that afternoon, but Jeremy didn't have anything scheduled. Lindsay was hoping they would be able to spend some actual time together, maybe play one of the new games they had bought.

With the weather still hot and sticky, they decided to spend the morning back at the pool. In the water, the kids acted like kids, and Lindsay could imagine them as the sweet young children they used to be, even if they wanted nothing to do with her. Lindsay opted to lounge in the shallow end, watching the kids and making sure they didn't get into too much trouble.

The pool was crowded, and Emma was able to join a group of other kids who were playing a game of some kind. Jeremy swam near some older kids, but they didn't pay him any attention, so he just floated along on his own. Lindsay's heart went out to him. She knew it was hard at his age to be the new kid, to not have any friends around. Kids could be so cruel, and with his own temper, Jeremy could be quick to snap or resort to taunting if others did something to bother him. He had always had trouble making friends. But Lindsay knew he wanted to be accepted. He enjoyed being around other people. She hoped he would make some connections in the activities they had lined up this summer. Maybe the basketball program would help, since that was multiple sessions a week for a few weeks. He was bound to get to know people then.

After a couple of hours in the pool, they headed back to Pine Valley to dry off and have lunch. So far so good.

"Okay, so after lunch, Emma has her art class, and Jeremy, I thought you and I could hang out here and play a game or something." Lindsay put their plates on the dining table, and the kids sat down to eat.

Jeremy gave her a look as if that was the stupidest idea she could come up with.

"What? We bought those games to play. You approved them."

"Yeah, but that was for family time or whatever. Or when we were with Gran and Pops."

"So we can only play when Emma is around?"

Jeremy shrugged.

Lindsay sighed. "Well, since Emma will be in her art class, she won't be using her phone, so the same will apply to you."

"What the hell?" Jeremy stood up, a scowl on his face.

"Watch it," Lindsay scolded, giving him a pointed look.

"I didn't use my phone the entire time we were at the pool, and you said we can't use them while we eat. Why can't I have it after lunch?"

"You may use it for a short while after lunch, but once we drop Emma off, you'll take a break while she's in her class. You guys can have some screen time later."

Jeremy sat down again, his face still in an angry pout. "That's bullsh—"

Lindsay cut him off. "I suggest you watch the language if you want to use your phone at all today."

The pout never left his face as he ate his burger, but at least he was quiet. After eating, he shoved his chair back, snatched his phone off the end table and went upstairs.

Emma watched the interaction in silence, calmly eating her burger.

"You okay, Em?"

Emma nodded. "I hate when he gets like that."

"Me, too." Lindsay took a bite of her own burger. "Are you looking forward to your art class?"

Emma's face lit up, and she nodded eagerly. "I think this one is going to be my favorite. I love painting, but I've never tried watercolors. They look so peaceful, though."

Lindsay smiled and squeezed her daughter's hand. "I hope you enjoy it. I used to like watercolors when I was younger."

"I've never seen you paint. Or do anything artsy."

"It's been a long time since I've painted. But I used to create things for my work. I would design ads and flyers and stuff."

"Yeah, but that's different."

"I guess it is. Still creative, though. Like you with your animations and avatars."

Emma shrugged. "I guess." After chewing another bite, she added, "maybe they have classes for adults, too."

Lindsay cocked her head to one side. "You know, I never thought of that. I've been so focused on making sure you and Jeremy have enough to do, I haven't thought much about things for me. But I have to start working next week, so I'm not sure how much time I'll have."

"I'm sure other grown-ups have to work, too. Maybe they have stuff at night. Or at the library or something."

"Maybe."

"You should ask when you drop me off."

Lindsay chuckled. "Okay, maybe I will."

By the time they reached The Art Spot, Jeremy was scowling again, but at least he wasn't arguing. Emma looked happier than Lindsay had seen her in a while. While she was part of an art club at school, she didn't have much other time to explore her creativity. Summers were usually filled with traditional day camps, with some arts and crafts, but nothing very in-depth. The specialized camps were shorter hours, and usually more expensive. Lindsay was grateful she could give her this opportunity.

As they turned to leave after waving good-bye to Emma, Lindsay remembered the conversation from earlier. It wouldn't hurt to ask about classes for adults, would it? Or if they didn't have classes, maybe she could at least get some art supplies and do her own thing.

Lindsay returned to the front counter, where Addy was greeting more students. She welcomed them and gestured toward the classroom, where another young woman was handing out supplies. Then she turned to face Lindsay.

"What can I do for you?"

"Hi." Lindsay suddenly felt shy, which was ridiculous. This woman was younger than her and not at all intimidating. But she was out of her element here. When was the last time she had thought about a hobby? Or trying something new? "Um, I was wondering if you also offered classes for adults."

"I'm so glad you asked! We don't have too much, since adults' availability can vary so much. But we have a few things. We have paint nights once in a while, when we show you how to make a particular painting. And a local artist is going to be starting an introductory drawing class, which should be fun. Then we always have the paint-your-own pottery and the community mural."

"Community mural?"

"Yeah. Let me show you." Addy walked them over to a canvas hanging on a side wall. She explained as she walked. "A local artist sketches out a picture on a big canvas, and then members of the community can stop in whenever they're free and give it some color. I have a cart set up with paints and brushes and palettes, and people can kind of do their own thing. Some people choose to just color in sections, and some will get a bit more involved with shading and textures and all that. I wasn't sure how it would go, but it's been popular, and the results are better than I expected. Some of our locals are pretty skilled with a brush, and they bring it all together."

Lindsay examined the canvas and watched as an older woman used careful brushstrokes to fill in the trunk of a tree. Lindsay's fingers itched to pick up a brush, but she suspected Jeremy wouldn't want to sit and watch. And she couldn't see him getting involved; art had never been his thing.

"That's great," she said after a moment. "I'll have to see if I can find time to stop by and work on it. When did you say the classes were?"

Addy handed her a couple of flyers, and Lindsay folded them and put them in her purse. She would look at them later, when she had more time. Maybe her parents would be willing to watch the kids so she could participate in one. Or stop by and work on the mural. Now that Emma had planted the seed, Lindsay found herself anxious to get started.

"Thank you so much," she said to Addy. "We'll be back in an hour to get Emma."

"See you then!"

Jeremy had spent the last few minutes looking around with a perpetual scowl on his face. But at least he hadn't been complaining or grumbling, for which she was grateful.

"Thank you for behaving in there," Lindsay said when they were back on the sidewalk. "I appreciate your humoring me."

"Whatever."

"So, since you nixed the game idea, what do you want to do?"

Jeremy shrugged. "I guess we can play a game. I don't have any other ideas."

"Okay. Maybe next time we can bring a game with us and play on one of the tables in the park or something, so we don't have to drive back to the house."

"Whatever."

Lindsay resisted the urge to roll her eyes. "This weekend I was thinking maybe we could go to a museum or something. There's a science center in Hartford that's supposed to be pretty good. I thought you would like that."

"We could do that."

Lindsay smiled to herself. That almost sounded like enthusiasm.

Chapter 20

Now that they had decided to take a break from the motel, Sylvie was almost giddy with anticipation. Should they take a vacation? Go on day trips? Start new hobbies that didn't involve staying in one place?

They didn't have money to blow on frivolous expenses, but the library had passes that could get them into several attractions around the state. Heck, even going for a long drive would be a treat at this point. Maybe the kids would like to go down to the beach. Sylvie wasn't much of a beach person, but it had been so long it might be nice.

As long as they could afford it, the possibilities were endless. And perhaps stepping back from it all would offer some perspective, and they could actually figure out what they should do.

Lindsay and the kids were coming over after Emma's art class, so Sylvie busied herself making a salad and whipping up a batch of cookies. She was curious to hear how the last couple of days had gone. Phone conversations had been brief, and Sylvie had sensed awkwardness since she had mentioned taking a break. Perhaps Lindsay was having trouble processing. After all, she wasn't the one who'd been stuck in place for four years. Sylvie hoped Lindsay would eventually come to understand her reasoning. And if not, well it was her life. She needed to take back control of it.

Lindsay pulled into the motel parking lot at around three. It was too early for dinner, but she was anxious to discuss the situation with the motel more in depth. She was trying to understand but failing to see the logic in cutting off potential income, however small, when money was already tight. Hopefully spending time with her parents would clarify things a bit.

As she was parking, Lindsay saw a man taking pictures of the outside of the motel. Apparently, the kids noticed, too.

"What's that guy doing?" asked Jeremy, temporarily putting down his video game.

"I have no idea. But I'm going to find out. You guys go inside. If you see Pops, send him out."

The kids ran into the motel office, and Lindsay got out of the car to greet him. When the man saw her, he walked over, grinning broadly.

"Great little place you've got here," he said, putting away the phone he had been using to take pictures and extending one hand to Lindsay.

"Um, thanks?" Lindsay replied, taking his hand reluctantly.

"This is your place, right?" he asked, gesturing toward the building.

"My parents', actually."

The man nodded. "Gotcha. Well, my name is Christopher Parker." He handed her a business card. "I represent a client over in Westin who is very interested in your parents' property."

Lindsay looked at the card. Christopher here was apparently a real estate agent. Had her parents put the motel up for sale already? Without even mentioning it to her? "And, uh, how did your client learn about my parents', uh, property?"

The man flashed her another grin. "Let's just say he has his eye on lots of these little places around the state. Checks on them once in a while. He saw the reservations had been put on pause indefinitely and thought it might warrant a conversation. Are your parents looking to sell?"

Well, at least it hadn't been listed yet. Lindsay wasn't as in the dark as she had feared. "Nothing has been decided yet." She attempted to give Christopher his card back, but he held up a hand in refusal.

"Keep it. My client is very motivated. If your parents do decide to sell, he'll make them a very nice offer. Just give me a call." He tipped his head in farewell. "It was a pleasure meeting you, Ms. —"

"Thank you. Have a nice day, Mr. Parker."

He grinned again. "You, too." Then he got into the only other car currently in the parking lot, a shiny black Mercedes.

Lindsay rolled her eyes. She never trusted men who smiled so much. Her husband had been like that in the beginning: all charming and slick. She had learned her lesson. But, ultimately, it wasn't her call. So she tucked the card in her pocket and turned, just in time to see her father stepping out of the office.

"Who was that?"

Lindsay fished the card out of her pocket and handed it to him. "Realtor. Said he has someone who wants to buy the motel if you're selling."

"Huh." Ed glanced at the card, then put it in his pocket without another word about it. "You coming in? Mom won't let me have a cookie until you've been served."

Lindsay smiled. "Ah, I see. You didn't come out to save your daughter. You just wanted cookies."

Ed put one arm around her shoulders. "I know you can handle yourself. But those cookies won't eat themselves."

"I guess you're right." Lindsay put her head on her dad's shoulder, and they walked into the motel. She wondered what he thought about the realtor. Did he want to sell the motel? Was he on board with taking a break, or had that all been her mother? Sometimes she wished her father didn't keep his cards so close to his chest. She would love to know how he really felt. Maybe tonight's conversation would shed some light.

Chapter 21

The event committee met in the program room at the library. Jake knew it would have been tight in his apartment, and Cherise, the children's librarian who was also on the committee, had graciously reserved them the space.

Jake was nervous. He didn't usually present to groups of people. He was better one-on-one. But he needed more people to bring his vision to life. So he did his best to push down his nerves.

The other members chatted amongst themselves until Jake saw everyone had arrived. Taking a deep breath, he stood up and cleared his throat. When the room quieted down, he attempted a smile.

"Hello, everyone. Welcome. Thank you so much for coming tonight. I, uh, know I spoke to you all individually about this, but I thought it would be helpful to kind of give an overview of what I was thinking, and then we could start discussing." Jake paused and took another deep breath.

"So, as you all know, I am a police officer here in town. And over the last couple of months, I've noticed a bit of an uptick in petty crime. Speeding, small-scale robberies. And at least some of the crimes, if not all, have been linked to our younger residents, teens ages sixteen to eighteen." Jake could feel his nerves settle as he warmed to his subject. "Now, the police can handle the catching and pun-ishing part, but I got thinking about how we could try and stop it before it even started. And I suspect that at least part of the problem is a lack of activities for this demographic. The library and parks and rec department do a great job for the younger kids, but I know it's notoriously difficult to get teens interested. So I thought maybe an event that would appeal to them could offer an alternative."

Sandeep, a doctor who had an office in town, raised a hand. "Sorry to interrupt, Jake, but if you're talking about a single event, I fail to see how that would keep them out of trouble the rest of the time."

Jake nodded. "I admit, the more I thought about things, the more I wondered the same thing. I thought we could discuss having multiple events, or getting the teens involved in the planning and set-up. Or both."

Cherise put up her hand next. "While I love the idea of getting the teens involved, I'm afraid the kids who volunteer to help aren't the ones who are likely to cause trouble in the first place."

"A valid point. Any suggestions?"

"Well," Cherise continued, "during the school year, high school kids have to fulfill a certain number of community service hours to be able to graduate. That won't help you over the summer, though."

"True, but I like your thinking about the community service hours. It's not uncommon for juvenile delinquents to have to fulfill community service as part of their consequences, especially for minor violations. I could bring it up with my chief. Thanks for the idea." He made a note on the pad of paper he had set in front of him.

Conversation then shifted to the type of event, how many, and when they would be held. By the time they decided to end for the night, Jake's head was swimming. They hadn't actually decided much, but he had appreciated getting others' input. And he had learned two things: putting together an event, especially with a group of people who hadn't worked together before, would be incredibly difficult, if not impossible, before the end of summer. And they would really benefit from having teens on the committee, to help them figure out what would draw fellow teens in and make them actually want to participate. But where would they get teens? He would have to discuss the community service idea with the chief. He wondered how Sherry was doing with the robberies case. Had she found any leads?

As Jake pulled into his parking spot back home, he went through the discussions of the evening over and over in his mind. It wasn't until he went to open the front door of the building that he noticed something looked different.

Jake stepped back and looked over the front of the building. Smiley faces had been painted on all the first-floor windows, including the glass door. He sighed. Looked like he had another crime to investigate.

Chapter 22

"No, your building wasn't the only one hit, and no, I don't have any leads," Sherry said as Jake walked into the office the next day. "And no, I don't have leads on the robberies, either." She sounded frustrated. "I can't believe we're being outsmarted by a band of hooligans. And yes, I'm convinced it's a band since there's no way a single vandal could have tagged all those buildings in such a short amount of time. All together five buildings were hit. I'll get you the addresses. I was hoping you could check with businesses while you're on your rounds, see if anyone caught anything on camera. Times like this I sure wish we had traffic cams in town."

"You got it."

Jake was grateful for having something proactive to do. As much as he believed Sherry could get things done, he hated waiting on others. He hated having nothing to do even more. He just hoped they could finally catch a break.

Unfortunately, as he had encountered when investigating the robberies, he struck out when asking about camera footage. One business had a camera that caught part of the sidewalk, but all he could see that could potentially be relevant was a blurry image of a hooded sweatshirt. Frustrated, Jake decided to head to the gym after work. He really needed to punch something.

Maybe it wasn't just boredom that was getting these kids to act out. Maybe they needed a physical outlet, for energy or whatever. Maybe if they had a gym in town, or a karate place or something. Not that he was prepared to open either said establishment, but they could invite businesses in surrounding towns to put on demonstrations or sponsor booths at the community event they were planning. Transportation could be an issue, but, as evidenced from the speeding frenzy that spring, at least some of them had cars.

Jake thought back to all those speeding tickets he had written back then. They may not have any leads on the robberies or vandalism, but they had names and addresses from those speeding tickets. And if, as he suspected, it was the same group of teens who had escalated their efforts, maybe keeping tabs on those speeders could lead them to the current culprits. It was worth a shot, anyway. He texted Sherry his idea, and she replied she would look into it. At least it was something.

Lindsay looked at the notes, ideas, and plans she had put together for the motel. Even after their initial conversation about taking a break, Lindsay had continued to work on the marketing plan. She had been having too much fun to stop, and the ideas just kept pouring out of her. Now, after the conversation with her parents the night before, she wondered if it had been a waste of time after all.

Lindsay felt bad for her mom. Her dad could keep himself busy, find maintenance that needed doing or projects to take on. But her mom thrived on socialization, and the paltry business that trickled in just wasn't enough. Lindsay tried encouraging her to get away from the motel, even if just for a few hours, but Sylvie had said she felt guilty being away from the office without someone to watch the desk. Ed could handle questions or maintenance issues, but he wasn't great with making reservations or dealing with the computer system. What if they lost business?

From that perspective, Lindsay could understand her mom's desire to shut things down for a bit. If nothing else, she needed to breathe, to be around other people and live a little. Lindsay just wondered if Sylvie would want that freedom to be permanent. Would they call that slick real estate guy and sell to the client who would supposedly make it worth their while?

Lindsay looked at her notes again. She would miss the motel. It was such a big part of her childhood. She had so many memories of running around the grounds, meeting interesting people, and her mom smiling. It hadn't always been easy, but it had never been dull. And her mom had been so happy. She wished she could bring that smile back to her face.

Turning on her laptop, Lindsay pulled up the website she had been working on. The realtor's visit had given her the push to take pictures of her own, and she had gotten some great shots with the sun setting in the background. She uploaded them now and fiddled around with them on the site. From the right angle, the motel looked appealing, like it did back in its heyday. If they spruced things up, maybe added some more landscaping to the outside and updated decor on the inside, it wouldn't be so bad. She suspected even that would be outside her parents' budget, though. She had taken another look at the books the night before, and things were bad. If they didn't sell, she wasn't sure how long they would even be able to survive. There was no money for improvements.

Unless Lindsay chipped in the money. But that was out of the question. Her own budget was tighter than she would like, and she dreaded her next credit card statement, after everything she had spent money on while being in Pine Valley. Where would she get the money to fix up the motel? Take out a loan?

You could sell the house. The thought came out of nowhere. But it was ridiculous. She couldn't sell the house. Where would they live? Stay here? Move into the motel? Yeah, that would go over well. The kids didn't even want to spend the summer in Pine Valley, never mind move here permanently. And space was tight for now. They would need a bigger place, which would mean more money she didn't have. And she would probably lose her job, since her boss had only agreed to working remotely for the summer. So she would lose her source of income. Not to mention what would her ex say? She may have full custody of the kids, but Kyle would still need to approve their moving across state borders. Not that he saw them now anyway. What difference would it make to him? But legally she had to let him know.

Lindsay rubbed her face with both palms. She had started the summer with a lot to figure out, and now, instead of figuring those things out, she was adding more dilemmas to her plate. She was moving in the wrong direction.

Still, it had been a pretty good day with the kids. Emma had loved her art class, and Jeremy had actually smiled a couple of times while they were playing their game. Only because he was kicking her butt, but still. He had been enjoying himself without a screen. Now they were having a bit of screen time before they headed to the park for a picnic. Lindsay had had to push a bit for them to go with it, but not as much as she had expected. Maybe they had just needed to get used to the idea of doing other things. They both had a coding class that afternoon at the library, and then they were heading to a drive-in movie a couple of towns over. It had been years since Lindsay had gone to a drive-in movie. She hadn't known they still existed.

Okay, technically coding and a movie were screens. But it was different somehow. Learning new things, connecting with other people, connecting together as a family, they were more meaningful. Not perfect, but getting there. Maybe she was moving in the right direction after all.

Chapter 23

Having a guest made all the difference in the world. Seeing people moving around the property, having someone besides Ed to greet in the morning, being able to make small talk, Sylvie loved it all. And, she had to admit, if she had more guests, she would be less inclined to want to leave the motel. But things were just too discouraging as they were. She couldn't rely on steady guests, and the project to revive the motel was just too monumental. And beyond the scope of what they could do right now. Sylvie would be grateful for the guests they had, look forward to her break, and accept that that might be the end.

Lindsay was taking the kids to the Connecticut Science Center for the day on Saturday, but she had stopped by before they headed up. She had brought plants of all things, suggesting that Ed spend the day planting them around the front of the motel. He, of course, had thought it was a brilliant idea. Sylvie hadn't seen the point. Lindsay tried explaining that regardless of if they decided to sell or keep the motel, making the outside look friendly and inviting would benefit them. Ed had grinned and patted her on the shoulder, then started lugging the pots out of the car and deciding where they should be planted.

Sylvie wouldn't complain. He was happy, and it kept him busy. The weather was relatively mild and dry, and she thought she might spend some time outside, too. Maybe she would even help him with the planting. Wouldn't that be interesting? It had been a long time since she had gotten her hands dirty with anything other than bread flour. And maybe if she seemed interested in what he was doing he would be more open to discussing the motel situation and what they should do on their break. She couldn't be the only one to decide.

She did wonder how Lindsay had bought the plants. She knew money was tight on her end, too. And she didn't like the thought of Lindsay spending her own money to pay for things at the motel. It was a parent's job to take care of their kids, not the other way around. But what was done was done, she supposed. Now she just had to decide if she wanted Lindsay to take on the other suggestion she had made.

Lindsay wanted to watch the desk at the motel one day that week so Sylvie could go out and do something with the kids. She supposed Ed would participate, too. Lindsay said she could work anywhere, and it would give Sylvie and Ed the chance to have fun. Sylvie had to admit the idea was tempting. They hadn't had help in the office for so long. But why was Lindsay acting as if nothing had changed? Sylvie would have plenty of time soon enough to do whatever she wanted. Why take a day off now?

Too many decisions, that was the problem. Too many life-altering decisions. Sylvie liked things to go smoothly. She wasn't afraid of hard work, but she liked to know what to expect. She wanted to be able to plan ahead. But barring the ability to do that right now, she would do what she could with what she had. And apparently what she had was plants that needing planting.

Now that the thought had occurred to her, Lindsay couldn't get it out of her head. The thought of moving back to Pine Valley was appealing in many ways. The kids had started settling down, she felt less frantic than she had in ages, and they had actually started doing things together as a family. And it had only been a week! A week ago, she had felt hopeless, convinced she was a horrible mother who had made a mistake in coming back here. Now she felt like they might actually have a future.

But it had been a week. She was on vacation; the kids were on summer break. There was no way this would continue all summer. And if she even suggested they stay permanently? All progress would be lost, and her kids would hate her more than before.

So why couldn't she let it go?

Thoughts and ideas kept spinning through her mind as they explored the Science Center. Jeremy was in his element, and he seemed to love everything, from the space section to the hands-on engineering exhibits. Emma seemed to be enjoying herself, too, though she was drawn more toward the nature-themed sections. Lindsay was glad she had splurged on tickets. And on the plants for the motel, though she cringed at the thought of how much they had cost. While she hadn't been wrong to get them, she probably should have held off. At the rate she was going, she would have to sell the house just to pay the credit card bill.

And it had only been a week.

Lindsay sighed. She was dreading going back to work on Monday, remote or not. While she didn't dislike her job, this time away, when she had been able to rediscover her marketing roots, had made her long for something different. But she certainly couldn't afford to leave her job, so not returning to work was not an option.

And neither was moving to Pine Valley.

She doubted there were many job openings for marketing executives around here, and the cost of living wasn't so much less that she could take a pay cut. Heck, the cost of living might even be more. Connecticut wasn't known for being affordable. Though she wouldn't have to work in Pine Valley, even if they lived there. People commuted all the time. She was sure plenty of companies in Hartford were looking for marketing people, and other areas, too. It wasn't unreasonable.

Lindsay sighed again and tried to focus on the exhibits and what the kids were doing. At the moment, they appeared to be trying the hurricane simulator. Watching them squeal in delight as Emma's hair whipped around them made her smile. It had been a long time since she had seen them like this. But why? They had this kind of thing in Pennsylvania, too. Why didn't they ever try any of it?

Maybe that was the real problem. It wasn't where they were located; it was the effort she was putting in, the time they were spending together. Why couldn't they do this back home? And if her parents sold the motel, they could even move closer. They wouldn't have to be so far apart. It was something to consider, anyway.

Lindsay snapped a picture of the kids before they exited the simulator, then put away her phone. She wondered what it would be like to work the desk at the motel. Assuming her mother took her up on the offer, that is. She wondered if she would get any insight, if the experience would have her looking at the situation differently. Either way, she was looking forward to it: a change of pace, trying something she hadn't done in ages. And maybe the time on her own would help her settle the argument she kept having with herself.

Chapter 24

Sherry had pulled the info for all speeding tickets over the last two weeks for drivers under twenty. There were twenty-three all together, with several for repeat offenders. Jake would start with those. While he couldn't really stalk them, he would see what he could do in terms of keeping an eye on them. He was off duty this weekend, but first thing Monday morning he was going to see what he could find out.

Days off were usually filled with errands, laundry, and whatever cleaning he had to get done. If the weather cooperated, he would go for a hike. If it didn't, he would stay inside and play video games. Sometimes he would meet up with a few coworkers at the bar, or hang out with friends, but many of his friends had families of their own, so they were usually occupied with other things. The days were pretty low key, and, if he was honest, they tended to drag.

By the time Monday rolled around, Jake was glad to be back at work.

Just after lunch, a call came through on the radio about another vandalism report. Great, just what they needed.

"Copy. What's the address?"

"Pine Valley Motel."

Jake sighed. "On my way."

Everything looked in order when he approached, but he could see the woman he had met on the trails hovering near one corner of the building, so he suspected the situation was just out of view.

"Hey," he said as he approached her. Was it Leslie? No, Lindsay. And she did not look happy, though he couldn't blame her. "What seems to be the trouble?"

Lindsay sighed and gestured for him to follow her as she went around to the side of the building. As he turned the corner, Jake could see more faces painted on the side of the building. This time, though, instead of smiling, they were frowning. Was that significant in some way?

"Any idea when it happened?"

Lindsay shook her head. "I can't be sure. I thought I heard something earlier, but it could be unrelated. I was just taking a walk around after lunch and happened to see it."

"So you didn't see anything suspicious? No one lurking around the premises? Spray cans left behind?"

Lindsay shook her head again. "No, sorry."

"Okay. I'm going to search the perimeter, see if anything got tossed in the woods or the dumpster."

"Okay."

Lindsay watched Jake head toward the woods, then she sighed again and headed back to the office. Of all the days.

She had expected a calm day. Her parents had let her watch the motel so they could enjoy a leisurely breakfast in town and do whatever they wanted for a few hours before picking the kids up before lunch. Jeremy was in the basketball program, and Emma was at her art camp, and she was back to work. It should have been smooth sailing. Her parents were going to take the kids to lunch and see what they wanted to do. And now this. Should she call them? She was thinking "no." It wasn't like they could do anything about it at this point. Why ruin their day?

At least it was on the side of the building. She could break it to them gently rather than have them see it as soon as they pulled in. Though they did usually park at the back of the building... Which side did they use? It must be the other side, right? The vandalized side was closer to the woods.

Lindsay was back at the desk, trying to get some work done, when Jake entered the office a while later. He carried an evidence bag that held a can of spray paint, and he held it up to show her.

"I found this in the woods. I'm going to take it with me to check for prints. No luck finding anything else, but hopefully this will offer a lead. This wasn't an isolated incident, so I don't think it was personal. I don't expect the vandal to return."

"Okay." Not an isolated incident? What did that mean? Who was going around Pine Valley vandalizing buildings? She had always thought of it as a sweet, law-abiding town. Of course, things could happen anywhere. But still. How many incidents had there been?

"Do you by any chance have cameras monitoring the outside of the building?"

Lindsay nodded. "A couple, but they're focused on the front of the building, or the back where room entrances are located. I don't think they would show the side, but you're welcome to check."

Lindsay showed Jake where the security system equipment was. She should really get back to work, but she had to know. He rewound the recording to the beginning of the day, then played it at an accelerated speed while checking for movement. Lindsay could see her arriving, her parents leaving. No other traffic, since they had no guests. Wait, what was that? In the corner?

Jake had seen it, too, and he rewound and replayed it more slowly. There was definitely someone on the property, and they were heading to the side of the building. It was so hard to make out any details, though. Her parents' system wasn't exactly the newest model, and it had limited features on top of somewhat grainy video. But something about the figure was familiar, which was ridiculous. She didn't know anyone in Pine Valley.

Jake rewound and replayed the video multiple times, trying to zoom in, play it more slowly, try to catch any details. The shirt. That's what was familiar. She knew that shirt. Jeremy had one just like it. Wait. Had he been wearing that this morning?

Lindsay felt her entire body get weak. Her hands started shaking. "I think you might have been wrong about it not being personal. I think that's my son."

Chapter 25

Jake could only stare at Lindsay. "Are you sure?"

Her eyes were still glued to the screen. "I can't be positive, but I know he has a shirt like that, and I'm pretty sure he was wearing it this morning."

"Do you know where he is now?"

"He – he was supposed to be at a basketball thing, and then my parents were going to pick him up. They should have him by now, and they haven't called to say there was any problem, so I assume he's with them."

"Can you call them?"

"Uh, yeah." Lindsay reached for her phone on the front desk and tapped a few things on her screen.

Jake could see Lindsay's hands shaking, and his heart went out to her. He really hoped she was wrong, but, at the same time, it would be a big break in the case. But they had only been in town for a little while. And Jake knew her son couldn't have been acting alone. How could he have gotten wrapped up in this mess so quickly?

"Hi, Mom, it's me." Lindsay's voice broke the silence that had fallen in the office. "Well, um, something happened, and I hate to mess up your day off, but do you think you could bring the kids to the motel?" She paused. "Okay, no problem. I'll see you soon." She disconnected the call and turned to Jake. "They were about to play mini golf over in Westin, so they'll have to drive back. Shouldn't be too long, though. They hadn't started playing yet."

Jake nodded. "Okay. Do you mind if I hang out while we wait?"

"No, that's okay. Um, do you want anything? Coffee or something?" Her hands were still shaking.

"No, I'm good. I'll head back outside and see if there's anything I missed."

"Okay."

Jake was pretty confident he hadn't missed anything, but he didn't want to hover. He couldn't imagine what Lindsay was feeling right now. He suspected she would want some time to compose herself before they had to confront her son, and he needed to prepare himself, as well. He was not looking forward to what was next.

Lindsay saw her parents' car pull into the parking lot, and Jake reentered the office at almost the same time as Sylvie did. Sylvie looked frantic, and her eyes bounced from Lindsay's to Jake's and back again.

"What is going on? Why are the police here? Was there a burglary?"

Lindsay took a deep breath. "No, no burglary. But something happened. We need to wait for Jeremy to come inside."

"Jeremy? What's he got to do with it? He was with us."

Ed came in then, with the kids behind him. Lindsay's eyes went to Jeremy. His ears were red, but his eyes were glued to his phone. Typical. She looked at Jake.

He cleared his throat. "Well, this is a bit of an unusual circumstance, based on the order of events, but I suppose we should start by identifying the crime."

"Crime!" Sylvie was still looking frantic. "What crime?"

"If you would all like to follow me," Jake said in response, leading the way outside. He walked to the side of the building.

Sylvie gasped when she saw the faces painted on the windows on the side of the building. "When did this happen? Who would do such a thing?"

"I noticed it around lunchtime, when I took a walk," Lindsay replied. "So I called the police, and Jake here came out to investigate."

"I found a can of spray paint in the woods, and then reviewed the security footage to see if I could gain any insight into what had happened."

Lindsay's eyes stayed glued on Jeremy. He was still looking down at his phone, but she could see him tense up when Jake mentioned the security footage. He probably figured there hadn't been anything tying him to the crime. She blinked away tears. She couldn't believe her son had been involved in a crime. And involving her parents' motel. What had he been thinking?

"I've been meaning to update the security system," Ed interjected then. "I know it's not the greatest quality."

"No worse than others I've seen in town, and, while the image was a little grainy, we did catch something that offered a clue."

"The suspect was wearing your shirt, Jeremy," Lindsay said then, her voice quiet.

He looked up to meet her gaze. He seemed to be battling with himself, unsure if he should lash out in anger or break down in tears.

Sylvie, Ed, and Emma all turned to look at Jeremy, mouths hanging open.

"Vandalism is an act of criminal mischief," Jake said. "And we take it seriously."

"What if we don't press charges?" Ed asked.

"Unfortunately, it's not just up to you. Vandalism is considered a public offense, and, considering there have been other acts of vandalism around town recently that bear a striking resemblance to this act, we will need to investigate."

"What does that mean?" Lindsay asked, turning to Jake.

"It means I need to bring Jeremy into custody." He met Lindsay's gaze, and she could see sympathy in his eyes. "I'm sorry." Jake turned to Jeremy. "Jeremy, based on the evidence we have seen, I'm going to need to bring you down to the station. I'd like to ask you some questions. You have the right to remain silent. And you have the right to a lawyer if you want one. What happens next will be up to a judge."

What followed passed in a blur. Before she knew it, Jeremy was in the back of the police cruiser, and she was following in her car. Emma would stay with her parents until they knew what was going to happen. Lindsay didn't even know what to think. She had never expected to be in this position. She knew Jeremy could be rash, impulsive, could lash out when upset. But something like this seemed so deliberate, calculated. Where had he gotten the spray paint? Why hadn't he been at the community center, where he was supposed to be? How had he even gotten this idea?

There had to be some logical explanation, and she really hoped Jake could get to the bottom of it. Not to mention, he had said there were other acts of vandalism. She doubted Jeremy had had opportunity to do those, so he couldn't be involved. Could he?

Lindsay wiped tears from her eyes as she tried to focus on her driving. Oh, Jeremy. What did you do?

Chapter 26

Sylvie watched the cars leave the parking lot, then followed Ed and Emma into their apartment. She couldn't make sense of what had just happened. Jeremy had been arrested? For vandalizing the motel? It seemed so unlikely, so impossible. Why? How?

Today was supposed to be a good day, a carefree day. She and Ed had had a wonderful morning, having a leisurely breakfast at the cafe, taking a walk around town. She had felt freer than she had in a long time. They had picked up the kids, taken them to lunch at the diner. Then they had driven into Westin to play mini golf. Nothing had seemed off. The kids had been glued to their screens for the most part, though Ed had insisted they put them away at lunch. Maybe Jeremy had been a bit more subdued? She had taken it as defiance for losing his precious phone. But maybe his mind had been elsewhere.

Sylvie sighed. She felt drained, exhausted. She didn't know how she would be able to rest until this whole mess was figured out, but she felt like she needed to lie down.

Ed looked up when she entered the living room. His brow furrowed. "You feeling okay, Sylvie?"

Sylvie shook her head. "How could I be? But I think I just need to lie down for a bit. All this drama has worn me out."

"Okay." She could feel him watching her as she went into the bedroom.

He came to check on her about ten minutes later with a glass of water. "How are you doing?"

Sylvie sat up to accept the water, but the room swayed around her, and she fell forward. Ed caught her.

"Sylvie?" There was panic in his voice.

"I think – " Sylvie tried to calm her own panic as she swallowed. "I think you need to call an ambulance, Ed."

Lindsay watched her precious baby boy get fingerprinted. Though not always necessary in juvenile situations, with the can of spray paint in evidence, as well as evidence already in police possession that they believed was linked to the string of vandalism, they needed to know if Jeremy could be tied to any of it. And that meant comparing fingerprints.

While that was getting processed, Lindsay and Jeremy sat in a room that she was sure would be used for questioning. She didn't even know what to say to him. And he seemed to feel the same. His phone had been taken away, so he just sat, staring at either the floor or the table in front of them. He hadn't succumbed to tears yet, but Lindsay could tell they were near the surface.

He wasn't a bad kid. Lindsay knew that. He had a short fuse, and he could do things he definitely shouldn't, but he wasn't a bad kid. If she had to guess, she would say he probably thought he was doing something that was no big deal. Paint could be washed or scraped off, right? He wasn't breaking anything or hurting anyone. It could have been a whole lot worse. But this was pretty bad.

Jake stepped into the room after several minutes and took a seat across from them. Taking a deep breath, he put a folder on the table.

"Well, Jeremy. Your fingerprints matched those found on the can of spray paint that had been in the woods by the motel, and that paint matched the paint found on the windows at the motel."

Jeremy's shoulders sagged, and Lindsay could see a single tear roll down his cheek.

"Your fingerprints did not, however, match those found on other evidence we had in possession, and the paint was a different color than that used in the other acts of vandalism. At this time, we have nothing to tie you to those crimes, though we cannot rule it out, either. I spoke with my supervisor, and unless additional crimes have been committed, we don't feel it's necessary to bring this specific incident to court, though you will need to attend a meeting with the review board to determine consequences."

Lindsay released a breath and felt her shoulders relax. No court was good, right?

"While we are determining the best course of action for dealing with this incident, I was hoping to ask you a few questions. I will again remind you that you have the right to remain silent, and you have the right to have a lawyer present."

Lindsay looked at Jake. "Should we have one? If it's not going to court, I mean?"

"That is not my call to make. I cannot sway you one way or the other. Since the case isn't going to court at this time, if you choose to have a lawyer, it would be at your expense, or you can seek legal aid. Public defenders are only appointed if deemed necessary when a case goes to court."

Lindsay turned to Jeremy. "Jeremy? I have never been in this position before, and I don't know what we should do."

Jeremy met her gaze, looking so lost her heart broke. Tears welled in her eyes, and she turned back to Jake.

"Can I think about it? And could I get info about legal aid? Just in case?"

"No problem. Let me see what I've got. I'll be right back."

Jake left the room, and silence fell again. After a moment, Lindsay's cell phone rang.

"Oh, geez. Sorry. Let me just – " Lindsay pulled out her phone and looked at it. It was her dad's number. There was no way he would be calling unless it was an emergency. She answered the call. "Dad? What happened?" Being in an interior room of a police department was not great for reception, and Ed's voice kept breaking up. Lindsay stood up. The call disconnected. "Jeremy, that was Pops. I – " She felt ready to burst into tears. She didn't want to leave her little boy alone, but she had to know what was going on. "I'll be right back, okay?"

Lindsay left the room and went out into the impossibly bright sunshine. What else could go wrong today? She called her father back. He answered after one ring.

"Lindsay?"

"Dad! What happened? I couldn't hear you. We were inside the police station."

Ed's voice was still breaking, but it had nothing to do with the reception. "Your mother. She –." Lindsay heard a muffled sob. Was her dad crying? He never cried. "She's in the hospital. They think she had a heart attack."

Lindsay collapsed onto the sidewalk. The tears flooded down her cheeks. "What? Is she going to be okay?"

"I don't know. They're running some tests. I just –. I don't know what to do. I can't lose her."

"I know, Dad. I know. I –. I can't leave right now. Jeremy's fingerprints were found on the spray paint, and I have to decide if we want a lawyer, and –. Where's Emma?"

"She's with me. We're at the hospital."

"Okay." Lindsay had never felt so torn. But she had to be here for Jeremy. There was no way she could leave him alone. "I'll get there when I can. Let me know if you get any updates."

She disconnected the call and tucked her phone back into her purse, then she wiped her cheeks and took a deep breath. Her thoughts were swirling, and she didn't know how to feel. But one thing kept rising to the surface.

They never should have come back to Pine Valley.

Chapter 27

Jake grabbed a business card for a local legal aid office, jotted down some additional information, then returned to the interrogation room. He was surprised to find Jeremy alone.

"Where's your mom?" he asked.

Jeremy shrugged. "She got a phone call."

"Oh, okay. I'll wait until she gets back. Be back in a bit."

Jake stepped back out of the interrogation room. He didn't want there to be any chance of perceived impropriety. When he saw Lindsay re-enter the station, he began approaching, then paused. She looked upset. Was it just the situation with Jeremy, or had something else happened? He watched her take a deep breath, square her shoulders, and walk back toward the room that held Jeremy. He stopped her before she entered.

"It's not your fault, you know."

Lindsay looked up at him, confusion on her face. "Excuse me?"

"I know you had been having concerns, about failing as a parent or whatever. You mentioned it that day on the trail. But it's not your fault this happened."

Lindsay's lower lip wobbled. "Thanks. That's not why I stepped away, though."

"Jeremy said you got a phone call. Is everything else okay?"

He could see tears welling in her eyes, and she shook her head. "No. My mom is in the hospital. They think she had a heart attack."

"Oh my god." He wanted to put his arms around her, but he wasn't sure how that would be received – or perceived by his coworkers. "I am so sorry. Do you have to go?"

Lindsay shook her head again. "No. I have to be here for Jeremy. They're running tests right now. My dad will keep me posted."

"Are you sure?"

She nodded. "I'm sure."

"Okay." He took a deep breath and handed her the card and paper. "This is the legal aid info. I can give you some time to discuss with Jeremy, see what you want to do. You can call legal aid first, if you want. I'll check on you in a little while."

Lindsay took the card and paper, nodded once, and entered the room. Jake sighed. His heart went out to both of them. Jeremy seemed obviously remorseful. It had probably just been a stupid act of rebellion or getting roped into something he didn't fully grasp. One of the first things he wanted to ask was where he had gotten the idea. He knew other people had been involved in the previous incidents. Had Jeremy just heard about them, or had the perpetrators dragged him into it?

Lindsay closed the door behind her and sat next to Jeremy again. She decided that unless he directly asked, she was not going to tell him about the heart attack. She did not need to put any additional burden on him right now. But they did need to decide what to do.

"Okay, so I have the legal aid info, but I'm undecided on if we should have a lawyer here or not. I think it would help a lot to know what actually happened, and if things are going to get even worse."

Jeremy was back to staring at the floor. He was bouncing one knee up and down, and Lindsay had to hold herself back from grabbing the knee to keep it still.

"Jeremy? Did you paint those faces on the motel windows?"

The knee stopped bouncing, but Jeremy didn't respond. After a moment, Lindsay could see his shoulders shaking. Was he crying?

"Jeremy?"

He still didn't answer, so Lindsay scooted her chair closer to his and put an arm around his shoulders. After a moment, his opposite arm came around and grabbed her in a firm hug.

"I'm sorry, Mom," he said after a moment, his voice coming out in choked sobs.

"Oh, honey. What happened?"

"I just want to go home."

"I know. But we can't. We have to deal with this."

"I mean home home. Back to Pennsylvania. I don't want to be here. It sucks. There's nothing to do, and the kids are mean, and –"

Lindsay closed her eyes and took a deep breath. "And what?"

Jeremy sucked in a deep breath. He pulled back and looked at Lindsay with wet eyes. "I was at the basketball thing, right? I figured since I had to be here for the summer, I should at least try and meet people or whatever. But everyone had their groups of friends all set, and the leaders had to get me onto a team, which was embarrassing, especially when no one would pass me the ball. And I don't totally suck. I know sports aren't my thing, but I can be okay when I try. So in the drills and stuff, I was trying. I actually kicked ass at H.O.R.S.E. But they didn't care. So when we stopped for a water break, I just left."

Well, that explained that, at least. But her heart ached for her poor, rejected son.

"Where did you go?"

"I just walked. Saw Gran and Pops at one point, but they didn't see me, so I headed the opposite way. And there were these guys, a little older than me, and they called me over. They asked me my name, and what I was up to. They seemed nice. And I was still mad, and they asked if I wanted to let some of that madness out, so they showed me some graffiti they had done. They said it was great for burning off some steam, and that no one knew it was them, so they couldn't get into trouble. They gave me a can of paint, showed me how to use it. Asked me where I'd like to try. And I was still mad, and I wanted to go home, and I knew Gran and Pops weren't at the motel, so I went there. They said to do the windows, since that could be scraped off. It wasn't permanent damage or whatever. They seemed to know what they were doing."

"Did you do anything else?"

Jeremy shook his head. "No. I swear. I painted the faces, then I drop-kicked the can of paint into the woods. The guys laughed at that. But they patted me on the back and said I probably felt better, and I said I wasn't as mad. They said I should find them if I ever wanted to let off some steam again. And then they left. And I walked back to the rec center so Gran and Pops wouldn't know I had left."

Lindsay released a breath. She hoped that was the whole story. She really did. She wished he hadn't done it in the first place, but it didn't sound malicious, and he obviously regretted it. "Okay. Thank you for telling me. It doesn't sound like we need to drag lawyers into it, so we'll see how we do without one, okay?"

Jeremy's shoulders sagged in apparent relief. "Okay."

"But you will need to tell the police officer what you just told me."

"Can't you just tell him?"

Lindsay shook her head. "No. You did this, and you need to face up to it. For what it's worth, Officer Jake seems like a nice guy. I think it'll be okay."

Jeremy nodded in resignation and sighed. "Okay."

"I'll go see if I can find him so we can get this over with."

Lindsay stepped out of the room, closing the door softly behind her. Taking a deep breath, she looked around the station. Catching Jake's eye on the other side of the room, she gestured to the closed door with her head, then nodded. He was by her side a moment later.

"What did you decide?"

"We will forego the lawyer. And Jeremy's ready to talk."

Chapter 28

When Sylvie woke up, she felt disoriented. She felt cool sheets under her fingers, but something else, too – a kind of clamp on one finger. And there was a beeping near her right ear. What had happened?

She turned to see Ed sitting in a chair by what appeared to be a hospital bed. She was in the hospital? That's when she remembered. Shortly after suggesting Ed call an ambulance, she had passed out. She could only assume the ambulance came and brought her here. But what had happened?

"Ed?" Sylvie's voice was raspy, and her throat was scratchy.

Ed's chin had been resting on his chest, but when she said his name, his head jerked up. "Sylvie?" She could see unshed tears glistening in his eyes. "Oh, honey, are you okay?"

"You tell me. What happened?"

"You had a heart attack. Scared the living daylights out of me. They said it was mild, but it didn't seem mild to me. They ran some tests. We're waiting on the results to see if you'll need surgery."

"Oh my."

"How are you feeling?"

Sylvie tried taking a deep breath. "Tired. Weak. Sore."

"Any pain?"

Sylvie shook her head gently, then wished she hadn't. "Not really. Thirsty, though. Could I have some water?"

Ed poured her a cup of water from the pitcher on the bedside table and held it to her mouth.

Sylvie took a sip, then held up her hand when she was done. Ed put the cup down on the table. "Did they say how long it would take?" Her mouth felt like it was filled with cotton.

"They've been gone a while, so hopefully soon." Ed glanced at the door. "Can I bring Emma in? She was really worried, too."

"Oh, no. Emma. Poor thing. Of course she can come in."

Ed gathered Emma from the hallway and led her into the room. When Emma saw Sylvie, tears began to glide down her cheeks.

"Gran!" Emma ran to the side of the bed and wrapped her arms around Sylvie.

"Gentle, Emma," Ed reminded. "She's still weak."

"Oh, Emma. I'm okay." Sylvie patted the untethered hand on Emma's back for a moment, until Emma stood up and wiped her cheeks.

Ed cleared his throat. "Emma here might have actually saved your life, you know."

Sylvie looked at Emma in surprise. "Really? What happened?"

Emma's cheeks reddened, and she looked down to the floor in embarrassment.

Ed continued. "I called the ambulance as soon as I could, but when you passed out, I didn't know what to do. It was Emma who thought it might be your heart, and she started doing CPR. I don't know where she learned a thing like that."

"I took a babysitters course a while back. That was part of it," Emma said quietly.

"The EMTs said it greatly improved your chances." Ed turned to look at Emma and put an arm around her. "I'll never forget it." He kissed the top of her head.

Sylvie smiled and reached for Emma's hand. Squeezing it, she said, "thank you, sweetie. I'll never forget it, either."

A knock on the doorframe broke up the emotional scene, and a doctor holding a clipboard entered the room. "Glad to see you're awake, Sylvie. How are you feeling?"

"Like I had a heart attack."

The man chuckled softly. "Understandable. Any pain?"

"No. Just tired. And I feel weak."

"That's to be expected."

"Ed said you ran some tests. Do I need surgery?"

The doctor shook his head. "It doesn't look like it. From what I can tell, there isn't a blockage, so surgery shouldn't be necessary at this point. Of course, we'll have to monitor things, see how your heart heals. I understand you've had high blood pressure for a while now, and that you've been under a lot of stress?"

That was putting it mildly. "Yes, they've been monitoring my blood pressure. They had me on a low-dose medicine, but I keep forgetting to take it. Stupid, I know."

"Well, not the best move. You'll need to start taking it. And I'll be upping the dose a bit, at least until you're in a better position. Maybe set yourself an alarm so you don't forget to take it. We'll have to take a look at diet and exercise, too, and we'll have to see what we can do about reducing your stress levels."

So much easier said than done. At least she had the time off coming up. They just wouldn't be having any stressful conversations until she was feeling better. But she acknowledged the doctor's evaluation.

"We'll be keeping you in the hospital for a day or so to see how you're doing, and, if all goes well, we can release you Wednesday morning. Sound good?"

"Okay," Sylvie said, swallowing back emotion.

The doctor promised someone would check on her soon, to see if she needed anything, then he left the room.

Sylvie took a deep breath and closed her eyes. What a day. It had started off so promising, and then that whole business with Jeremy. Sylvie's eyes flew open. "Jeremy! What happened with Jeremy?"

The machine beside Sylvie began beeping louder and more insistently.

"Sylvie, you need to settle down," Ed said, just as a nurse came into the room.

"What's going on in here?" the nurse said, glancing at the machine's monitor, then taking Sylvie's wrist to check her pulse. "Are we getting wound up? That won't help your heart, now, will it?" She paused to take the pulse, then released Sylvie's arm. She looked into Sylvie's eyes. "Are your visitors bothering you? Should I have them let you rest?"

"No, no, it's okay," Sylvie assured her. "I just remembered something distressing. I'm okay. Really." Sylvie tried to take more deep breaths to calm herself down. "I'm okay."

The nurse gave her a skeptical look but didn't press the issue. "Okay. I'll be back in a little bit to take your dinner order and run through the plan for the night."

"Okay. Thank you."

The nurse left, and Sylvie turned back toward Ed and Emma. "What's going on with Jeremy?" she asked, trying her best to keep her voice even.

"Lindsay said they took his fingerprints and were able to link him to the graffiti on the motel. I haven't heard anything since. Now that you're awake, I should probably call her to let her know what's going on here, too. I'll see if I can get any updates. I just hate to disturb her. I'm sure they're in the middle of things."

"Maybe just send her a text, let her know what's going on and ask how they're doing. If she's busy, she'll get to it when she can."

Ed took out his phone and tapped out a message to Lindsay. Sylvie could see his hands shaking. Poor Ed. She can't imagine what he must have gone through. She couldn't imagine how she would have felt if the situation had been reversed. And Jeremy... Oh, Jeremy. What was he thinking?

Lindsay heard the notification on her phone just as Jeremy was finishing up his statement. She really wanted to check it, but she needed to be alert to make sure she knew what was going on with Jeremy, too.

"Thank you for letting us know what happened, Jeremy," Jake said. "Do you have names or contact information for the guys who gave you the spray paint?"

Jeremy shook his head. "Not their real names. There were three of them. One called another one 'Jack,' but it sounded like a nickname. He seemed like the one in charge. And another one they called 'Pinky.' I don't remember hearing a name for the last one."

Jake made some notes. "Okay. Do you think you would be able to identify them?"

Jeremy shrugged. "Maybe. We weren't together for very long, and my brain was all messed up, you know?"

"I understand. Where did you first meet up with them?"

"Just on one of the side streets, not too far from the main road. I don't know any of the names, though."

"That's okay. Do you remember any landmarks? Anything that stood out?"

"Not really."

"Okay." Jake made more notes, then put down his pen. "I think that's all I'll need from you today. If you think of anything else, your mom knows how to get ahold of me. In the meantime, I will work on getting a meeting with the review board scheduled. I will let you know when that meeting will be. You'll need to be at that meeting on time, and you'll need to take it seriously. You may need to go over some of the same things we just talked about again. The review board will then decide what your consequences will be. In the meantime, you are free to go."

Lindsay took a deep breath. Finally, they could get out of this place. She turned to look at Jeremy. He looked dejected. "Come on, honey, let's go." She held out her hand for him, and after a moment he took it. She couldn't remember the last time she had held his hand, this little boy who was now as tall as she was.

They walked out of the station together, Jeremy's head hanging and his sneakers scraping against the floor. When they stepped outside, Lindsay closed her eyes and took another deep breath. Then she took out her phone and looked at the message from her father.

"Gran's awake."

Jeremy looked up at her. "What do you mean 'awake'? Why was she asleep?"

"Gran had a heart attack, right after we got here."

Jeremy's mouth fell open, and his face took on a frantic look. "Because of me? I gave Gran a heart attack?"

"No, Jeremy, you did not give Gran a heart attack. She's been under a lot of stress, and she's had high blood pressure for years."

Jeremy's body relaxed, but only slightly. "Is she going to be okay?"

"I hope so. Let me call Pops, then we'll go see her, okay?"

He nodded, and Lindsay called her father back. They caught up on the basics of each other's news, and Lindsay told him they were coming up to the hospital and could discuss more then. After disconnecting, she looked back at Jeremy. "How are you holding up?" she asked.

Jeremy shrugged. "I don't know."

Lindsay nodded in agreement. "I get that. Let's go see Gran."

Chapter 29

Jake watched Lindsay and Jeremy leave, then went to Sherry with his notepad.

"What did you find out?" she asked as she pulled a file folder from the pile on her desk.

"Not a lot, but hopefully something." He filled Sherry in on everything Jeremy had said.

"So we're looking for a Jack and a Pinky, but those aren't their real names."

"And there's a third, unnamed member of the group."

"Did he say how old they were?"

"He said they looked a little older than he was, maybe juniors or seniors in high school."

Sherry sighed. "Well, that's something, I guess. Think he could ID them?"

"He said 'maybe.'"

"Okay, here's what I'm going to do. I'm going to get us a copy of the high school yearbook. We're going to cross-reference names from those speeding tickets and put together a picture line-up. We'll see if Jeremy recognizes anyone."

"Sounds good."

Finally. A possible lead. Jake really hoped Jeremy's memory was up to the task. Even if they couldn't tie the teens to the vandalism, if it was the same group of kids who had committed the robberies, as he suspected, they could get them for those charges. From what Jeremy had said, these kids had no remorse and had acted very deliberately, with premeditation. Jeremy might stay out of the courts for a single act that he had been coerced into, but there was no way these repeat offenders would. The only question was: could they be remediated, or would they end up in juvie? Or worse, tried as adults? Some of their suspects were eighteen, with the others not far behind. It could go either way.

Jake returned the keys to the police cruiser and got ready to go home. He was done for the day, and he was grateful. It had been quite the day. He wanted to work out his aggravation at the gym, grab something to eat, and get to bed early.

As Jake headed to the gym, his thoughts drifted to Jeremy. That was the kind of kid he was trying to save: not perfect, but still open to making better choices. He hoped the older kids could be remediated, as well. Of course he did. But he wanted the ones who were borderline, or starting to dabble with bad choices, to know they had options. They could be more successful and happier – by choosing a straighter path.

He still had to talk to the chief about getting kids eligible for community service to be able to help with his event. He thought Jeremy could be an excellent candidate for the program. But it occurred to him that he didn't want to encourage just the kids who had already committed crimes. He wanted to get to them before they got to that point. Maybe he should delay the event after all, if for no other reason than to bring in all those teens needing community service hours for school, as Cherise had mentioned.

If they could wrap up the open case, maybe he wouldn't feel so pressured to hold the event as soon as possible and he wouldn't mind delaying. Then he could give it the attention it really deserved. Delaying would give them more time to really come up with a plan, to figure out not only the ultimate goal, but how to get there. They needed to determine what kind of event they wanted, how to get teens interested, and how to get teens involved. Would the event be just for teens? Or a big community event, open to everyone? Or did they want to try both?

Jake was feeling ambitious, especially now that they had a lead on the crime spree. And he was feeling more optimistic, rather than pressured. He was looking forward to the next committee meeting on Thursday. Hopefully they could actually start figuring out some details, rather than simply brainstorming and discussing. He had to believe it would all come together. Eventually.

Jeremy's footsteps slowed as they approached Sylvie's room, until Lindsay had to stop and turn to make sure he was even still following her.

"Everything okay?" she asked.

He nodded, but he was almost at a stop at this point. Lindsay waited for him to catch up.

"They already know what happened, so we'll just focus on Gran."

"I know, but I –. I don't think I can face them."

Lindsay put an arm around Jeremy's shoulders. "Do you regret doing it?"

Jeremy nodded again and looked down at the floor. His ears turned red.

"Then tell them that. Say you're sorry. Tell them you're going to clean it up. Promise to never do it again. If you're sincere, they'll believe you. They love you, Jeremy."

"I know. And it was stupid. I don't know what I was thinking."

"You were upset. We all do stupid things when we're upset. All we can hope to do is learn from it and do better next time."

They resumed walking until they reached Sylvie's room. Then Lindsay knocked gently and opened the door.

Sylvie was lying in bed, with Ed and Emma in chairs by her side. She looked pale, but she was smiling, so Lindsay smiled back. "Hey, Mom. How are you feeling?"

"I've been better, but I'm doing okay. Better than I was."

"That's good." Lindsay dragged a couple more chairs over, and she sat down. She turned to look at Jeremy, who was still standing by the door. "Jeremy? Do you want to join us?"

He moved closer to the bed but didn't sit down. Ed, Emma, and Sylvie all looked up at him. Lindsay could see concern in their eyes, but she wondered what Jeremy saw. Would he think they were angry with him?

After a few moments of silence, Jeremy stepped to the edge of the bed and said, with his lower lip trembling, "I'm sorry." His voice came out in a whisper. "I was mad, and it was stupid. And I promise I won't do it again." He was on the verge of tears, and Ed stood up to put his arm around his grandson.

"We forgive you, Jeremy. We're not happy about it, but these things happen. We hope you learned a lesson."

"I did. I promise."

"Good. Then let's see what we can do to move past it, huh?"

"Okay." Jeremy sat down then, and conversation flowed with general small talk and chitchat.

It wasn't until the nurse came in carrying Sylvie's dinner tray that Lindsay thought to look at the time. She gasped when she saw it was after six. She took out her phone and saw missed calls and texts that must have come through after she got into the hospital and silenced her phone. She opened her emails. Message after message from her boss, looking for updates, asking where she was, wanting to know why she wasn't responding.

Lindsay closed her eyes and leaned back in her chair. Her boss had already been reluctant to let her work remotely. Would he let this slide when she explained what had happened? Or would he give her a hard time? After everything that had already happened today, she couldn't lose her job, too.

Excusing herself from the room, Lindsay decided to go outside, where she would have more privacy. Then she took a deep breath and called her boss.

Chapter 30

Lindsay was gone a long time, and by the time she returned, visiting hours were nearly over. They said their good-byes, and then Sylvie was alone with a quiet room. She was grateful they had turned down the volume on the incessantly beeping machine, but at least it would have been something to keep her company. She hadn't been completely alone at night since she and Ed married forty-something years ago. Of course, she supposed she wasn't really alone now. The hospital was filled with other patients, and doctors and nurses keeping an eye on things. Somewhere babies were being born and people were breathing their last breaths. And nurses would be coming in to check on her periodically. She wasn't really alone.

But it felt like she was.

Alone with her thoughts and fears and insecurities. She had almost died today. Her grandson had almost gone to prison. Who knew what was going on with Lindsay. She had returned to the room distracted and pale. Sylvie hoped it wasn't more bad news. She couldn't take much more.

Ed had gotten her a novel and a book of crossword puzzles from the gift shop, but Sylvie left them on the bedside table. She couldn't focus on them just now. Her thoughts were drifting to all the stories she had heard of people with near-death experiences, who used them as a wake-up call to make changes, or to live life to the fullest. They came out of them feeling invigorated, full of passion and enthusiasm for life. Sylvie wondered if that feeling set in right away, or if it took a while. Because right now she was still feeling weak and unsure, scared and alone. Would she feel differently tomorrow? Or the next day? She hoped so.

Should she take this as a sign that it was time to give up the motel? That it had become too much? Too much stress, too much worry? Selling would definitely be easier. But would she feel relieved, or would she miss it? Or both? Was it possible to miss something that you were glad was no longer there?

Sylvie sighed. If they sold, they would probably move closer to Lindsay. That would mean leaving behind everything she knew, everyone she knew. Not that she saw them much these days, but she would be starting over. They didn't have to move, of course, but it would make sense. Lindsay could use the support, and it would be nice to see them more often. But regardless of where they lived, what would she do with herself? The same thing she did now, hang around at home, not doing much of anything? Of course, she would have more freedom, more flexibility. She could go out and do other things, maybe volunteer or join some club or another. She could find new hobbies and interests. They might be able to take the occasional trip, if the sale and the move left them with enough funds to do so. How much *would* they get for it? Maybe they should find out so they could make an educated decision.

Sylvie shifted on the bed to try and get more comfortable. She wondered how much sleep she would get that night. Between the awkward position and her wandering thoughts, she suspected it would be a long night. And they wanted her here all day tomorrow, too. She just wanted to go home. No matter what stress it had caused her, the motel was still home. And she really wished she were there now.

Lindsay brought the kids back to the rental house, picking up fast food on the way. They ate, then went their separate ways to wind down for the night and get ready for bed, leaving Lindsay alone with her thoughts.

Her boss was a nice-enough guy, but he believed work should come first. And he had very high standards for the people who worked for him. Usually, it wasn't a problem. Lindsay had high standards for herself, and she had found ways to maintain them, even when the kids were younger and more demanding. Kyle had been more involved then, albeit reluctantly, and had been able to pinch hit a couple of times when she really couldn't leave work. So when she had disappeared for an afternoon, her boss knew that it was uncharacteristic. But that didn't mean he was happy, especially since she was already working remotely.

Lindsay had explained the situation as best she could, and he had agreed to give her one more chance, but he had made it clear that it would be her last chance. She had missed a client meeting and had already been behind from her vacation. The work was piling up, and soon it would be affecting not only her but the other people on her team.

So, despite the long, trying, exhausting day, Lindsay found herself opening her laptop to try and get some work done. If she could make up at least a little of the time, then tomorrow wouldn't be so bad. She hoped.

She had a presentation to put together, numbers to analyze and compile into charts, and recommendations to make following some advertising tests. But the data swam in front of her, blurring until she rubbed her eyes to try and wake herself up. She didn't want to do this. Not just now, but in general. But what choice did she have?

She had originally set up her workstation on the dining table, but, seeing Jeremy getting settled into bed, Lindsay picked up her laptop and carried it outside to the back deck instead. The air had cooled, and a light breeze blew, bringing peace with it. The sun had set, leaving the only remaining light from her laptop monitor. Lindsay settled herself onto the deck chair and placed the laptop on top of the table, lifting it to set in front of her. She was ready to work.

Focusing wasn't any easier out here, though. She suspected mosquitoes would be attacking her soon enough, but for now the quiet tranquility of the night had her leaning back and closing her eyes. She breathed in the cool night air, relaxed her shoulders, and fell asleep.

Chapter 31

rue to her word, Sherry put together a picture line-up that included the teens with speeding tickets as well as other random kids that were the same age and had similar characteristics. Jeremy had remembered a few vague details – hair color, general height – so she put together a valid selection for him to work with. If none of them looked familiar, they would be back to square one, but at least for now, Jake had hope something would pan out.

Lindsay had indicated she wouldn't be able to bring Jeremy by until after five, but he didn't mind. He was working the late shift that day, and he could spend the earlier part of the day patrolling the center of town and looking out for a group of three teens who looked ready to cause trouble. By the time Lindsay and Jeremy entered the station, Jake hadn't had any luck, but he was more than ready to tackle a line-up. He beckoned Sherry over, then went to greet Lindsay.

She looked terrible, exhausted and drawn.

"How's your mom?" he asked after greeting them.

Lindsay sighed. "Not too bad, all things considered."

"That's good." He turned to Jeremy. "Are you ready?"

Jeremy looked uncertain, but he nodded.

"Okay. We'll be going into the same room we were in before. A detective named Sherry is going to be joining us. She's been working the case, plus some other things that might be related."

They entered the room. Sherry was already seated, but she stood up and introduced herself before gesturing for them all to sit.

"Okay, Jeremy," she said, opening a file folder. "Based on the information you gave us, as well as some information we had previously, we've put together a list of possible suspects. Some are in this stack of photos. I'm going to spread them out so you can get a good look at them. If you recognize any of them from the group of kids who approached you, let us know. But if you don't, that's okay. The important thing is to be as honest as possible."

Jeremy nodded, looking nervous. He fidgeted in his chair, then scooted to the edge of the seat to look at the pictures as Sherry spread them out.

"Take your time, Jeremy," Jake said. "We're not in a hurry here. We're more concerned with accuracy, okay?"

Jeremy looked at the pictures one by one. "Definitely not these two," he said after a minute, pointing to the two pictures on the left side. Sherry removed the pictures. "Or this one."

Jeremy took his time, and Jake was glad that he was taking it seriously. While he had been hoping for a quick, assured confirmation of the suspects, he knew that Jeremy's memory of the incident was a bit hazy.

"This one," Jeremy said after a couple of minutes, pointing to one of the pictures in the middle of the rows. "That's Pinky. I remember he had that weird thing in his ear."

Jake looked down at the picture that Jeremy had pointed to. He didn't recognize the kid, but he hadn't really recognized any of them. He could see how the gauge stuck in the kid's left ear could be distinctive, though.

Sherry took the picture and put it to the side.

"Wait, can you put that picture next to this one?" Jeremy asked.

Sherry did as requested.

"Yeah, I think that's the third one, the one I don't know his name. I remember thinking he and Pinky looked like they could be brothers. See how they both have that hair thing sticking up?"

Jake noted the cowlick that stuck up near the back of each teen's head. And the teens did look like they could be family. Jeremy had a good eye. "Any sign of Jack?"

Jeremy shook his head. "I don't think so."

"No problem. You've done very well, Jeremy. Thank you." Sherry gathered the pictures and tucked them into the folder, leaving the two Jeremy had identified paper clipped on the top of the stack.

"Is that it?" Jeremy asked, looking from Sherry to Jake.

"That's it," Jake confirmed. "You're good to go."

Jeremy's shoulders sagged in relief. "Thanks."

"Thank you," Jake replied. "I'll walk you out."

He led Jeremy and Lindsay to the front door. "I don't have a date with the review board yet, but I should have one in the next couple of days. I'll be in touch when I know more. In the meantime, try not to worry too much. You have cooperated with us and shown remorse for your crime. Both of those things will go a long way with the board."

They said their good-byes, and Jake went back to meet up with Sherry.

"So? How did he do?"

"Well, the two pictures he picked match two of our speeding culprits."

"That's great."

"I'm guessing the third guy, Jack or whatever his name is, is the ringleader. He probably gets the younger kids to do the dirty work. We'll bring these two in and see what we can dig up. I'm not expecting to get them on the vandalism charges unless they confess, but if their prints match any of the stolen goods, we can tie them to that. And, of course, they still have to pay their traffic fines."

Lindsay left the police station and wished she could just go back to the house and crash. She was exhausted. After falling asleep on the deck the night before, she had woken up at about midnight, itchy and stiff. She had dragged herself inside and tried to go back to sleep, but the rest of the night had been mostly spent tossing and turning. She had put in a full day's work, but she knew it wasn't her usual caliber. She had no idea how her boss would react.

But, for now, Jeremy had done what he needed to. While she was working that morning, Jeremy had scraped paint off of the windows at the motel, and washed them all when he was done. Emma had been able to attend her art camp, then she had hung out at the motel with them while Jeremy and Lindsay each finished their tasks. It had been surprisingly relaxed and companionable, despite the fact that Lindsay wished she had been sleeping instead.

They had dropped Emma off at the rental house before she and Jeremy had gone to the police station. Now they were picking her up, then heading back to the hospital to check on Sylvie and give Ed a break. He had been there all day, as soon as the visiting hours had begun. Lindsay suspected he hadn't gotten much sleep the night before, either. It had been a long couple of days.

They drove in silence for a bit before Emma asked, "what do you think Jeremy's punishment is going to be?"

"Shut up, Emma," Jeremy said, pushing her with one hand.

"Hey, it's a valid question. Do you think he'll go to jail?"

"Shut up!" Jeremy's voice was louder, angrier.

"Emma, that is enough," Lindsay scolded from the front seat. "Jeremy won't be going to jail. I don't know what the punishment will be, but he doesn't have to go to court, so there won't be any jail time. My guess would be community service. He probably would have been told to clean the graffiti, but he already did that, so he's a step ahead."

"He wouldn't have to be a step ahead if he hadn't been such an idiot," Emma continued.

"Emma, shut up!" Jeremy yelled again.

"Emma, I said that is enough." Lindsay's voice rose to match the volume of her children. "I am much too tired and too stressed to be dealing with this garbage today. Please cut it out."

Silence fell before Emma asked, "are you going to have a heart attack, too?"

"What?" Lindsay couldn't follow Emma's train of thought. "Why would you think I was going to have a heart attack?"

"Because Gran had a heart attack because she was really stressed. And she got super tired before she passed out."

Lindsay took a deep breath. "No, Emma, I am not going to have a heart attack. I am tired because I did not sleep well last night. I've had a lot on my mind. I'm stressed because of everything that has happened over the last couple of days. But I am healthy. It is normal to be stressed sometimes. It is normal to be tired after a rough night. It doesn't mean I'm going to have a heart attack."

Emma stopped asking questions, but Lindsay could see in the rearview mirror that she was still thinking. Lindsay hoped she didn't need to start worrying about Emma now, too.

Chapter 32

The days were moving both quickly and slowly, Sylvie thought. The hours seemed to drag, but the days passed in a blur. She had been dismissed from the hospital with a new prescription and dietary guidelines, so she was back at the motel, but still undecided about what to do. The new enthusiasm for life she had been hoping for had yet to materialize.

Despite the lack of excitement, however, everything seemed different, off somehow. Though Lindsay and the kids still slept at the rental house, and Emma still had her art camp, they spent most of their time at the motel. Lindsay had taken to getting her work done in the office, and Ed had taken Jeremy under his wing, showing him how to maintain the grounds and take care of any maintenance that needed addressing. Jeremy seemed sullen and withdrawn, but he didn't complain about the work. Maybe he considered it his penance. He wasn't even on his phone as much as he had been.

The days fell into a routine, with Sylvie no longer tied to the office since Lindsay was there, but still feeling unable to leave somehow. She didn't feel strong enough to take walks, despite the doctor's assurance it would be good for her. Yet she didn't feel tired enough to rest. She was left somewhere in between, wanting to be active, but convincing herself she couldn't be. Lindsay had taken over most of the cooking, trying to make meals that followed the new guidelines, but, regardless of how tasty the meals turned out, Sylvie found herself picking at her food, unable to eat more than a few bites.

Lindsay was worried about her mother. Though she had stayed tied to the motel, Sylvie had always been active, moving about the property or their apartment, cooking or baking, working on one project or another to stay busy. These days she seemed a shell of her former self, and between Sylvie and Jeremy, Lindsay didn't know what to do. It didn't help that she was wrapped up in work herself, trying to not only catch up but get ahead. Jake had let them know that the review board that would settle Jeremy's case had set a time for the following week, and Lindsay had no idea how much time the meeting and whatever consequences that resulted would take up. She was already on thin ice and feeling anxious; if she let the situation affect her work anymore, she might have another thing to worry about.

The motel had a guest staying over the weekend, and Lindsay had hoped Sylvie would perk up with the company. But it had been Lindsay who handed over the key and answered questions while Sylvie stayed in the apartment. While Lindsay had wanted to be on hand to help her mother, she began to wonder if her presence was doing more harm than good. Would Sylvie be more active if she had no choice? But what if she wasn't?

Maybe it was time for Lindsay to take charge. Though she had a project to finish up over the weekend, she would have considerably more time to get everyone out of this funk. And at some point, they needed to make plans for the future. Would it cause Sylvie undue stress to discuss it? Or would it be good to have something to focus on, to give her a kick in the pants to actually *do* something?

On Saturday, she told her dad to take Sylvie out for lunch. Lindsay would watch the motel, not that there was much to do. While they were gone, Lindsay figured out how to forward all motel calls to her cell phone. It would be easy enough to switch the setting to her mom's or dad's phone, so Sylvie wouldn't feel so chained to the motel office. And she wrote down all the steps so her mom could turn it on or off as needed. Next, she changed her parents' sheets, swept and vacuumed floors, and put a cake in the oven. By the time Ed and Sylvie returned, the apartment was clean, and both kids were ready and waiting at the dining table to play a board game with their grandparents.

"I have to finish my project for work, but I want you guys to have some fun. Play a game, then go for a walk. The weather should have cooled off enough by then."

Sylvie seemed torn between what to do.

"You need to start being present, Mom. You didn't die. Stop acting like a ghost."

Sylvie turned to her with startled eyes. "That is what it's been like, isn't it? Like I'm not really here." The look in her eyes broke Lindsay's heart.

Lindsay squeezed her mom's hand. "But you are here. We want you here. And we want you to be happy. So play a game. The kids picked the silliest one. Laugh a little."

Sylvie gave her a small smile. "I can do that."

"I know you can."

Lindsay watched them get settled at the table, then returned to the office. She would stay out here to keep an eye on things, despite the fact that the forwarded phone hadn't rung once.

With Jake having regular duties to worry about, Sherry had taken on the brunt of the casework for the teen criminals they had identified. But, he reasoned, that was her job, even if it had him itching to do more. Maybe he should look into being a detective. He knew it wouldn't be easy to pass the exam, but he suspected he would like the work. He enjoyed figuring things out, looking for clues, trying to think one step ahead. Paperwork was no fun, but he had his fair share of that already. What was a little more?

Despite his lack of active involvement, Sherry kept him up to date on the case. Both of the identified culprits had been brought into custody, fingerprinted, and questioned. They were minors – aged sixteen and seventeen – so their parents had been informed, but had not been present at the questioning. Prints for the young man identified as "Pinky" matched prints on several of the stolen items, which led to his arrest. His court date was scheduled for the following week, the day after Jeremy's case review appointment. So far they didn't have any leads on the third member of the group – or on any other possible members, since some of the stolen items didn't have any matching prints. Pinky – otherwise known as Peter Dinkle – and his brother, Michael Dinkle, had been tight-lipped when it came to sharing information. Jake hoped something would come to light during or after the court appearance.

For now, though, he had traffic duty.

As Jake directed traffic while a construction crew worked, his thoughts drifted back to the event committee meeting that had taken place a couple of nights ago. It had been a productive meeting, and Jake was glad others were getting interested and involved. They were starting to work out details, and Jake hoped that soon they would be able to send out a general invite to teens – and adults – who might want to volunteer. He had discussed the possibility of having the event be a community service project with the chief, and he had seemed on board. Jake hoped that after the review board determined Jeremy's consequences, Jeremy could be their first volunteer. If he was interested, of course. For all Jake knew, Jeremy would prefer to pick up trash at the park.

They had decided to start with a relatively small-scale event and schedule it for the fall. It would be a trial of sorts, so they could learn how to work together and see what worked and what didn't. It would be open to all ages, but they would pay particular attention to making sure there were enough activities and attractions to bring in the older kids and teens. What those would be were yet to be decided, but he hoped the volunteers would be able to help come up with a list of options.

The biggest hiccup would be funding, which Jake hadn't even considered. He was used to working with a budget that was already set, not starting from scratch. One of the committee members had suggested inviting vendors to set up tables – for a fee. That would help bring in working capital so they could do things like rent tents and tables and chairs, since they had decided to hold it outside. The town also had a rental fee to reserve the town green, though one member of the committee was going to see if they could get it waived, since they were holding a community event. Without a reputation or any idea on number of attendees, however, they had no idea how much to charge vendors, and Jake couldn't in good conscience charge very much, since this was all an experiment. They could charge for some of the activities, but that would only help for future funding, not what they would need for this year.

Jake had to admit, planning an event of this size was a lot more complicated than he had thought. But he had brought together all of these people, and he had all these ideas on how he wanted it to go. He couldn't possibly give up now. He just hoped it would all come together.

Chapter 33

Lindsay could hear chatting and laughter coming from the apartment, and it made her smile. She was glad she had pushed the issue. Her mother needed to be active to get better, both mentally and physically. After the game, Sylvie balked at the idea of going for a walk, but it was Emma who insisted they go.

"We'll go slow, Gran. It's not like we're in a rush."

Sylvie had finally agreed, and the group passed Lindsay on their way out, checking to be sure she would be okay on her own.

In truth, Lindsay was grateful for the solitude. She hadn't had much time to herself at all over the last couple of weeks, always worrying about the kids or her parents. The little time she'd had had been filled with tasks and responsibilities, so there had been little time to savor the quiet except for stolen moments outside. She thought back to that hike through the woods she had taken what seemed like forever ago. She should do that again. Not the getting lost part, but the taking time for herself. Maybe once her mother was feeling better, she would feel able to enjoy time away.

For now, Lindsay put aside her work project, grabbed a notebook and pencil, and stepped outside.

The sun was sinking lower in the sky, reducing the oppressive heat that had been present earlier in the day. It was actually pleasant out now, with a light breeze blowing. Lindsay sat in one of the Adirondack chairs her parents had tucked on the sides of the office and placed the notepad on her lap.

Her mind had been filled with ideas and inspiration since she had been spending so much time at the motel. She could picture improved landscaping and a revitalized recreation area. They had space for a gazebo, maybe even a pool, though she knew those could be more hassle than they were worth. The plants she had bought were thriving, and she was pleased with the bursts of color they provided along the front walkways. She could do so much with this place – and that was just the outside! Her ideas for the rooms were just as plentiful. She would love to update and refresh them, with new bedding, maybe new carpet, new artwork. They could replace light fixtures and faucets, give everything a facelift.

Lindsay sketched as she thought, letting her mind wander and dream and imagine. She knew it was pointless. She would go back to Pennsylvania, and her parents would probably sell the motel. They needed a life beyond the motel, especially her mom. The heart attack may not have killed her, but it looked like she was dying a slow death just by feeling chained to this place. Lindsay wished she could explain that it didn't have to be like that. But without help, what were the options? Her parents taking turns keeping an eye on things while the other went out and had a life?

If Lindsay stayed, they would have more options. She could revive the motel, and her parents would have more time to travel or just go out and do things. But that was wishful thinking. It just wasn't that simple. Even if business picked up, the expenses to fix things up would be astronomical. That didn't even take into account a salary for her. How could she and the kids survive?

And, of course, speaking of the kids: with everything that had happened with Jeremy, why would they even want to stay? Jeremy had expressed in no uncertain terms how miserable he was here. Emma seemed to be doing okay, but Lindsay knew she missed her friends. They would never agree to staying. She would be lucky if they made it through the summer. Even if they had seemed to develop a rhythm, Jeremy was far from happy.

Lindsay let the notepad drop to the ground and sighed. She leaned back in the chair and closed her eyes, letting the breeze glide over her. If the kids could be happy, and she could make the money work, would she want to stay? She had never even considered taking over the motel. Pine Valley had never been an option when she thought about the future. She had to admit, her creativity had been reignited here. Her ideas to bring life back to the motel – not just in terms of renovating the place, but really bringing it to life, with community connections and new offerings for guests – made her feel alive, too. But how long would that last? Once she had made the changes she thought of, would she get bored? Would they even work? Would she wish she hadn't given up security for such a crazy scheme?

She didn't know. All she knew was that when they went back to Pennsylvania, she would miss the Lindsay she had rediscovered in Pine Valley.

Sylvie enjoyed the walk and spending time with her family, even if she did get tired quickly. They weren't able to go far before she asked to go back, but the fresh air had done her good, as had playing the game with the kids. And, more importantly, she had seen Jeremy smile again. While she didn't condone what he had done, she knew it had been a mistake, and one he regretted. He seemed to have learned his lesson. She only wished she knew what had prompted it in the first place. Lindsay hadn't wanted to go into detail, saying it was Jeremy's story to share if he wanted to.

When they reached the motel again, Sylvie saw Lindsay lounging on one of the chairs near the front. The kids went inside, most likely to play on their devices again, and Ed wanted to relax and watch TV, so Sylvie sat beside her daughter.

They sat in companionable silence. While the walk had invigorated her, Sylvie was glad to be sitting. "Thank you for pushing me," she said after a while.

Lindsay turned to look at her. "You're welcome." She smiled. "You know I just want what's best for you."

Sylvie scoffed. "Who, exactly is the mother here?" But she softened the scold with a smile. "I know you do." Sylvie patted Lindsay's hand. "And I want what's best for you."

"I wish I knew what that was."

"Me, too."

"Have you given any more thought about what you want to do with the motel?"

Sylvie sighed. "I feel like that's all I've thought about. That and Jeremy."

"Jeremy will be okay."

"Will he?"

Lindsay nodded. "I think it was good for him to realize that there are consequences to his actions. It wasn't an easy lesson to learn, but it could have been so much worse."

"This is true."

"So...what about the motel?"

"Oh, I don't know. I really need to talk to your father about things, but he's been tiptoeing around me these days, afraid to cause me any kind of upset, so we just wander around each other, making small talk or watching TV."

"What are *you* leaning towards?"

Sylvie sighed again. "I don't know. I go back and forth. Selling would be so much easier. But then I think about all the memories. And then I think about what will I possibly do with myself without the motel? And then I think about how little I've done because of the motel. And that makes me think selling would be easier again. But then I think I'll get bored. It's really a vicious cycle."

Lindsay nodded. "I get that."

They fell into companionable silence again.

"I really wish I had a crystal ball," Sylvie said after a few moments.

Lindsay laughed. "Me, too."

Later that night, when they were settled back at the rental house and the kids were ready for bed, Lindsay paused before heading upstairs. She went over to Jeremy and sat on the edge of his bed. He had been staring at the ceiling, but he turned to her when she sat down.

"Hey, kiddo," she said.

"Hey."

"It was good to hear you laughing today. I haven't heard much of that in a long time."

Jeremy shrugged.

"How are you holding up?"

He shrugged again. "Okay, I guess."

"I know it's been a rough week. But I wanted to let you know I'm proud of you for speaking up, admitting what you did, and trying to fix it."

"Thanks."

"I'm sorry you hate it here so much."

"It's not that I hate it. I mean, I love Gran and Pops. I just feel, I don't know, like I'm stuck in the middle of nowhere and no one wants anything to do with me."

"I want you around."

"You're my mom."

"Yeah, but I still like you. I still want to spend time with you."

"It's not the same."

"I know. You miss your friends."

"Yeah. I miss knowing where I belong."

"I get it." Lindsay let silence fall as she thought. "I'm sorry basketball didn't work out. And I know you didn't feel like doing anything else this week, but maybe next week you can try some of the other things we signed up for. As long as they don't interfere with your meeting. I'll have to check the calendar. But you seemed to enjoy those."

"They were okay."

"The kids were nice in the other programs?"

Jeremy shrugged again. "I guess."

"Well, that's something. And those were more up your alley, anyway. Maybe you just didn't have anything in common with the basketball kids."

"Maybe."

Silence fell again. Just as Lindsay was going to say goodnight, Jeremy spoke again.

"Mom?"

"Yeah?"

"Why do you care so much if I make friends here?"

"I just want you to be happy."

"We're still going home at the end of the summer, right?"

"That's the plan."

"Okay. Good. I can suck it up for another month and a half. I'll be busy anyway."

Lindsay wished Jeremy goodnight, then climbed the stairs to get herself ready for bed. If she had needed confirmation that Jeremy did not want to be in Pine Valley, she had just gotten it.

Chapter 34

Sylvie opened her eyes Monday morning and stared at the ceiling. It was the same ceiling she had been waking up to for over thirty years. What would it be like to wake up to a different one?

She had decided that today would be the day she and Ed discussed the future of the motel. They were officially on vacation, she was feeling stronger, and Lindsay and the kids would be spending the day elsewhere. It was time.

Ed had always been an early riser, and Sylvie found him in the kitchen, drinking a cup of coffee and playing a game on the computer.

"Good morning," she greeted, giving him a kiss on the cheek. "Did the kids get you hooked on something?"

Ed grunted. "I can see why the kids spend so much time on these stupid things. They're addicting."

Sylvie laughed. "Well, when you can pull yourself away, let me know. I was hoping today would be the day we sit down and start making some decisions."

Ed grunted again but didn't respond. Fine. If he wasn't ready to discuss it, she would start working on her own lists. She had decided that was the best way to figure things out: with a whole bunch of lists. She was going to start with a list of pros and cons, then break those down into their own lists. Like when she listed "more time to do other things" as a pro for selling, she would make a list of what those other things could be. Would she have to sell to be able to do them, or was she using them as an excuse? Did she actually want to do those things?

Of course, she wanted and needed Ed's take on everything, but Sylvie figured she had to start somewhere. And getting her own thoughts in order was a great place to start.

The weather was beautiful this morning, so Sylvie opted to take her notepad outside. There was nothing like fresh air and a warm breeze to free the mind.

Her thoughts were interrupted by sirens not far away. Not long after, another siren sounded, this time moving in a different direction. What was going on? Shaking her head, Sylvie tried to focus on her lists. She hoped everyone was all right.

It had been less than two weeks, and Jake was already feeling the difference from going to the gym. Between that, the progress on the petty crimes case, and the progress on the community event, he was feeling pretty darn good. Of course, decisions still had to be made, and plenty was still in limbo, but everything was moving in the right direction.

Feeling confident, Jake walked into the station. He had given it a lot of thought over the past few days, and he felt the time was right to apply to become a detective. He had been an officer for a while now. He had the interest and had shown the capability by helping on not only this most recent case, but cases previously, both in Pine Valley and in Waterbury. What was he waiting for?

When he entered the main office, officers and detectives alike were moving about in a frenzy. Jake's confident smile slipped.

"What's going on?" Jake asked a fellow officer, Ron, who was walking past.

"Everything," Ron replied. "Or at least it seems that way."

What was that supposed to mean? But Ron was already walking away. Jake approached Sherry's desk. She was on the phone but held up a finger when she saw him.

"All hell has broken loose," Sherry said after a moment, putting the phone back on its cradle. "The phones have been ringing off the hook. Reports of robberies, more vandalism, even a bomb threat. So far, officers checking out the calls have reported them as false alarms, but each call needs to be checked out just in case. I suspect someone just wants to keep us busy today."

"What can I do?"

Sherry gestured toward a desk along one side, where assignments and notices were usually posted. "All calls are getting put on the board. Grab one and investigate. Call in your report. Then, if that one's closed, come grab another one. This has been going on for two hours. It's going to be a long day."

"Any idea where the calls are originating?"

Sherry shook her head. "Still working on it. Whoever is doing it is using a spoofer, so it looks like they're coming from all over town."

Jake had a strong suspicion about who was behind it, but without any evidence, it would be hard to prove. He was going to have to keep his eyes and ears open as he investigated his calls.

The morning became a blur of driving, questioning, writing reports, and starting again. One thing was for sure: these guys had way too much time on their hands. But they were also racking up the offenses. Filing a false police claim was a crime, and with the number of calls made just this morning, the list was getting considerable. Jake wondered if the offenders knew the effects of their efforts and didn't care, or if they thought it was a harmless prank. He was getting the feeling that there was something malicious going on, at least from the ringleader. It was possible the others that got dragged into it, like Jeremy, didn't know how much trouble they were getting themselves into.

By the time Jake paused for lunch, the department had processed over twenty false claims. The phones had fallen silent, and everyone hoped the perpetrators were done. But it was possible they were just breaking for lunch, too.

A couple of other officers were in the break room when he headed back. Not surprisingly, conversation centered on the drama of the morning. Jake wondered if any progress had been made on identifying the origin of the calls, but as he thought about that, he picked up snippets of the conversation nearby. Something was starting to click.

Chapter 35

Lindsay finished compiling the data chart she had been working on, then rocked her head back and forth to stretch her neck. At least that was done. She opened her email and composed a message to a coworker to submit the chart. Just as she hit send, an email from her boss appeared in her inbox.

One of their biggest clients had been pleased with the results of their latest ad campaign. Always a good thing. They wanted to schedule a meeting to go over the findings. In person. In Pennsylvania. Not a good thing.

Lindsay leaned back in her chair and sighed. This had been the one concern with having her work remotely. Despite the digital nature of most of her work, clients occasionally wanted face-to-face meetings. They wanted real-time assurances and something tangible to show for the thousands they were spending. She supposed she could make it work, though it would be exhausting. Drive five hours the day before, attend the meeting, make a presentation, then drive back. If her parents could watch the kids, it wouldn't be so bad.

Lindsay read the email again. The client was requesting the meeting be scheduled for Thursday. Jeremy's case review meeting was Wednesday. That made things trickier. Could she make it work? Maybe, if she left right after Jeremy's meeting. It all depended on how long Jeremy's meeting lasted.

Of course, she also had to put together the presentation for the meeting, but she could take care of that easily enough. She just had to compile the data and make more charts. Such fun.

Lindsay stood up and got herself a glass of water. The kids had been quiet, though they usually were when they were on their devices. With Emma's camp done, and the motel on hiatus, they had all been home that morning. It had been nice to have their own space after spending so much time at the motel the past week. Though a bit tighter than they were used to, the little rental house had started feeling comfortable. She wondered how it would feel to go back to their house in Pennsylvania. Especially without the kids, when she went for her meeting.

Calling to the kids to turn off their devices, Lindsay opened the fridge to figure out lunch. She needed to go grocery shopping. But they had some nuggets and fries, so she preheated the oven and prepped a cookie sheet. Maybe they would get pizza for dinner. She wasn't in the mood to tackle the grocery store. To be honest, she wasn't in the mood to tackle much of anything. Definitely not the presentation that had just been added to her list. She was tempted to fill the rest of the day with busywork and push the presentation until the following day. But she knew she would regret that tomorrow.

Even with the stress and anxiety of coming to Pine Valley, having the kids mad at her, and learning about the state of the motel, having that week off from work had been nice. And being back at it made Lindsay realize how little interest she had in her job.

She wondered now if that was part of the reason she had been feeling so overwhelmed at home. Yes, the kids' extracurriculars, combined with all of the housework and regular responsibilities at home, did leave little time for fun, but dreading going into work made everything that much more challenging. She wasn't just busy; she was unhappy.

Lindsay let that sink in for a moment. Since taking the time to breathe, to find moments of calm, and to tap into her creativity, she had felt invigorated and ready to tackle anything. Considering all that she had had to deal with this past week, that was nothing to sneeze at. If Jeremy had gotten into trouble with the law back home, she likely would have either dissolved into tears or exploded in anger. If her mother had had a heart attack then, Lindsay wouldn't have known what to do. Sure, these things had affected her. She got emotional just thinking about them. But she had been able to tackle them with a clear head.

Had she just needed a vacation?

Then again, here she was, still here but working again, and she couldn't even tackle the grocery store.

She wondered how it would feel to go back, to settle into their normal routines after the summer away. There would be cleaning and laundry to do, but not like after a typical vacation. She had had to do all that here. Going back to work in person would be tough, and for the kids, going back to school. She had liked the rhythm they had gotten into when they were spending their days at the motel. She would get some work done, the kids would be off working on projects. It had been laid back, low pressure.

It wasn't real.

She had to keep reminding herself of that. Nothing that had happened over the last two weeks was sustainable. She couldn't just not work, and her job would not support them and a failing motel. And if they revived the motel, the laid-back, low-key days would be no more.

The oven beeped, and Lindsay called the kids to eat. With nothing on the agenda for the afternoon, they would have to find something to do.

"We have that thing at the library tomorrow, right?" Jeremy asked, dunking a fry in ketchup.

"Yes, you both have a program tomorrow. Coding again, I think."

"Okay. I think I'll see if I can finish my book, then. Get me some raffle tickets."

Lindsay put one hand on her chest, then leaned toward Jeremy to put the other one on his forehead. "Is this my son? Are you feeling okay?"

Jeremy swatted her hand playfully and stuck his tongue out at her. "Hey, I read."

"Not usually by choice." She turned to Emma. "What are you thinking of doing?"

Emma shrugged. "Dunno. I might read, too. Or I have a painting I was working on."

"The weather is really nice today. One or both of you could go outside to read or paint."

Emma shrugged again. "Maybe."

"Either way, it sounds like a good plan. I have to put together a presentation." Lindsay stuck her tongue out this time.

"Ooh, have fun with that," Jeremy replied, cringing. "I do not envy you."

"Gee, thanks, kid."

Jeremy grinned. "Any time."

They all finished eating, and Lindsay took a good look at her kids. When had this easy camaraderie set in? She couldn't remember the last time they had been able to banter like this. Was it from spending more time together? Had everything that happened brought them closer? Or was it just the slower pace that had calmed them all down?

She was being very introspective today, Lindsay thought as she cleared away the lunch dishes. Maybe that's what happens when you realize you dislike the job you've been doing for the last ten years. And maybe that's why the idea of staying in Pine Valley and renovating the motel had been so appealing.

Maybe what she really needed was a new job. That was an interesting thought. But what would she do with it?

Chapter 36

The calls were traced to a burner phone, which got them no closer to finding the culprit. They would have to try a different approach.

Sherry was trying to examine the order of the calls and their locations in an attempt to discern any patterns. One of the other detectives was listening to recordings of the calls to check for clues in the caller's voice or background noises. Between the two of them, the hope was they would be able to identify where the calls were made.

Jake looked at the list of calls. Only one had been a bomb threat, while the others had been more along the lines of the petty crime he had been investigating. Was that significant somehow? Or had the culprit just realized that bomb threats were a bigger deal, so he didn't do more? Jake was considering the first option.

The bomb threat had been made to a building close to the center of town, but far enough away that the center wouldn't have been the focus. The building housed a flower shop, a pharmacy, and a law office. Was there a tie to one of those businesses? The law office perhaps? It wasn't uncommon for criminals to threaten lawyers who had put them away. But Pine Valley saw so little crime, who could possibly be targeting them?

It was a theory, though. He had been away from Piney Valley for a while. Maybe something had gone down while he was away and the criminal was just released. He would ask Sherry when she paused her line of investigating.

In the meantime, he would check to see what else was going on. Maybe someone had a lead or at least something else that needed doing. As he walked back to the assignment desk, he was called over to reception. The officer working the front desk handed him a slip of paper.

"You got a phone message when you were out earlier. Something about a review board meeting."

Jake took the paper. "Thanks, John." It looked like Jeremy's meeting needed to be rescheduled due to a conflict. It had gotten pushed to Thursday. No problem.

Sylvie had made excellent progress on her lists, even without Ed's help. He had gone from playing on the computer to puttering about in the yard to having lunch to taking a nap. It appeared he was taking the idea of taking a break to heart.

By the time dinner rolled around, they still hadn't discussed anything of substance, but Sylvie was hopeful they would be able to chat over her roast chicken and potatoes, one of Ed's favorite meals. As they sat down and began to serve themselves, Sylvie decided to break the ice.

"I had a very productive day today."

Ed laughed. "I didn't."

Sylvie smiled. "Well, we are on break, so you're allowed to relax."

Ed gave her a pointed look. "So are you. And you *should* be relaxing. And resting. You need to be taking it easy."

"Actually, if you'll recall, the doctor said I should be resuming regular activities. As long as I don't overdo it, I should be up and active. I need to regain my strength. Besides, it's not like I did anything strenuous."

"What did you do, then?"

"I made a whole bunch of lists."

Ed guffawed, nearly losing a mouthful of chicken. "We're on break, and you made lists? Of what? Places to go? Things to do?"

Sylvie did not appreciate his tone. She scowled at him and took a bite of her own dinner. "It was a bit more involved than that, though that was part of it. I would have liked your input, but you were too busy *relaxing*."

"It's our first day of the first break we've taken in a very long time."

"I know. But it's not like we were so busy before that you needed to recuperate!"

"I know. I'm sorry. Not for relaxing, but for poking fun. Now, tell me about your lists."

"I don't know if I want to tell you now."

Ed rolled his eyes. "Fine."

They ate in silence for a while, until Sylvie sighed. "I was making lists to try and get my thoughts in order, to try and figure out what to do about the motel."

Ed leaned back in his chair. "And what did you figure out?"

"Well, nothing concrete. I do want to discuss things with you, you know. And bounce some things off you. I know we can't keep going the way we have been. At the very least, the money is running out."

"I know. And I thought the plan had been to have Lindsay come up with a plan to bring in business again, but then you started talking about wanting to sell instead. I can't keep up."

Sylvie sighed again. "Me, neither. I've been so torn. That's why I made lists. Pros and cons, and trying to cover all the bases."

"And?"

"And I don't know. If I'm honest, I realized that I have used the motel as an excuse for a lot of things. When I made the list of things I could do if we sold, I had to admit that with a little planning, I could do most of those things now. Lindsay showed me how to forward calls to my cell phone, and, really, if we didn't have guests, we could easily let calls go to voicemail. It's not like there were that many to begin with. I just started getting so paranoid that we would lose business that I convinced myself I had to stay."

"I tried telling you that. Many times. You didn't want to listen, so I gave up."

"I think I needed to figure it out for myself. But even if I figure out the boredom thing, or the lack of a social life, we still have to figure out the money thing."

"Selling is definitely the easier route for that."

"Yes, it is. Especially since we already know someone is interested."

"It would be hard to let go of this place."

"Yes, it would. And Lindsay had shown me some of the ideas she had to bring in traffic. I know she's worked on a website, and she has all these visions for sprucing things up and making them look as good as they did back in its heyday. And she was talking about building connections with the community, offering packages and things for dinner in town. I have to admit I started getting excited seeing her vision."

"But all of that costs money. And takes time to put together. We don't have the money to put in right now. That's the problem."

"So you think we should sell."

Ed thought for a moment. "You know I don't mind putting in the work. I've done my best to keep things in tiptop shape around here."

"And you've done a great job. I will never fault you for that. I can't imagine what this place would look like without your constant attention."

"But..."

"But some things need replacing. And bringing in more people will draw attention to that. We give the guests we've had our best rooms, the ones with the newest bedding and amenities. But there's only so much 'best' to go around. If we get more people, like we did back in the fall, we will run out of the good stuff. And unlike those guests, who were desperate and just grateful to have a roof over their heads, regular visitors will want the good stuff."

"And we don't have the money to give it to them."

"Exactly. But let's think about this for a minute. Even if we have a wonderful website, and even if we put together amazing packages, chances are we won't get a ton of people right away. So conceivably we could use the money from the first couple of guests to update more rooms, so as business grows, so does the number of decent rooms."

"Possibly. But we still need to keep the lights on, Sylvie. We won't be able to use all the money to buy new stuff."

"No, but we could use some. We could make a list of priorities, to decide what needs to be done first. Actually, I think I already made one. I'll dig it out later."

"Oh, Sylvie." Ed chuckled.

"I was trying to think of everything."

"I know. My concern is that we'll spend all the time, and whatever money we have, and the business won't follow. Or we'll be too worn out to enjoy it. As you said, we're not exactly young anymore. When we first bought this place, we had all the energy in the world to fix it up. Plus two strapping kids who could help us. Lindsay and the kids are going back to Pennsylvania at the end of the summer. Lindsay might put together a plan, but it will be up to us to implement it. What if we don't have the strength? Or we try and it ends up being a waste of time and money?"

"Or what if we sell and wish we hadn't?"

Ed sighed. "I don't know, Sylvie. I just don't know."

Chapter 37

Lindsay got off the phone with Jake and sighed. One more hiccup. Was this a sign, or was she just looking for any excuse to be miserable with work?

Jeremy's review board hearing had gotten moved, and it was now in direct conflict with the client meeting she had to attend. There was no physical way she could do both. Even if the client agreed to a Zoom meeting – highly unlikely – the timing would overlap. She had to make a choice.

She looked over to where Jeremy was reading his book. He seemed relaxed, but Lindsay suspected there was a lot of tension and anxiety hiding beneath the surface. She knew he was nervous about the meeting. There was no way she could just not go. Even if her parents were willing to take him, he needed her support. He needed to know she would help him get through this.

That meant she couldn't go to the client meeting. She had already indicated she would attend, but maybe she could say she had an unexpected conflict? That she needed to reschedule? She wasn't sure how her boss would respond. And there was a very real possibility that this would be the last straw and she would lose her job.

She wasn't nearly as upset about it as she probably should be.

The last couple of weeks had caused a shift in her. Actually, the last several months had caused a shift in her. She had realized she didn't want to settle for just surviving, making it through each day at any cost. She wanted to enjoy life, to see both herself and her kids thrive. And with all of her recent thoughts of disgruntlement over work, maybe it was time to make a change. The thought of being without a steady paycheck terrified her. But the thought of not having to return to work didn't. In many ways, it would be a relief.

But she couldn't be without a job. And that meant jumping into full job-hunting mode as soon as possible. From a distance, that would be a challenge. And time-consuming. She could kiss the laid-back time in Pine Valley goodbye. She could kiss time with her kids goodbye. Job hunting these days was like having a full-time job. Just one that didn't pay. She supposed she would probably get unemployment for a while if she was let go. That would offer a cushion. Would it be enough to let her enjoy the rest of the summer? Or would the stress just keep eating at her, destroying any tranquility she might otherwise have gained?

Maybe if she lost her job, they could cut their time in Pine Valley short and just head back early. She could job hunt in person. Of course, that posed its own set of problems. Jeremy's legal consequences might require him to stay local for a time. And, of course, there was the whole situation with the motel. She wanted to be on hand for her parents, in case Sylvie needed health support, or in case they needed helping with either selling or revitalizing the motel.

What a mess.

Maybe she was jumping the gun. She might not lose her job. Her boss might be willing to work with her. The client might be flexible. Strangely, the thought of keeping her job was more disheartening than that of losing it.

"Hey, kiddo," Lindsay said after a moment. "Your meeting got pushed to Thursday."

Jeremy looked up from his book. "Okay."

Lindsay opened her laptop again and began an email to her boss. Might as well get it over with.

Jake approached Sherry's desk after getting off the phone with Lindsay. He wanted to pitch his bomb threat theory, and it appeared she had taken a break from her exploration of the calls, if the closed eyes were any indication.

"I have a theory to run by you. Well, an idea, at least."

Sherry opened one eye. "Will it cause me more headaches?"

"Hopefully not. I take it you haven't found any leads?"

Sherry shook her head. "Nothing that I can make sense of. Locations seem random, a mix of business and residential, in no apparent order."

Jake gestured toward the other detective working the case, who still had headphones on at his desk. "Tim having any luck?"

"Not that I'm aware of. So if you have an idea, spill it."

"Okay. So I was having lunch, and the guys next to me were discussing the situation, of course, and they were discussing how only one of the calls was a bomb threat, with the others being small potatoes. So I decided to explore that a little more."

"And what did you find out?"

"Not a lot, but I'm hoping you can help with that. The building the bomb threat was for holds a flower shop, a pharmacy, and a law office. I know lawyers have been targets before, if they sent someone to jail or whatever. I thought you might know of something that could be connected."

Sherry leaned back in her chair and thought for a moment. "Usually retaliation threats have a bit more substance to them, not just a call. Bomb squad didn't find anything that even hinted at a bomb. The only result was inconvenience. And I can't think of any cases that would be big enough to result in something like that anyway. The only case of note in the time I've been with the department is the apartment collapse last year. That was a whole fiasco, and the guy responsible ended up in jail, but he wouldn't be getting released yet."

"Could someone be acting on his behalf? A friend or family member maybe?"

"It's a long shot, but I can do a little digging. I'll let you know if anything turns up."

"Thanks." Jake left Sherry to her work and headed toward the chief's office. The day may have gotten a bit sidetracked, but it had actually cemented his resolve to do something about it. What better time to express his interest in becoming a detective?

Chief Ortiz was seated at his desk, practically buried beneath a mountain of paperwork.

Jake knocked on the doorframe.

"What do you need, Figueroa?"

Jake cleared his throat. "I realize it may not be the best time, Chief, but I wanted to let you know that I have decided to apply to become a detective."

The chief looked at Jake over the top of his reading glasses. "After a day like today, you still want to be a detective?"

Jake nodded. "Yes, sir. I think I can be a valuable addition to the team."

Ortiz chuckled. "About damn time."

Jake furrowed his brow. "Excuse me, sir?"

"Jake, you have been showing the signs of being a detective for months now. You read into everything. You go a step beyond writing a report to come up with theories and look for clues and offer suggestions. Sherry was surprised you hadn't applied before."

"Really?"

"Really. Application's online, in the department database. Let me know if you have questions."

"Yes, sir. Thanks, Chief."

The chief waved him away and returned his attention to the stack of paperwork in front of him.

Jake left the office feeling lighter, with his confident smile returning. Maybe it hadn't been such a bad day, after all.

Chapter 38

They may not have come to any decisions the night before, Sylvie mused the following morning, but at least they had talked about it.

Ed seemed to be in much the same boat as she was, weighing the options and trying to figure out what would make them happier. The one thing they had decided was to call the realtor who had approached them and find out how much his buyer was willing to pay for the motel as is. They needed to truly know what their options were.

Sylvie called Christopher, the realtor, and set up an appointment with him and his buyer for Wednesday. She told him they didn't know if they would be selling, but they would consider whatever offer he made. Now they had to wait.

Sylvie had always been terrible at waiting. One would think that after spending the last four years waiting for the phone to ring that she would have gotten used to it. But she hadn't. She had just gotten used to keeping busy.

She decided to spend some time exploring the motel. Though she felt she knew the place inside and out, the truth was she hadn't stepped foot into most of the rooms since the guests from the apartment building had checked out last fall. Ed went into them all periodically, airing them out and checking for any issues, but she tended to focus on the few rooms they checked out most often. She wondered how bad the other rooms had gotten. Better to find out now than when the realtor was here.

Sylvie started with room number one, located in the front of the building on the left side. This was one of their "in between" rooms – not the best, but not too bad. They had once had a family staying in this room that was from California. Every year they travelled to a different state and tried to find places to stay that were off the beaten path. She had always thought that was a neat idea.

Travelling was definitely on the list of things to do if they sold. While she could find a way to do most of the other items on the list, that one eluded her. Unless, of course, the motel's business picked up so much that they could hire staff again. But Sylvie wasn't counting on that, especially anytime soon.

The room wasn't as bad as she had expected. The sink in the bathroom had some wear and light staining from the hard water. The carpet had some areas that were getting a bit worn. Artwork and comforters were faded. But aside from some light dust due to not being used, everything was clean. If she were to stay here, how would she feel?

Sylvie tried closing her eyes and imagining she was a guest. Perhaps she was visiting Pine Valley for the first time. It was a small town, but surrounded by nature, beautiful and serene. She wouldn't expect the accommodations to be new and modern. She would expect them to be lived in. And that's what the motel was. Lived in. Worn but comfortable. It could use a refresh, but it could definitely be worse. Of course, she hadn't seen the rooms in the back yet. Those didn't get much use.

The rest of the rooms at the front of the building were much the same as room one. Some had less wear than others, so they tended to put guests in those, but, Sylvie realized, since those were being used more often now, they were getting just as worn as the others. Not horrible, but not as nice as she would like.

Maybe that was the problem: Sylvie's standards were just too high. If she was honest, the rooms weren't that bad. They were worn, yes, but there weren't any holes in the carpets, comforters, or walls. No furniture was broken. Everything was in working order. Maybe she shouldn't feel bad about encouraging guests to visit. Maybe they could start small, build up business again, and take things one step at a time.

But were they up to that? Thinking about her health scare gave her pause. If Lindsay hadn't been around, Ed would have had to run the motel by himself when she was in the hospital. What if it happened again, to either of them, once Lindsay returned home? What if business was up, and they had several rooms booked, and one of them was out of commission? What would happen then?

This latest train of thought made her worry. If they decided to save the motel, they would need to put together a back-up plan, people they could call at a moment's notice to step in. Who would they even get for something like that?

Ed met up with her as she rounded the side of the building to check out the rooms in the back.

"Hey," he said with a smile. "What have you been up to?"

"Investigating the rooms. And thinking."

"Uh oh. That's always dangerous." He grinned. But Sylvie wasn't in the mood for joking around.

"Ed, I think we should sell the motel."

Chapter 39

Lindsay's boss wanted her to call him, and she already knew how the conversation would go. She would have to make a choice. But really, there was no choice to make. If it came down to her job or her child, she would choose her child every time. Even if she had loved her job. There was no contest.

But she called anyway, just to make sure everyone was on the same page.

"Lindsay, the client is not willing to move the meeting time."

"I understand. I will unfortunately not be able to attend, then."

Her boss, Mr. Collins, sighed. "You know how important this client is. We cannot afford to lose them."

"I would be happy to put together the presentation and send it over to someone who is able to attend. All of the information will still be available." Happy might be stretching it, but she had to at least try.

"You are the one who knows the information inside and out. I need *you* there."

"I'm sorry, Mr. Collins, but as I explained in my email, I have an unexpected conflict that has come up. I am no longer able to attend the meeting."

"Not able or not willing?"

Lindsay paused. "Both."

"We talked about this last week. You assured me that this job was a priority, that you were committed to getting things done."

"It is a priority, but not my only one. And my family will always be my top priority, Mr. Collins."

"And this company is mine. If you are not at that meeting, Lindsay, I will have no choice but to let you go."

"I understand. I will not be at that meeting. But I will send all of the relevant information to you so you can be prepared to meet with the client. And I will forward you everything else I have for other clients, as well. I will consider Wednesday my last day, so I can tie up any loose ends."

"You were a valuable employee, Lindsay, but I don't know that I can give you a positive reference after this."

Lindsay swallowed. That would make things harder. But she still had no choice. "I'm sorry you feel that way. I have given this company a lot over the last ten years. I'm sorry it didn't work out."

By the time she hung up, Lindsay felt numb. Had that really just happened? Had she just quit her job? Well, not quit. She had technically been let go. And that meant she could claim unemployment. She hoped. But that was logistics, and she would have to figure that out later. For now, she had to make sense of what had just happened, get her work affairs in order, and figure out how to break the news to her kids.

With Chief Ortiz in his corner, Jake suspected he would have no problem making the step up to detective as long as he passed the exam. But even getting to the exam was going to be tough. The application was no joke. Not only would he need to submit proof of his college degree and graduation from the police academy, but he would need to write a letter of interest, answer a slew of questions, and share an updated resume that offered highlights of cases he had assisted with. Then, assuming his application was accepted, the exam came next, with a written test, physical assessment, and psychological evaluation. He had no idea how long the process would take, but he was not looking forward to it. He knew it would be worth it, though.

With the application process swimming in his mind, he walked into a much calmer office on Tuesday. Like all of the other crimes committed by this band of petty criminals, the false claim calls had ended as quickly as they had begun. Jake assumed it was the same group of teens. Everything lined up, at least to him.

"I hear you're finally going for detective," Sherry said as he approached her desk.

"Yeah. I expect it will take a while, though. Have to jump through a few hoops first."

Sherry barked out a laugh. "You'll have plenty of hoops to jump through after, too. Don't expect the job to be a cake walk."

"I don't. Speaking of, any progress on our mystery caller?"

"I did some digging into that lead you suggested. The only recent case of note for that law office was the suit against the deadbeat who brought about the building collapse last year. But turns out there may be something in it after all. That deadbeat had a kid. And guess who happens to be nineteen and on our list of speeding offenders?"

Jake felt like punching the air in excitement, but he restrained himself. "And I'm guessing he didn't end up in the yearbook because he had already graduated?"

"Yup. But I dug through some older yearbooks, and it looks like he may have been buddy buddy with the Dinkles. They were in some candid shots together and in some club together. I'm working on putting together the rest of our speeding culprits, see if there are any connections. Think you can get your informer Jeremy to come in and identify 'Jack,' otherwise known as David Malloy?"

"I will give his mom a call and see what they say."

Jake left a voicemail for Lindsay, then went out on his route for the day. He really hoped the rest of the pieces would fall into place.

Lindsay saw the call from the police station but let it go to voicemail. If Jake was calling to say the meeting had been changed again, she didn't know what she would do. She could not crawl back with her tail between her legs. But even if she could, she wouldn't want to. The initial numbness had given way to relief, and she didn't want to go back. Even if she knew the road ahead would be a rough one.

Lindsay had decided to wait until after Jeremy's meeting to break the news to the kids about her job. She needed to explore her options a bit, and she needed to know the results of Jeremy's case before she even knew what all of those options were. She suspected they would have to stick around Pine Valley while he completed whatever kind of sentence they imposed, so she figured she had time.

The kids went to their coding program at the library, and Lindsay decided to hop on one of the public computers while she was there. It didn't make sense to rush back to the house to work when most of her work would be getting passed along to someone else anyway. She just had a few final reports to finish up, and those could easily be done later.

The library hummed with activity: patrons checking out materials or asking questions, kids checking in for summer reading or signing up for programs, friends greeting each other and catching up on news. Lindsay didn't mean to eavesdrop, but she couldn't help it. She heard about prospering gardens and disappointing children, a new baby and an upcoming wedding, graduations and college prospects. She loved feeling the pulse of the community. While she supposed she could hear similar conversations if she were to sit in a cafe back home, the feeling was different. There was less rushing here, more connection.

It was probably the location, Lindsay reasoned. People went to a library when they had time, not when they were grabbing a coffee or lunch on the run. People made connections everywhere. Could she replicate this feeling back home?

Absorbed with her thoughts, Lindsay puttered around online for a bit. Maybe she should see what jobs were out there. She groaned inwardly. She would have to update her resume. And write cover letters again. It had been so long since she had applied for jobs. She imagined everything was different now. Would she have to go to classes or something to even get up to date on *how* to apply for jobs? Discouraged, Lindsay logged off the computer. She didn't know what the future held. But she did know that she didn't want to spend the next few days stressing out. She needed to think things through rationally. And she wanted to retain that sense of peace and serenity she had started feeling during her vacation week. She would have plenty of time to worry about the future later.

Chapter 40

Sylvie and Ed greeted Christopher and his client, Zachary White, on Wednesday afternoon. He greeted them with a big smile and a firm handshake and told them to call him Zach. He was younger than Sylvie had expected, and she wasn't sure if she liked that or not, though she supposed he would have to be young and energetic to really whip this place into shape. But why was he so eager? That part confused her.

They walked around the property, looking inside each room. Zach was interested but didn't seem overly concerned with any of the work that needed to be done.

"This is a great place you've got here," Zach said once they had done an initial walk-through and were sitting together in the motel office. "Chris showed me the pictures he took, but it's even better in person."

"Thank you," Sylvie responded, handing Zach the folder of business documents he had requested.

"I have to ask," Ed said as he flipped through the documents, "why are you so interested in the motel?"

"A valid question, a very valid question," Zach replied, nodding his head in agreement. "The truth is, I'm an investor. And my niche is hospitality. I find properties that could use fixing up but have a lot of potential, and I turn things around."

"Do you sell them afterward, or do you run the businesses?"

"Some I sell; some I keep. It all depends on the location, and if the project is something that speaks to me. I have a soft spot for these little towns, and I know the right business can boost the local economy and really make a difference for residents."

"Have you done this a lot?" Sylvie asked.

"I've renovated about a dozen or so properties. I still own a handful. The money I make from the ones I sell goes right back into more properties. I'd be happy to give you references if that would set your mind at ease, get you in touch with some of the prior owners or current managers of my existing properties."

Sylvie and Ed shared a look. He was saying all the right things, but it was a big step.

"We haven't made any final decisions about selling yet," Sylvie said. "So we'll have to give it some thought."

"Of course. It's not a decision to take lightly. I tell you what. Now that I've seen the property, let me crunch some numbers, and I'll have Chris reach out to you with a formal offer. I'll also tack on that list of references, just in case."

"Sounds good," Ed replied, and they all stood up.

"Out of curiosity," Sylvie added, "what do you envision for this place?"

Zach looked around. "Updates, for sure. Modern amenities, updated domestics and appliances, a refresh on carpet, paint, and all that. Then it becomes about getting people comfortable, so they want to stay and come back. Coffee maker and pastries in the lobby, welcoming outdoor spaces for gathering and entertaining. I'd have to see what felt right, how we could use the natural setting to our advantage. Maybe offer family events, things like that. S'mores around a campfire, guided hikes. The possibilities are endless."

Sylvie could picture what he was saying, and she liked it. Maybe he would be good for the motel, offer a fresh perspective that brought it back to life. It would be easier to walk away if she knew that their efforts hadn't been wasted, and that the motel would be in good hands.

They bid Christopher and Zachary goodbye, then turned to face each other. After so many years together, the looks they exchanged spoke volumes. It was a big decision, but if the price was right, this sounded like a very good offer.

Lindsay and Jeremy walked into the police station and asked for Jake. It felt strange, being a regular at a police station. It was not a good feeling.

"Welcome back," Jake greeted them with a smile. "Sorry to drag you back down here, but you're the only one involved in this mess that's actually helping us. The entire department appreciates it, especially since this case has really been stumping us. It looks like the pieces are finally falling into place, though. We just want to see if you're able to identify the last person in the group." Jake cringed. "Sorry, that probably sounds like we're putting all the pressure on you. Honestly, it's not like that. It would be great if it works out, but anything you do will help us proceed. As with the other lineup, we'll offer you several pictures. Let us know if anyone looks familiar."

Sherry was waiting in the interrogation room, as she had been before. They all sat down, and Jeremy took a deep breath. Lindsay could tell he was nervous. Despite Jake's assurances, he did feel the pressure. And he was ready to put this whole mess behind him.

Sherry spread out the pictures, and almost instantly Jeremy pointed to the one in the middle. "That one. That's Jack."

Jake and Sherry shared a look. "Are you sure?" Jake asked. "That was really fast."

Jeremy nodded. "Yup. I remember thinking he looked kind of like a bird, with that pointed nose and beady eyes. Like he reminded me of some of my gamer buddies back home, but kind of creepy, too."

"Okay, then. That was easy. Thank you so much for coming in, Jeremy." Jake stood up and held out a hand for Jeremy to shake.

Jeremy shook Jake's hand, and Lindsay could see him standing a little taller. Despite this whole mess, she was proud of him. He had really grown up in the last couple of weeks.

They left the interrogation room, and Lindsay put an arm around Jeremy's shoulders. "I'm proud of you, kid."

"For what, being a criminal?"

"No," Lindsay replied, stopping and turning to look at him. "For doing what's right, even if it's hard. For accepting what needs to be done. I know you're not looking forward to tomorrow, or to any of this, but you're taking it in stride and not letting it get you down. That takes guts."

"I just wish I hadn't done it in the first place."

"I know. But, hey, everything happens for a reason, right? Maybe you had to get roped into this so you could blow the whole case wide open. Who else would be willing to identify those creeps, huh?"

"I guess."

"Own it, kiddo. Despite doing bad, you did good. Now we just have to get through tomorrow."

Chapter 41

Though she knew the juvenile review board meeting wasn't taking place in a courtroom, it was more informal than Lindsay was expecting. They met in a conference room at the town hall, with Jeremy and Lindsay on one side of a long table, and four people lined up on the other side: Jake, as the arresting officer; Linda, a member of the town's youth services department; Jerome, a local social worker; and Keisha, a representative from the district juvenile court. Even lined up like a firing squad, they looked like friendly professionals, and they smiled at Jeremy as he entered the room.

Keisha began the proceedings. "Welcome. We are here to discuss the case regarding Jeremy Powell, accused of vandalizing private property in the form of spray-painting graffiti on windows. Is that correct?"

Jeremy swallowed nervously. "Yes, ma'am."

"Okay, Jeremy. Now, this meeting is less formal than a court hearing, so it's going to be more about asking questions and having a conversation, okay?"

Jeremy nodded. "Okay."

Keisha looked at the file in front of her. "Now, it is my understanding that you confessed to the crime in full and since the crime took place, you have repaired the damage and further assisted the owners with additional work on the property. Is that correct?"

Jeremy nodded again. "Yes, ma'am."

"And, beyond that, you have assisted with bringing your co-conspirators to justice. Is that also correct?"

"Yes, ma'am."

"I commend you for taking responsibility for your actions and taking steps to make amends."

Jeremy's ears turned red, and he mumbled a thank you.

"Now, the purpose of these kinds of meetings is to ensure you have learned your lesson, and to set you on a straighter path so as not to repeat the behavior. I can see that you have taken your actions to heart, and I think my fellow board members would agree with that sentiment." Keisha looked to her right and left, accepting nods in response. "I would like to open up the meeting for discussion on how best to proceed from here."

The review board members chatted amongst themselves, discussing possible options. Since they did not live in town, Keisha asked Lindsay how long they would be in the area, and if there was anything else they should consider when determining consequences. Lindsay explained that they were scheduled to leave at the end of summer but had no other restrictions. After the board finished conferring, they turned to look at Jeremy again.

"The board is in agreement that the punishment for the crime as mentioned should be community service. Since retribution has already been made to the owner of the vandalized property, and vandalism is considered a public crime, service must be completed for the benefit of the public. The board has determined that eighteen hours of community service over the next six weeks should suffice. Officer Figueroa has a suggestion he would like to run by you as a possible solution to at least some of those hours. Officer Figueroa?"

Jake cleared his throat. "Several townspeople and I have started putting together a community event. While the event will take place in the fall, after you've left, I believe you could assist with the planning and preparation. Our intent in putting together this event is to put together activities that encourage safe, legal fun amongst the teen population in town. We will be attempting to recruit other teens to volunteer on the planning committee and also offer it as a community service option for those who have gotten in trouble with the law. Our hope is that others, like you, Jeremy, will realize that turning to crime to alleviate boredom or upset emotions is not the solution. We need teens to help us come up with the list of activities, plus help us plan and prep for them. I think you would be a perfect candidate to join our committee. The choice is yours, however. There are plenty of other community service projects you could select instead."

"Do I need to let you know now?" Jeremy asked.

Jake shook his head. "Not at all. Give it some thought, and let me know. Wherever you decide to complete your service, there is an official form that will need to be filled out and signed by your supervisor. I have a copy here." He slid a piece of paper across the table, and Lindsay and Jeremy both looked it over. It seemed straightforward enough. "If you decide not to help with the event, or if you decide to split your time among different locations, I would be happy to give you some suggestions as to where to go. Your mom knows how to get ahold of me."

"Thanks."

The meeting wrapped up, and before Lindsay knew it, they were back outside in the sunshine. "Well, that was quick."

"Thank God," Jeremy said, shoulders sagging in relief.

Lindsay put an arm around his shoulders. "And the punishment doesn't seem to be too bad. It only works out to three hours a week, though I bet you could do it faster if you wanted to."

Jeremy shrugged. "Whatever. It's not like I have much going on anyway."

"Hey, maybe you'll even like this community service thing and decide you want to keep it up. That kind of stuff looks great on college applications, you know."

"Don't talk to me about college. I'm not even excited about starting high school." Jeremy made a face.

"I know, I know. We'll take it one step at a time. I'm just saying it's something to consider."

They walked to the car, and Lindsay took a deep breath of the fresh air. One thing done. One *big* thing done. Now onto the next. Emma had been staying with her grandparents, and they were all going to get together for lunch. Lindsay had decided it would be the perfect opportunity to let everyone know about her job situation. She had no idea how it would play out, but it had to get done.

Sylvie watched the car pull into the motel parking lot and called out to let the others know Jeremy and Lindsay had arrived. They were earlier than expected, but, Sylvie thought, wringing her hands, that wasn't necessarily a bad thing. She hoped Jeremy's meeting had gone well. And she hoped Lindsay was in a good mood. She honestly had no idea how Lindsay would take the news about the motel.

The offer had come in, as promised, and it was higher than Ed and Sylvie had expected. Not exactly enough for them to retire on completely, but certainly enough to buy a little house somewhere and set some aside to save and grow. They could get easy part-time jobs to keep them going as long as they wanted and actually live a little. They hadn't accepted the offer yet, but Sylvie felt pretty confident they would. Zach's vision for the motel had helped set their minds at ease. Now they just had to get Lindsay on board. Not that it was her decision, but they had dragged her into this mess; the least they could do was make sure she was okay with what was happening.

They all said their greetings, then retreated to the apartment. Lunch was still in the oven, but everyone wanted to know what had happened in the meeting, so they sat and chatted for a bit. Lindsay filled them in on the review board's decision. All things considered, it could have been much worse. And Jeremy had already undone the damage he did to the building, so Sylvie was glad he hadn't been punished too harshly. She shared a look with Ed. Should they share the news now, while everyone was together? Or should they wait until the kids were on their devices and it was just them and Lindsay? They opted to wait. The kids likely wouldn't care, anyway.

Once news about the kids was done, they went into the living room and took out their phones. Now the grown-ups could talk. But Sylvie was nervous. Looking at Lindsay, she was surprised to see that Lindsay looked nervous, too.

Was it just because of what had happened with Jeremy? But surely that was progressing as well as could be expected. Well, she would find out if and when Lindsay decided to tell her. In the meantime, she couldn't hold her news in any longer.

"Your father and I have some news," Sylvie began.

Lindsay met her gaze and then looked away. "So do I, as it happens."

"Oh, okay. Would you like to go first?"

"No, no, it's okay. It'll wait. What's your news?"

"Well," Sylvie said, looking at Ed, who nodded, "we have decided to sell the motel."

Lindsay's gaze shot back to her, then darted to Ed. "I thought you were still trying to figure things out."

"We were. And we talked about it, and we hemmed and hawed and decided to meet with the realtor and his client to at least get information, so we would know all of our options. But..." Sylvie's voice faded, and she took a deep breath. "I had to admit that my health scare, well, scared me. What would have happened if you hadn't been around? And your father had to take care of things on his own? What if, heaven forbid, something worse had happened? To either one of us? And if we spruced up the motel and had a lot of business? It would have been even worse. Then we would have had guests to worry about, and taking care of business. When you go back home, it will be just us again. And I – we – didn't know if we could handle it."

Lindsay nodded, but she looked sad. "I get it. I do. Even before your heart attack, you were concerned about your age. And I know it's hard on your own." She sighed. "Have you accepted an offer?"

"Not yet. But we have received one, and we felt it was generous. It would help us be comfortable, if not completely set."

"Wait, you said 'the' realtor. Was it that slick guy who was over here taking pictures?"

"His name is Christopher, and he's really quite nice."

Lindsay didn't look convinced. "He was a bit too cocky, if you ask me. I know his type."

"He's one of the top real estate agents in the state."

"That just means he's a good salesperson. That doesn't mean he's a good person. And what about this client of his?"

"His name is Zach, and he seemed very nice, too. He's an investor, and he's apparently done this kind of thing elsewhere too, fixing up properties."

"So he's a property flipper."

"With some of the properties, yes, but he's kept some, too. He finds places that are in need of some TLC and renovates them so they can thrive and benefit their communities."

"Is that what he told you? He could just be feeding you a line. Did you look into him at all?"

"I'd like to think I'm a pretty good judge of character. And your dad liked him, too." Sylvie looked at Ed to confirm. "He seemed to know his stuff."

Lindsay sighed again. "You can't just take someone's word for it, though, Mom. Can I at least look into him a bit before you accept his offer? Make sure he's legit?"

"If that would make you feel better, sure. But he was telling us a bit about his plans for the motel, and a lot of it aligned with what you had been thinking, too. I really think he would be a good fit."

"Get me his info, and I'll see what I can dig up. If he's everything you say he is, then I'll be happy for you. But better to know now if he isn't."

"Okay. He gave us some references, too. I'll forward you the email he sent us."

"Thanks."

"Now, you said you had some news, too?"

Lindsay took a deep breath. Her parents' news had thrown her for a loop. She had thought they were still in the thinking and debating stage. She hadn't expected them to decide to sell without talking to her first. Though, she supposed, they kind of had. Getting an offer wasn't the same as signing a contract. And they had agreed to let her look into this supposed perfect buyer.

But now she had to let them know her own news, and she wasn't looking forward to it. She hadn't told the kids yet, and she had debated telling everyone at once. But she had decided that her parents would likely offer a calmer reaction, and possibly practical solutions to her dilemma.

"I lost my job."

"What?" Sylvie's reaction was much the same as Lindsay's had been a moment before. Ed looked just as shocked.

"What happened, Lindsay?" Ed asked.

"Well, my boss hadn't been too keen on my working remotely to begin with, but he was willing to let me try. When everything happened with Jeremy, and then you, Mom, I kind of dropped the ball with work. I wasn't even thinking about it. I explained the situation to my boss, but he wasn't thrilled. He made it clear I was on thin ice. So earlier this week he told me about a big client requesting a meeting. The meeting had to be in person, and it was scheduled for today. Originally Jeremy's meeting was scheduled for yesterday, so I thought I could go to his meeting, then drive to Pennsylvania for the night, attend the meeting today, then drive back. But when Jeremy's meeting got moved, there was no way. The client wasn't willing to reschedule the meeting, and I had to make a choice. Obviously I chose Jeremy."

"Oh, Lindsay," Sylvie said, moving to sit next to Lindsay and give her a hug. "I am so sorry. What are you going to do?"

Lindsay felt close to tears. "I don't know. To be honest, I had already been thinking about how I wasn't really enjoying my job as much as I used to. Brainstorming ideas for the motel had reminded me how I liked the creative side of things, rather than the analytical. So I was thinking of making a change. But I thought I had time." Lindsay sniffed. "I thought I had more time."

"Have you told the kids?" Ed asked.

Lindsay shook her head. "Not yet. I was hoping to have some kind of game plan in place first, but that hasn't happened. I was worried about Jeremy's meeting and doing research. I had thought I might take some time to work on the motel, if you guys were interested in trying some things that didn't cost much, if any, money. But if you're selling, that won't work. So I guess I'll have to start job hunting. I don't know how much is out there. I started thinking about how much has changed in even applying to jobs since I was last looking, and I got a little overwhelmed, so I didn't get too far."

"Will you be able to collect unemployment?" Ed asked.

"I don't know yet. Technically I haven't been let go yet. My boss said that if I wasn't at the meeting today he would have to let me go. The meeting started a half hour ago, so I assume I'll get my formal letter of termination sometime later today or tomorrow. Then I can apply for unemployment. But I was looking into it, and if the reason for losing the job was a result of my actions, I may not qualify. And I don't know if that applies in this situation. Is choosing to be there for your child a dismissible action?"

Sylvie shook her head. "I don't know what that boss of yours is thinking. Maybe he'll change his mind once he thinks about it and realizes how valuable you were."

"I doubt it. He's not known for changing his mind. And he made it quite clear that the company should be my top priority. Considering he's twice divorced, with adult kids who don't talk to him, I doubt he values family that much. And employees are replaceable. Even after ten years of loyal service." Lindsay played with the edge of the placemat in front of her. "To make matters worse, he said he wasn't sure he could give me a positive reference after this. So finding a new job might be even harder."

"Oh, Lindsay." Sylvie rubbed Lindsay's shoulder. "We'll figure something out."

"I'm not sure how I'm going to tell the kids without Jeremy feeling like it's all his fault. He already feels bad enough about the entire situation. If he knows his meeting led to my losing my job? I can't put that burden on him."

"Then don't. Kids aren't usually too worried about the details. They'll just want to know how it affects them."

"I guess." Lindsay took a deep breath and attempted a smile. "Well, that's my news. Any other life-altering information I should know about?"

Sylvie gave a sympathetic smile back. "I don't think so. We've covered Jeremy, the motel, and your job. I think that about sums it up. But lunch should be just about ready, so why don't you call over the kids, and I'll set the table?"

Lunch passed with small talk and general chatter. Lindsay wasn't sure when to tell the kids about her job, but she figured she at least had time for that. There wasn't much she could do about it at the moment, anyway. She had to wait for her termination notice, wait for Jeremy to complete his community service, wait until the motel sale was resolved. At this rate, she could wait until the end of summer to tell them. But she was already worried about money, and she knew she couldn't wait until then to figure something out. But what?

Chapter 42

What a day. Jake left the review board meeting and carpooled with Keisha to the district courthouse, where the hearing for Peter Dinkle was set to take place. He hadn't been sure he would make it for Peter's hearing, but the list of cases was apparently long today, and, according to Sherry, Peter should be set to meet with the probation officer sometime this afternoon. He honestly wasn't sure how that one would go. Peter didn't seem like the smartest kid, which was probably how he had ended up getting caught in the first place. His brother had practically rolled his eyes when he heard Peter's fingerprints had been found on the stolen items. Would he confess? Would the probation officer let him off easy or recommend the case go in front of a judge? Would Peter have heard about David Malloy's arrest?

Jeremy's identification of David Malloy's picture had been the verification they needed to make an arrest, and David had been taken into custody the day before. He had seemed surprised but defiant at being identified, and he had taken full advantage of his right to remain silent. Due to the laundry list of charges against him, he remained in custody until his own hearing the following week, but they needed to build a solid case against him before he went to trial. The evidence they had so far was circumstantial, with the only charge that could possibly stick that of coercing a minor into committing a crime. That wouldn't get them anywhere. Jake really hoped that the searching of David's property the day before had yielded something more substantial. He would find out when he met up with Sherry at Peter Dinkle's hearing.

What a day.

At least the review board meeting had gone well. Everyone seemed satisfied with the results. Jake figured that once they processed everything he would hear from Lindsay with questions or to set up Jeremy's first batch of hours. Until then, he would try to focus on the other cases he was handling right now. Whatever happened to Pine Valley being a quiet town with no crime?

Jake spotted Sherry outside the meeting room and went to sit by her. "How did it go yesterday?" he whispered, doing his best not to interrupt those around them.

"Pretty well, actually," Sherry responded. "But we can't talk here. I'll fill you in on the ride back to the station."

Jake nodded. Peter Dinkle and his father were sitting on a bench a bit further down the hall. His father did not look happy, but it was hard to tell if that was because his son had done something stupid or because he disdained the court.

Two hours later, Jake and Sherry were on their way back to Pine Valley, practically grinning from ear to ear. Not only had Peter Dinkle confessed to stealing the items in question, but he had also confessed to two of the acts of vandalism – and thrown his brother under the bus for two more. He had mentioned Jeremy, but Jake had advised the officer that they already knew about his involvement, and that matter had been settled. When Peter asked about a reduced sentence if he acknowledged other people involved, Jake's knuckles turned white from gripping the arms of his chair. Could this less-than-bright kid actually be the key to throwing the case wide open? Would he mention David Malloy's involvement? Did he know anything about the fake calls?

Yes. Yes to all of the above. And Jake could not keep the smile off his face.

"So, that was unexpected," Sherry said as they got on the road.

"You can say that again. I guess you should never underestimate the dumb kid."

Sherry burst out laughing. "Guess not. And his confession and statement will corroborate nicely with what we found at the Malloy house."

"That's right. What did you find?"

"Well, the mom still lives there with the kid, and she let us in when we showed her the warrant. She didn't seem surprised that her kid had gotten into trouble. Apparently, he takes after his dad. She had plenty to say about both of them, and went on and on about how her husband ruined her life. She's having trouble getting a job now and all her friends are giving her the cold shoulder. She said if her kid ends up in jail, she might just move and start over. Heck, she might do that anyway. 'He's an adult,' she said. 'He can deal with his own messes.' Whole family sounds like a piece of work."

"That tracks. Did you get any actual evidence, though, or just a possible character witness?"

"Oh, plenty of evidence. This David kid seemed pretty sure that we would never suspect him. Either that or he wanted to eventually be found. Practically had a manifesto set up in his room. White board with a list of names he blamed for his dad's trouble, articles taped up about the collapse and trial. We started running some of the names, and a bunch of them match the robbery victims. Vandalized buildings are workplaces of some of the tenants who had submitted complaints about issues in the building. False alarms were at others, plus, of course, the bomb threat at the law office. Looks like he was getting his friends to do some of his dirty work, though I suspect the calls were all him. Didn't find the burner phone, but with Peter Dinkle's statement, I suspect it's just a matter of time before we get some evidence to tie him to those, too."

"Man, what a day."

"How did the hearing go this morning?"

"Pretty well, as expected. The board opted for community service, no surprise there."

"Glad it went well."

They fell into a companionable silence. After all the excitement of the day, Jake wasn't sure he had the energy for anything else, but he had a committee meeting that night, and he was hoping they would work out more details. Specifically, he wanted to see what opportunities they would have for potential teen volunteers. If Jeremy took him up on his offer, he would need something for him to do. Jeremy didn't strike him as the kind of kid who would be outgoing and start spouting out ideas in a room full of strange adults. They needed more teens, to create a kind of sub-committee to come up with suggestions. Maybe he should suggest that tonight. He could oversee this sub-committee and then report back, or have one of the teens report back, to the committee as a whole. And then, as they came up with lists of tasks and projects that needed to be completed, the teens could take on some of those, too.

Pleased with his train of thought, Jake spent the rest of the ride brainstorming ways to get teens interested in volunteering. He hoped some of the other members had ideas, too. He would need all the help he could get.

Chapter 43

Since Lindsay had research to do on the proposed buyer of her parents' motel, it was easy to pretend she was still working on Friday. The kids thought nothing of her spending hours on her computer or making phone calls, plus they were busy on their devices, or, surprisingly, playing boards games with each other or reading.

Lindsay was thrilled that they had found something that worked for them, doing things together or exploring their individual interests. They had gotten into a routine, not just today, but over the last couple of weeks. Emma had taken to painting outside when Jeremy had programs at the library or community center, and Jeremy would read or work on coding projects on his tablet when Emma was at her programs or art classes. It was everything she had hoped for. Now she just had to get a schedule set for Jeremy's community service, if he would ever decide what he wanted to do. But while he was deciding, she had work to do.

So far, this Zachary White seemed to be everything he said he was. She had found numerous articles about property sales he had completed, and the subsequent renovations and reopenings of said properties. Everyone seemed happy with his work. But that was in the beginning. There had to be information about down the line. Shoddy work could lead to big problems, or shady business dealings could result in former owners being screwed over. She would have to call some of the people who had worked with him. But not the ones he had listed as references.

Lindsay made a list of people Zachary had purchased properties from and wrote down all of the information for properties he had renovated, both the ones he had sold and ones he continued to maintain. Tracking these people down would be her project for the next few days. She hated being cynical, but she did not want her parents being taken advantage of, and she did not want the Pine Valley Motel to end up hurting this community. She had grown up here, and being back had made her remember why she loved it. They had dealt with enough after the previous year's apartment building collapse. They didn't need more shady businessmen wreaking havoc on the town.

Satisfied with her work for the day, Lindsay closed her laptop and went to find the kids. She heard laughing coming from the upstairs bedroom, and her heart skipped a beat. She had missed that sound.

"Sounds like someone's having fun in here," Lindsay said as she entered the bedroom. The kids were sprawled on the floor, playing a silly card game they had found on their first shopping excursion. "Who's winning?"

"I don't think anyone is," Emma said, grinning. "This game is just ridiculous."

"Well, as long as you're having fun, that's all that matters."

"Did you want to play, Mom?" Jeremy asked.

"No, I'm good. I was just thinking I needed a break, and I was going to see if anyone wanted to get ice cream."

Lindsay couldn't help but laugh at how quickly the kids got up.

"Clean up the game first, then come downstairs."

The weather wasn't too hot and sticky, so Lindsay suggested they walk to the ice cream shop. To her surprise, the kids agreed, and they began a leisurely stroll toward the center of town.

"Oh, Mom, I forgot to mention," Emma said, pausing in a recap of her latest pottery class. "A couple of the girls in my class wanted to know if I could hang out this weekend. I said I would let them know. Can I?"

"I'm glad you're making friends, but who are they? And what would you be doing?"

Emma shrugged. "I dunno. Their names are Nicole and Kaitlyn. They're the same age as me."

"Well, why don't you get some more info, and we can discuss it."

Emma immediately took out her phone and began texting. Lindsay could only shake her head before turning to Jeremy.

"We have to discuss your community service hours."

Jeremy sighed. "I know."

"Have you given any thought to what you want to do?"

Jeremy shrugged. "I don't really care. I just want it over with."

"I know. Do you want to help out with that event Officer Jake was talking about?"

"I dunno. I'm not really good around other people I don't know. And I don't know what I would have to do."

"Have you made any friends in any of your programs? Maybe they would want to do something with you."

"You want me to force other kids to do community service?"

"Not force, just ask. And some people actually like helping others." She gave Jeremy a pointed look. "Believe it or not, some people actually volunteer to do community service."

Jeremy rolled his eyes. "Yeah, yeah."

"So, is there anyone?"

He shrugged again. "Not really. I mean, I talk to other kids, but there isn't anyone I'm really friends with."

"Okay. Well, then, this could be an opportunity to meet more kids. Maybe you'll find some you click with."

"I'll think about it."

"Okay. Either way, you should start working on something next week."

"I know."

"They said we could get pizza or something," Emma interjected. "I guess people hang out on the green when the weather's nice."

"Okay. If it's out in public, I don't have a problem with it. I just wouldn't feel comfortable with you going to someone's house when I don't know them."

"Okay. I'll see when they wanted to get together. Did we have any plans this weekend?"

"Not really. I was going to see what you guys wanted to do."

Silence fell as Emma finalized her plans via text and they all walked toward town. A few other people walked by them and waved. Lindsay waved back. This. This was what life should be like.

More waiting. Now that they had decided to sell, Sylvie had thought they could start making plans. But, no, Lindsay wanted to research. While Sylvie appreciated Lindsay's looking out for them, she was also getting antsy. But she was determined to enjoy her weekend, at least. She and Ed had looked into the museum passes from the library to see what options were available. There were some nice art and history museums around, some historic buildings, even a butterfly conservatory, though that was a bit of a drive. But they finally had the time and the freedom. It was time to live a little.

They decided to take the drive to see the butterflies, and Sylvie insisted on rolling down her window as they drove. Though it was quite warm outside, it had been forever since she had felt the wind in her hair like this. She savored the feeling of her hair whipping around her head, even as she knew it was getting impossibly tangled. Ed could only smile at her and shake his head.

Sylvie could feel herself relaxing. The stress of the last few years was starting to melt away. While she knew they would miss the motel, she also knew that selling was the right choice. It had become a burden rather than a joy, and that wasn't how she wanted to remember it. She wanted to remember the pleasant guests and the hub of social activity, her kids running around and meeting people from all over. Perhaps the new owner would bring it back to life. She hoped so.

She did worry about Lindsay, though. Sylvie knew that losing her job had been a shock, and she suspected that was part of the reason Lindsay was throwing herself into this background search of Zach. She needed a purpose, something to keep her busy. With the motel off the table, and her job no longer in the picture, Sylvie imagined she was feeling at loose ends.

Lindsay had always landed on her feet, but she had been going through a rough patch already. Sylvie hoped she didn't let this setback drag her back down when she had started perking up again.

Okay, there it was. The stress was coming back. Of course, a parent never stopped worrying about their children, but times like this were hard. Sylvie took some deep breaths and tried to slow herself back down. Dwelling on things that were out of her control wouldn't help anyone. Besides, things had a way of working themselves out. She just hoped it didn't take as long with Lindsay as it had for them.

Chapter 44

Jake finally heard from Lindsay Saturday afternoon.

"I was beginning to think Jeremy was skipping out on his community service," Jake said playfully. "After we had been singing his praises about cooperating."

Lindsay sighed. "No, but getting him to decide what to do has been like pulling teeth. He's nervous about doing something that has him interacting with a lot of people he doesn't know. That hasn't worked out so well for him here."

"Understandable. I can set him up with something simple, where he doesn't have to interact much with people, if he would like. It would probably be boring stuff, though, like picking up trash or weeding gardens."

"Let me see what he wants to do." Jake could hear a muffled conversation in the background before Lindsay came back on the line. "I'm going to have you talk to him."

"Hello?" The reluctant voice was undeniably Jeremy's.

"Hey, Jeremy. It's Officer Jake. Your mom and I were trying to set up your community service. She said you weren't thrilled to be around other people, so I offered some options where you would be mostly independent, but they're kind of boring."

"Yeah, she said picking up trash and stuff."

"Is that something you would prefer?"

"Um, not really?"

Jake couldn't help but smile. He remembered being an awkward teen. "Okay. What are you thinking, then?"

"I don't know. That's the problem."

"Okay. Well, let me go through a few options with you, and you can let me know what you think."

"Okay."

Jake went over the list of ideas he had available. In addition to the trash and weeding, he told Jeremy about the event he was planning, and how they needed a group of teens to help brainstorm activities and projects, then help with implementing the ideas. He described a project that the local senior center could use help with, building benches for the front of their building. Jeremy would have to work with a few other people on that one, a group of volunteers who were experienced in building. The library could use help with programs for the little kids, preparing supplies and helping the kids with projects. Or the police department could use help with passing out flyers promoting programs of their own they had going on, to help inform residents of services that were offered.

"I don't expect any of these to take the full eighteen hours, so you can do a combination of them, or start with one and then see what else might pop up. Does anything sound interesting?"

"Actually that one with building benches could be good. My Pops had me working on stuff at the motel, and he said I had a knack for it."

"Great. I'll get in touch with the group at the senior center, then, and I'll let you know the details. Do you want me to reach out to you directly on your cell phone, or go through your mom?"

"Uh, better go through my mom. She's better at organizing stuff."

Jake grinned again. "You got it. I'll be in touch."

They said their goodbyes, and Jake reached out to the senior center to make arrangements. While he was disappointed Jeremy hadn't jumped at the chance to help with his event, he understood. Though if he had a knack for building things, maybe they could recruit his help with building booths and displays. It would all depend on what ideas they came up with.

The meeting this week had been filled with brainstorming, and they had a list of ideas already, but they really needed that teen input. Some of the committee members were going to see who they could recruit to the cause, and they were going to reconvene on Tuesday for a status report. If they had teens interested in helping, they would be attending that meeting, too. Jake knew it was tough with vacations and school being out of session, though, so he wasn't sure what to expect. Maybe they should recruit Peter Dingle, Jake thought, chuckling to himself. He was being assigned community service, as well, and Jake had been surprised once by him. Who knew what else that kid had up his sleeve?

David Malloy's court hearing was scheduled for Monday. Jake would be there, though as a peripheral player in the case, he wasn't expected to testify. Sherry would be there to offer testimony on the alleged crimes Malloy had committed. With the long list of grievances, Jake fully expected the case to go to trial. It was a shame David had decided to follow in his father's footsteps. He was obviously intelligent, with an analytical mind that could have done great things if it had been focused on helping rather than causing trouble.

Sometimes Jake thought that was the toughest part of being a cop: having to accept that sometimes people made bad choices, no matter the circumstances or opportunities they were offered. Though he hoped Malloy turned things around, sometimes people didn't want to be saved. Only time would tell.

Finally, they were getting somewhere. Jeremy's first community service session was scheduled for the following day, Sunday, when the group of volunteers would start planning and building the benches for the senior center. Jeremy was to report to the senior center at ten in the morning, and he actually seemed interested. Maybe it wouldn't be too difficult to get him to follow through.

Lindsay had spent the morning making phone calls before calling Jake. She had been trying to dig up dirt on Zachary White, but so far nothing had panned out. Sure, some people said he had been stubborn, or a tough negotiator, but overall he had done well with his renovation projects. Some had done better than others, but all of the properties were still open for business, with no big complaints, and the communities seemed happy with the results.

Why was she so determined to find something wrong with him? Her parents had seemed happy with the offer, happy with the solution it offered. So why couldn't she just accept that?

Lindsay looked around at her kids reading on the sofa, at the beautiful scenery visible through the back windows of the house, at the drying canvas in one corner of the kitchen and the stack of notebooks filled with ideas on the counter. They had come back to life here, and the motel had been their connection. If her parents sold the motel, where would they go? Would they stay in Pine Valley? Would they move out of town, follow Lindsay and the kids back to Pennsylvania?

Without the motel, would she ever come back to this town, her childhood home and place of rediscovery?

Lindsay didn't begrudge her parents their happiness. They deserved it. But she couldn't help but feel a sense of loss, of uneasiness. With everything else up in the air, she had hoped the motel would remain the one constant. But, she supposed, change was inevitable. She had left years ago to forge her own path. What right did she have to make demands now?

With a sigh, Lindsay walked over to the dining table and picked up her pages of notes, contact information, and printed articles. She had to let it go.

Chapter 45

With Ed and Sylvie out gallivanting all weekend, Lindsay had to wait until Monday to concede defeat. She and the kids stopped by the motel with bagels and coffee, and Lindsay handed over a tote bag full of papers and notebooks.

"What's this?" Sylvie asked, taking the bag.

"This has everything I found on Zachary White."

"And?"

"And," Lindsay said with a sigh, "he seems legit. I didn't find anything that gave me doubts about his intentions. I think I just wasn't ready to let this place go."

"I know, sweetie," Sylvie said, putting the bag down and wrapping her arms around Lindsay. "It will be a tough adjustment for all of us."

After a moment, Lindsay pulled away. "The bag also has all of my ideas, sketches, whatever, for the motel, and a flash drive with the website mockup I had been working on. I'm sure Mr. White has his own plans, but I couldn't bring myself to throw them away, so they're there if he wants them."

"Oh, Lindsay," Sylvie said, giving her daughter another hug. "I know you had so many ideas."

Lindsay sniffed. "I did, but it's okay. Having it to work on helped me get my creativity back, so it wasn't a total loss." Even if she had no idea what she was going to do with it now. She had half-heartedly looked at job postings over the weekend, and the jobs she was qualified for no longer interested her. The creative jobs that sparked her interest all wanted design portfolios. All she had to offer were projects more than a decade old and ideas that had never left the runway. The inklings of panic were starting to set in, but she had been doing her best to push them down, telling herself she could always go back to the analytical side of things if she had to. If her boss – ex-boss – was willing to give her a positive reference.

For now, she had to accept being in limbo.

"So," she said as silence fell while they spread cream cheese on bagels. "Now that you won't have the motel anymore, what do you plan to do?"

Sylvie looked toward the living room, where Ed and the kids had taken their bagels and were watching TV. "We...don't know."

"You must have some ideas, at least."

"We do. We will probably travel a bit, spread our wings a little while we can. But we'll need a place to live, and we haven't decided where that will be. We were waiting to see what happened with you."

"What do you mean, 'what happened with me'?"

"Well, with you needing a new job, we weren't sure if you would be staying where you are in Pennsylvania, or if you would be looking elsewhere. We..." Sylvie looked at Ed and the kids again. "We thought you seemed pretty happy here. And with everything that happened this spring, with you being so unhappy there, we thought maybe you would want to stay."

Lindsay swallowed a bit of her bagel. It wasn't as if the thought hadn't occurred to her. "I don't think the kids would go for that. Jeremy in particular has made it clear he wants to go home. Their friends are there, our house and all our things are there. With the motel selling, once Jeremy's community service is done, there won't be any reason to stay."

Sylvie nodded. "Okay. Good to know. Just keep in mind that stuff is just stuff, and friends can be found anywhere. You need to ask yourself where you will all thrive, not just where is comfortable."

Her mother's words ran through Lindsay's mind as they drove back to the rental house. There was a magic show at the library that night, but until then, they were free. Since she still hadn't told her kids about her job, she had to at least pretend she was working, so she turned on her laptop, worked on her resume, and perused job listings. She looked in central Pennsylvania, where they lived, and just for the heck of it, she looked in Connecticut, too. Then, because she had been enjoying being home with her kids, she opened her search to remote opportunities, as well. There were plenty of openings, and many sounded interesting. But with her lack of a portfolio, and the competition she knew was out there, she didn't bother applying to any of them.

Frustrated and discouraged, Lindsay closed her laptop. The kids were doing their own thing today – Emma was painting outside, and Jeremy was working on a coding project on his tablet. "I think I need a break," Lindsay announced.

Jeremy's head bounced up to look at her. "Ice cream again?"

Lindsay laughed. "No, not today, kiddo. I think I'm going to just take a hike and unwind a bit. Did either of you want to join me?"

The kids were settled into their activities, so Lindsay grabbed her phone and keys and went out on her own. Though she had taken plenty of walks, she hadn't been in the woods since that first time, when she met Jake. She hoped she didn't get lost this time.

The air was peaceful, cooler among the trees. She could hear birds and other animals, the rustling of leaves, the crunching of branches beneath her feet. She closed her eyes and took a deep breath. Though they didn't live in a city, they didn't have anywhere like this near them. She would miss being so close to nature. She had forgotten how much she enjoyed it.

Lindsay was amazed at how quickly everything had changed. The summer wasn't even half over, and she had already turned her life upside down. If Jeremy didn't have to finish his community service, what would they be doing? Would they stick it out through the summer, or would they end things early and head home? They still could, if Jeremy finished his hours quickly. Maybe she should discuss it with him and see what he wanted to do. Once the sale of the motel went through, they would have no reason to stay.

Well, that wasn't entirely true. They hadn't come here because of the motel. They had come to get away from their hectic lives and try to regain their sanity. But they seemed to have accomplished that. Sort of. Still, the rental was paid for, so she might as well enjoy the peace while she could get it. Who knew what would happen when they went back.

Lindsay found a fallen log and sat down. It had certainly been an interesting summer so far. And the kids thought it would be boring! Maybe now that they had gotten the drama out of the way, they could really relax and figure things out. Maybe she would get some answers about where to go from here. She could hope, anyway.

Chapter 46

The hearing of David Malloy led, not surprisingly, to a trial. Jake was glad they had not only witnesses but hard evidence that linked him to many of the crimes he was being charged with. And while Sherry was handling the case, Jake was back to his regularly-scheduled duties. And filling out the detective application. This case had to look good on his resume, especially if the ruling went in their favor, so he was feeling pretty confident.

With David Malloy in custody, however, and the teens involved in the petty crimes working on their community service, the streets were pretty quiet. While Jake was grateful the crimes had been solved, he once again found himself with too much time on his hands. His gym routine was progressing nicely. The event committee was making excellent progress. and they had even had a few teens show up on Tuesday night, so that was good. But the rest of the time he was back to overthinking and twiddling his thumbs.

While he was hoping his application would go through and he would become detective, he had to acknowledge that in a town as small as Pine Valley, interesting cases were relatively few and far between. That, combined with all of the time he had been spending on his own, made him wonder if he should start looking into larger towns, larger departments, for more action. It wasn't that he wanted more crime, but he wanted to be useful, and he wanted to put his skills to the test. While he didn't think he would jump into another city, there were suburbs with substantially larger populations than Pine Valley that would offer more cases, and a greater variety. Maybe he should see who had openings.

Then again, if he was applying for detective, did it make more sense for him to get approved here, then try to transfer? Or did it make sense for him to go elsewhere, work a bit as an officer, then try to make detective there? It was a valid question, now that he thought of it.

Jake loved Pine Valley, though. He supposed he could still live here and work elsewhere, but it wouldn't be the same. He loved being part of the community, building that camaraderie with locals. If he left, it would be like starting from scratch. New colleagues, new townspeople.

He would have to do some serious overthinking on that, too. At least he had the time.

Lindsay fell into the habit of taking a walk in the woods every afternoon. She found it helped clear her mind and bring her peace. She hadn't come any closer to figuring out her life, but at least she had moments of serenity that helped keep her grounded.

One afternoon, Lindsay returned to the house to find Alyson, the house's owner, juggling groceries and baby Nicholas. She rushed over to help. Though she wouldn't describe them as friends, she and Alyson had chatted on occasion, and Lindsay felt a kinship with her.

"Need a hand there?"

Alyson looked up, relief in her eyes. "Oh, Lindsay, thank goodness. I thought Jonathan or Katie would be home when I got back, but apparently they're both out doing who knows what. If you could hold Nicky for a minute, I would greatly appreciate it."

Lindsay took the smiling baby and returned his smile, giving him a little bounce before tucking him in her arm. He had grown up so much in just the few short weeks they had been here. Now he was holding his head up better and taking in the world with wide eyes.

"He is such a happy baby," Lindsay remarked.

Alyson laughed and grabbed a few grocery bags. "When he isn't screaming, sure."

"I haven't heard any screaming from our side of the wall."

"That's because his bedroom is against the opposite wall." Alyson grinned.

"Well, if you ever need any help, at least while we're still here, just let me know. I'd be happy to watch him, or Emma has done some work as a mother's helper, and she took a class and everything, so she could help, too."

"Good to know. I'll have to keep that in mind."

Lindsay followed Alyson into the house, holding Nicholas. "You have a beautiful home," she said, taking in the sunken living room, warm furnishings and comfortable decor.

"Thanks." Alyson put down the grocery bags and started putting things away. "Oh, that reminds me. I heard that the motel was getting sold. I hope that's a good thing. I haven't had a chance to talk to Sylvie about it."

Lindsay sighed. "Yeah, it's good for my parents. The business has been struggling, and my mom has been really stressed about it. Plus with her health scare, she didn't feel up to taking on the challenge of reviving the business."

Alyson nodded. "Yeah, I get that. Does them selling affect your plans at all? Are you still planning on being here through the end of summer?"

"That's the plan, though who knows? Anything can change. This has been the summer of change, and I feel like I never know what's going to come next."

"I get that. That was me almost a year ago, right about the time I found out that little guy was coming into my life." She smiled at her son. "The reason I ask, though, is that we're thinking of putting the house on the market, and I want to make sure we don't disturb you with showings and all that. We can wait until after summer."

"Are you thinking of moving out of Pine Valley?"

"Not if we can help it, and if we don't find anything we like, we probably won't sell, either. It's just with my dad moving out, and Nicky here taking over, and Jonathan working from home...this house just isn't the best fit for us anymore. So we're reviewing our options."

Lindsay nodded. "I understand." Nicholas was leaning against her shoulder now, and Lindsay's heart nearly burst. It had been a long time since she had held a baby. "He is so sweet. But I think he might be getting sleepy."

"It is getting to be that time. And the cold stuff is put away now, so I'll take him and get him settled. Thanks for your help."

"Any time."

They said their farewells, and Lindsay returned to the in-law apartment next door. She had felt a pang when Alyson mentioned they might be selling the house. She just couldn't figure out if it was a pang of loss or of envy. Maybe a little of both. This place had started to feel like home.

Chapter 47

The motel closing was scheduled for the last week of July. Though Zach had assured them it wouldn't affect the sale, he wanted to get a full inspection to know what he was getting himself into. And he wanted to give Ed and Sylvie time to get their paperwork in order and pack up all of their things. He had offered more time, but now that the decision was made, they decided they might as well get it over with.

Packing seemed a monumental task, and an emotional one Sylvie hadn't quite expected. Though limited space had limited the amount of stuff they could accumulate, and they had decluttered a lot when they renovated the kids' bedrooms into motel rooms, there still seemed to be too much. But it all held memories, and Sylvie found it hard to let anything go. But where would they put it? For now, it seemed like the best option would be putting most of it in a storage unit in a nearby town. They rented a portable storage container and spent the next couple of weeks filling it up. Lindsay helped when the kids were occupied with programs and events.

The one question that still hung in the air was where Ed and Sylvie would go once the motel sold. They wanted to travel, but they didn't plan on jumping into that right away. They needed to get settled first, have a home base. And they didn't want to go see the world when Lindsay and the kids were right here. Sylvie thought about them all taking a short trip, to get away from all the upheaval, but

Lindsay had to be tight with money, and Sylvie was reluctant to spend too much until they knew what they would need to start this next chapter of their lives.

It seemed everyone was in limbo.

Word spread about the motel selling, and within a week Ed and Sylvie had had more conversations with friends and neighbors than they had had in years – and had two offers of spare rooms for them to borrow while they figured out next steps. They accepted the offer from one of their long-time friend couples, Giuseppe and Maria, who owned the Italian restaurant in town. Soon, suitcases filled with clothes and other things they thought they would need for the foreseeable future were brought to Giuseppe's and Maria's house, and Ed and Sylvie were saying goodbye to the motel apartment. They still needed to do a final check to make sure they hadn't forgotten anything, but they wouldn't be staying there anymore, their furniture having been brought to the storage unit.

Sylvie spent the first night in a strange room alternating between crying and thinking. While she knew selling was the right choice, she still felt like she was losing a part of herself. And she didn't quite know who she was without it.

Lindsay tried not to dwell on losing the motel. It wasn't part of her real life, she reasoned. It was a part of her past. And once she went back home, she would probably forget all about it. It wasn't as if she had lost her parents. She would actually be able to see them more often now, regardless of where they ended up, simply because they would have more flexibility to visit. This was a good thing. Her parents were happy, and she could move on.

She still cried when she saw the empty apartment.

Maybe it wouldn't have been so bad if she felt settled and hopeful for the future. But she still hadn't found anything that clicked on the job sites, her unemployment application was pending, and she was running out of things to do to make it look like she was still working. She supposed she should just bite the bullet and talk to her kids. But they seemed so settled, she hated to ruin things.

Jeremy's community service had been progressing nicely. The benches for the senior center had been completed, but one of the leaders of the volunteer group had taken a liking to Jeremy and offered him another opportunity, repairing the gazebo on the town green. After one session there, though, Jeremy had approached Lindsay with a sheepish expression.

"Mom, do you think you could ask Officer Jake about that event thing he's putting together? I think I might want to join the group for that."

Lindsay was surprised. "Really? I thought you decided that wasn't your thing."

Jeremy rubbed a hand against the back of his neck. "Well, the guy who runs the volunteer group, his daughter Ashley helps out sometimes, and she said she's on the committee, and it's actually kind of fun. The event is meant for kids our age, so we get to come up with all of the activities they're going to have."

Lindsay suspected this girl Ashley had more to do with Jeremy's change of heart than the committee did. Did Jeremy have his first real crush? "Sure. I'll give him a call and see what he says."

"Thanks."

A moment later, Jeremy was texting someone on his phone. This was an interesting development, and one she would have to keep an eye on. At least it took her mind off work and the motel.

The day of the closing, Ed, Sylvie, and Lindsay met in a lawyer's office near the center of town. While Lindsay wasn't needed for any of the paperwork, she wanted to make sure everything ran smoothly and that her parents were taken care of. She had dropped the kids off at the library so they wouldn't get bored hanging around the office.

Zachary White wasn't using a mortgage to pay for the property, so the stack of paperwork was relatively short, and the process surprisingly quick. Paperwork was reviewed and signed, Ed handed over the keys, Zachary handed over a check, and they all just sat a moment, processing. Then Zachary shook all of their hands, thanked them, picked up his briefcase, and left. Ed, Sylvie, and Lindsay stood up and walked out of the office, thanking the lawyers and staff for their time and assistance.

It felt very surreal, stepping into the sunshine and realizing what had just happened. Ed and Sylvie were officially homeless, though they could go wherever they wanted with the check in Sylvie's purse.

They decided to start with picking up the kids and going out for lunch. It would be both a celebration and a farewell, the end of an era, and the start of whatever came next.

Chapter 48

Jake was surprised to hear that Jeremy was interested in joining the committee, but more than happy to have him. The group of teens – four in all, with Jeremy being the fifth – had been surprisingly resourceful. coming up with ideas he would never have considered. With a mix of interests, they had thought of everything from info tables on how to help the environment to a dunk tank with their teachers as the victims. While they wouldn't necessarily be able to offer everything, Jake knew that the more they offered in terms of variety, the more likely they would get a good turnout. And having the teens helped not only with manpower but also with spreading the word, as they told their friends and classmates. If the event would offer fun, exciting activities that the teen committee members were passionate about, they were more likely to get their friends excited, too.

The summer was passing quickly, though, and if they didn't want to have to push the date again, they were going to have to put together solid plans. This week they were going to finalize the list of activities and figure out exactly how to make them happen, including supplies they would need, the number of volunteers, and anything that would need to be constructed or require additional work.

Funding was still a concern, especially as they would need to buy or rent the supplies they needed. They had decided to invite vendors, which would help with costs, but Jake felt they needed something else to help with funding, too. Maybe a raffle? He wanted the event to be free to attend, so they wouldn't be selling tickets. Maybe they could just ask for donations, or sponsors, or something. They would need to decide that, too. And fast.

With the event planning in progress, Jake hadn't made any decisions about his job. He found the idea of leaving Pine Valley unsettling, especially as he was setting down roots, building more relationships with community members, and doing his best to make a difference. Did he really want to leave now, when things were just getting going? So he continued to work on the application, but he hadn't submitted it yet. He had time.

Lindsay felt like she was running out of time. Every time she paid bills, her savings dwindled a bit more. She wasn't sure how long she could make it last, especially if her unemployment didn't go through. She was going to have to make some hard decisions. And she was going to have to tell the kids.

A few days after the motel closing, Lindsay called a family meeting with her kids. She hoped it would go more smoothly than the last one, back in June. But she was just as nervous, if not more so.

She took a deep breath while both kids watched her expectantly. "So, here's the deal, guys. I got fired. I lost my job a few weeks ago."

The kids looked at each other, then back at Lindsay. They didn't seem to know quite how to react.

"What happened?" Jeremy asked.

"Well, my boss didn't like that I was working remotely, but he gave it a shot. And, unfortunately, it started affecting my ability to do my job the way he wanted it, so he let me go."

"So what have you been doing all this time?" Emma asked. "When we thought you were working?"

"Updating my resume, looking at job listings. It's a tough job market right now, and I've been trying to figure out what to do."

"So what does this mean?" Jeremy asked. "Are we going to lose the house? Are we going to be homeless like Gran and Pops?"

"I won't let it get to the point that we're homeless, but I will need to find another job, and how long that takes will determine what we have to do. We might eventually have to downsize or something. We'll definitely have to cut back on things."

"Why didn't you tell us sooner?" Emma asked next.

"We had a lot going on, and you guys actually seemed pretty happy. I didn't want to ruin things. And I think part of me was in denial, hoping things would just work themselves out. FYI, that never works."

"So do we have to go back home early so you can find a new job?" Emma asked.

"Jeremy needs to finish his community service before we can leave, and I want to make sure Gran and Pops are set, too, though they're probably in a better position than we are. Gran said they want to see what we do before making final decisions."

"Do they know about your job?" Jeremy asked.

"Yeah, I told them right after it happened. That was the day they told me they wanted to sell the motel."

"That was a long time ago," Jeremy said.

"Yeah, I know."

Silence fell as they all processed what this meant.

"I don't want this to put a damper on the rest of our summer. I just wanted you guys to know because it's possible that it will start affecting things. I've had to be tighter with money, for example. And I might seem a bit stressed out as I figure out my next steps. I'll be applying for jobs, and that's never fun. But we can still do things. A lot of the things we've been enjoying don't cost money, right?"

"Right," Emma said.

"Sure," Jeremy agreed. He seemed deep in thought for a moment. "Are we going to have to move?"

"I don't know. There are a lot of factors involved. I just don't have an answer to that right now. Would you be really upset if we did? I know you took it hard when I said we would be here for the summer."

Jeremy shrugged. "I don't know. I mean, I would miss my friends and whatever."

Lindsay sat up a little straighter. Was he saying what she thought he was saying? That he wouldn't mind if they had to move? "What about you, Em? What are your thoughts on the situation?"

Emma shrugged, too. "I dunno. I guess if we had to. It would probably depend on where we had to move. I mean, I wouldn't want to live in a bad neighborhood or anything."

Lindsay smiled. "I wouldn't, either. I just meant if we couldn't live in our house, or if we had to go to another town to be closer to whatever job I find."

Emma shrugged again. "I guess that would be okay."

"Okay. Well, I will keep you both posted, okay? And I won't make any big decisions without discussing it with you first."

The kids nodded, and everyone went their separate ways. Lindsay was proud of her kids. They had taken it all in stride, opening themselves up to the possibility of major life changes with calm and patience. No yelling, no arguing or demands. It certainly opened up options.

Chapter 49

Sylvie answered the phone call from the vaguely familiar number with a tentative "hello?"

"Sylvie? Zachary White here."

"Oh, hello, Is everything okay? Did we forget something, or did we leave something in the motel?"

"No, no, nothing like that. I was going through all the paperwork you left, and I came across a couple of notebooks and a flash drive. It looks like ideas for the motel, ways to boost business and all that. Were you working with a firm or something? There are some great ideas. They really seemed to understand the community here."

"No, no firm. Those came from my daughter, Lindsay. She's in marketing. We had asked for her help to boost business before we decided it would be better to sell."

"Hmm. I take it she wasn't interested in taking over the business?"

"We never really discussed it. We discussed renovations and ways to bring in more people, but she never expressed interest in running things. And she and her kids live in Pennsylvania, so I don't think they were interested in moving, regardless."

"That's a shame."

"Are you regretting purchasing the motel?" Sylvie bit her lower lip. Would he be able to back out of the sale once everything was signed and done? The check was already cashed, but they hadn't spent it yet.

"No, no, not at all. But I like her ideas and would love to have her as part of the team for this project. I wonder if she would consider consulting or something."

Sylvie perked up. "Well, I do know she's in the market for a new job."

"She is, huh? Hmm. Do you have her number handy?"

Sylvie grinned. "Of course."

Lindsay hung up the phone and blinked. She wasn't quite sure what to make of that conversation she had just had. She turned to see both kids staring at her.

"What was that all about?" Emma asked.

"I'm not entirely sure. But I think the person who bought the motel just offered me a job."

He had actually offered her multiple jobs, with the option to pick the one that spoke to her. Apparently he had seen her idea books for the motel and liked what he saw. She could be a part-time consultant for the motel, doing what she had started doing for her parents; she could be the general manager for the motel, helping with the renovations and then overseeing the business when he went on to other projects; or she could be a consultant for his business as a whole, offering plans and ideas for any projects he took on. Salaries varied from not-enough-to-live-on to decent to great, but there was a lot more to consider than money.

"You'd be working at the motel?" Jeremy asked.

"Well, he mentioned a few different options. One would be working pretty much anywhere, though I would have to at least visit periodically, but it was only part-time, and, possibly, temporary. I'm not sure how well that would work out."

"What about the other ones?" Emma asked eagerly.

"One would be helping with not just the motel but all of his projects. It sounds interesting, but it also sounds like it would involve a lot of travelling, and possibly for extended periods of time, so I don't know how well that would work out, either." Though the pay on that one was very tempting, as was the chance to be creative. "The last one would be working at the motel, first helping with any renovations and getting things up and running again, and then being the manager. That one would require being local, so we would have to move. So I'm not sure how well that would work out, either."

"Why not?" Emma continued.

"It would be a big adjustment. It's not just moving to a different house or a different town nearby. We would be uprooting our lives and moving five hours away. You would be leaving a lot of things behind. You probably wouldn't see your friends again. I didn't think you guys would go for that."

Emma and Jeremy looked at each other.

"It's not so bad here," Jeremy said after a moment. "We could deal."

Lindsay's mouth nearly fell open. "Seriously?"

They both shrugged.

"You need a job, right?" Emma said. "Would you like that one?"

"I don't really know. I guess I'll have to give it some thought."

The kids resumed the game they had been playing before her phone call, and Lindsay sat at the dining table to think. Would she like being manager of the motel? She hadn't ever considered something like that. She liked the idea of being able to oversee the remodeling and the guest experience moving forward, but being a manager also meant handling employees and any customer issues that popped up. If there was a problem, she would be the one to have to fix it. Did she want that responsibility?

At the very least, she would probably want to discuss it with her parents. Not only would they be able to offer insight into the inner workings of the motel, but she could find out if they would be okay with her even being involved with the motel. Would that be weird for them? It would certainly be weird for her. And that wasn't even considering her kids' reaction to the news. That was weirding her out even more.

Maybe she should make a pros and cons list for each option. Then she would schedule a dinner with her parents to discuss the situation. As Emma had said, she needed a job. But would this be the right choice for her?

Chapter 50

Jeremy was proving to be a valuable addition to the committee. As someone who did not usually take on volunteer opportunities by choice, he offered an interesting perspective. What would make kids like him want to volunteer to help? What would make them even want to attend the event? As he pointed out, even if they would have fun when they got there, getting them to actually get there would be a challenge. Could they offer an incentive of some kind? Maybe a big prize that anyone who came could win? Or something free that everyone would get?

While Jake wasn't opposed to the idea, it once again brought up the top of funding, and that was a sore spot. The committee decided that the best way to kill two birds with one stone was to look for sponsors. They could offer different levels, for different amounts donated. And they could ask all sponsors to donate a prize as part of their sponsorship. Prizes could be raffled off, with each attendee getting a ticket for a chance to win a prize. Maybe they could even require guests to be present to win, thereby encouraging them to stay for the full event.

It was an interesting train of thought that they likely wouldn't have started if it weren't for Jeremy's incentive idea.

He had ideas for activities, too, that hadn't been suggested before, like eating contests and video game contests. It seemed Jeremy liked opportunities to win, whether it was prizes or simply bragging rights. But Jake knew that could be a big incentive for other kids, too, especially the kids he was trying to target most: those who could get into petty crime for thrills and boredom busting. If those kids wanted to get their adrenaline pumping, contests could be a fun – and legal – way to do it.

When Lindsay picked Jeremy up from his second committee meeting, Jake pulled her to the side.

"I wanted to let you know that Jeremy is doing really well here," he told her. "He has contributed a lot to the conversation and has some great ideas."

Lindsay released a breath. Jake suspected she didn't often get positive feedback about her son. "That's really great to hear. I'm glad he decided to join, even if it was to impress a girl."

Jake lifted one eyebrow. "A girl?"

Lindsay chuckled softly. "He only expressed interest in joining when this girl Ashley – I guess she's the son of the head of the volunteer committee he was working with? – said it was fun. I got the impression he wanted to spend time with her."

Jake laughed. "Yeah, I can see that." He pointed Ashley out to Lindsay. She and Jeremy were chatting and laughing over something on Jeremy's phone. "But she's a good kid. He could do worse."

"That's good to know. But I am glad he's actually contributing, too."

"He's contributed a lot. Solved some problems we were having, too."

Lindsay looked over at her son again and smiled. Jake knew teens could be tough, and he didn't have to parent them. After the rough start Jeremy had had to the summer, Jake was sure Lindsay had had more than her share of worries. But they both seemed to be on surer footing these days, and he was glad. He had gotten to know Jeremy a bit better, and he was a good kid. Jake knew that if he could stay on the straight path, Jeremy could accomplish great things. He had a good head on his shoulders when he wanted to use it.

"Well, we should get going," Lindsay said after a moment. "Thanks again." She smiled at Jake, and they said their goodbyes before Jeremy and Lindsay left the building to go home.

It was a shame they were leaving at the end of the summer, Jake thought suddenly. Jeremy would never get to see the event that he was working so hard to put together.

"So, Officer Jake said you've been doing a great job," Lindsay said as they walked to the car. "I'm proud of you, kiddo."

Jeremy shrugged. "I've just offered some ideas. No big deal."

"Well, they were a big deal to him. Apparently, you've helped solve some problems, too, so they really appreciate it."

"Just trying to get my hours in."

Lindsay looked at Jeremy, seated beside her in the front seat now. While he may never have started volunteering if it hadn't been for his court-ordered community service, she suspected he was starting to enjoy it. But there were only a couple more weeks of summer and a handful of hours left to complete. She wondered how the rest of the time would go – and what would happen once it was over.

She still had to decide about the job offers Zachary White had given her. They were having dinner with her parents the following night, and she planned on discussing it with them then. But she kept going back and forth in her mind over whether or not she wanted to take it. She supposed, given her current situation, that she should at least accept the part-time consulting gig, but she wasn't quite ready to accept. Something was holding her back, though she couldn't quite say what. Maybe it was just knowing that she would still be stressing about money.

She had to decide soon, though, regardless of what her parents said. With the summer winding down, she needed to know what she was doing, where she was going, and what she wanted. The kids would be starting school, and they would need stability, especially with Jeremy starting high school this year. He would have enough to worry about without wondering if they would be losing the house or having to move in the middle of the school year.

She should probably just take the job. The manager job. Sure, it paid a bit less than she had been making, but it was enough to live on. The kids didn't seem to mind moving now, surprisingly enough, and before this whole mess, hadn't she been wishing they could stay? What was holding her back now?

Lindsay sighed. One thing at a time. She would talk it over with her parents, do her best to think objectively, then make a decision. She could do this.

Chapter 51

"The client is requesting you, Lindsay."

Lindsay blinked her eyes and tried to check the time on the clock by Emma's bed. She had been sleeping in a bit since she no longer had a job or other reason to get up early. But even so, it was barely eight o'clock.

"Mr. Collins?"

"I know you forwarded all of the information you had, but the client is requesting you. Vivian just isn't cutting it."

"You fired me, Mr. Collins."

"Technically, I didn't."

"You said if I didn't go to the meeting, you would let me go. I didn't go to the meeting." True, she had never received her termination papers, but he had been pretty clear. And she hadn't been working all this time. Did he honestly think she still worked for him?

"But I didn't actually let you go. We just took a break."

That was an interesting way of putting it.

"And now we need you back. The client is threatening to walk."

Lindsay sat up and tried to wake herself up. "What exactly are you saying, Mr. Collins?"

Mr. Collins sighed. "I want you to come back to work. No, I *need* you to come back to work."

"I'll need to think about it."

"What's there to think about? I saw you filed unemployment, so I doubt you've gotten another job."

"Not exactly, but I have gotten an offer."

Silence fell on the line.

"Mr. Collins?"

"I'll give you a raise. Ten percent."

Lindsay swallowed. Her old job had already paid more than Zachary White's offer. It was very tempting to just say "yes" and get on with things. But what about everything she had learned? About herself and her kids? "When do you need to know by?"

"Yesterday. I told you, the client is asking for you. I need to give him an answer, like now."

"I'll let you know by this afternoon."

"Lindsay, I need to know."

"I understand. But I need a minute to think it over. I'll let you know by this afternoon."

Lindsay disconnected the phone and put it back down by her futon bed. Well, this changed things.

"Who was that?" Emma's groggy voice drifted over from the bed.

"My old boss. He wants me to come back to work."

Emma rolled over to face her mother. "Well, that's good, right?"

"I don't know. I need to think. I think we'll need to have another family meeting after breakfast."

Lindsay got up, grabbed some clothes, then went into the bathroom to shower and get ready for the day. What was she going to do?

By the time Lindsay finished making pancakes and setting the table, Emma had told Jeremy the news.

"Does this mean we'll go back home?"

Lindsay sighed. "I don't know. There's a lot to consider."

"What's there to consider?" asked Jeremy. "You lost your job, now you got it back. Things will go back to the way they were before, and we'll go home like we planned."

"That is certainly an option. But we need to consider what that means. I know it was my decision to come here in the first place, but I did it for a reason. The way things were before wasn't necessarily the best thing for us. I thought you guys were happy here."

Jeremy shrugged. "Yeah, it's been okay."

"You both said you would be fine with moving."

"That was when we didn't think we would have an option."

"So you wouldn't want to move if you had the choice."

Neither kid responded. Lindsay didn't know what to do.

"Okay, so here's the deal. I have two job offers on the table: one is going back to my old job, and one is becoming manager at the motel."

"Technically you have more than that," Emma replied. "Didn't the guy who bought the motel give you other options, too?"

"Well, yeah, but the other options wouldn't work out long-term." Unless maybe she could do the part-time consulting in addition to her old job. Would that be enough to keep her creative mind working? Would she have enough time and energy to do both? She had felt so overwhelmed before with just one job. "Let me get a piece of paper, and we'll work things out."

Lindsay grabbed a notepad, and they discussed the situation while they ate.

"Old job pays more. We would live in our old house. New job pays less. We would have to find a place to live."

"That seems like a no brainer, then," Jeremy said, stuffing half a pancake into his mouth.

"With the old job, I didn't like what I was doing. I was getting bored, and I felt overworked and overwhelmed. I think that was part of the problem. Between work itself and the mental energy drain, I didn't have much quality time with you guys. I felt tired all the time, and the only time I saw you seemed to be when we were driving somewhere, eating, or I was hounding you to get up or go to bed.

With the new job, I would be able to be more creative, try different things, meet new people. I could be around for you guys more. We would get more family time."

"Except when we were in school," Emma said.

"Yes, of course, except when you were in school. But even so, I could see you after school, and, if some of my ideas for the motel panned out, you could bring your friends over and hang out. It wouldn't be embarrassing. There would be stuff to do."

Jeremy looked skeptical.

"With the old job, we would move back to Pennsylvania. Life would pick up where it left off. Nothing much will have changed. With the new job, we would move to Pine Valley. Things might be slower, but we could find a nice place to live and make new friends. Life would continue like it has been for the last month and a half."

Both kids were silent.

If it were up to Lindsay, she knew what she would pick. While it may have its challenges, she would pick the manager job at the motel. As long as she had her parents' blessing. She felt at home here, fulfilled here. She felt like she could breathe here, and it wasn't just the fresh air.

"I could make the decision for us, but I want to make sure everyone has a say. We all have to live with the decision."

"You want to stay here, don't you," Jeremy said. It wasn't really a question.

Lindsay took a deep breath. "I think we would have a better quality of life here. I know it can be hard to see the big picture at your age, but I think we could be happy."

"When do we need to decide?" Jeremy asked.

"I told my old boss I would get him an answer by this afternoon. I *might* be able to hold him off a little longer, but he was already upset that I was making him wait. I was thinking we could have lunch with Gran and Pops instead of dinner, if they're available, and discuss the situation with them. If they're really waiting for us to figure things out before they decide about their own lives, then our decision affects them, too."

The kids nodded and finished their breakfast in silence, then went to their separate areas to get ready for the day and get involved in their own activities. Lindsay cleaned up the breakfast dishes, put away leftovers, and ran the dishwasher. It was going to be a long day, but at least by the end of it, she would have some answers.

Chapter 52

"Hello, Sylvie, Ed," Maggie greeted with a smile as Sylvie and Ed walked into the diner. "How are you doing today?"

"Oh, we're doing just fine, Maggie. How are you?"

"Can't complain. Table for two?"

"Actually, it will be five. We're meeting Lindsay and the kids."

"Oh, that's nice! Let's head over to the corner booth."

They walked to the specified table, and Ed and Sylvie slid in.

"Jordan will be waiting on you today. He'll be right over to get you started."

"Thanks, Maggie."

Sylvie slid a menu out from behind the napkin dispenser, but she couldn't focus on the words. Her mind was whirring with possibilities that would explain why Lindsay had needed to move their meal together up from dinner to lunch. Linsday had been very secretive on the phone, insisting they would discuss it when they got together. What could be so urgent that it couldn't wait a few more hours?

Maggie approached the table again carrying a tray with glasses of water. "Jordan's occupied with another table at the moment, so I'll just drop these off while you're waiting for the kids." She set the glasses at the place settings, then tucked the tray under one arm. "How's life without the motel?"

"I can't decide if it's boring or peaceful," Ed said with a chuckle. "I certainly have more time on my hands."

"Oh, I understand. Just that brief time when the diner was out of commission had me going stir crazy. But I'm sure you'll settle into new routines and find new things to keep yourself occupied."

"That's the hope," Sylvie replied. "We just have to figure out next steps."

"Are you sticking around Pine Valley or moving to be closer to one of your kids?"

"Matthew is clear out in California, so I don't think that's happening. But maybe Lindsay. We'll have to see what she decides."

"I didn't know there was anything for her to decide."

"Oh, Maggie, I could fill you in, but it would take all day. One of these days I'll stop in during a slow time, and I'll get you up to speed."

"Ooh, the anticipation." Maggie laughed. "I can't wait."

Just then Lindsay and the kids arrived, and Maggie went to show them to the booth.

Ed and Sylvie shared a look. They, too, were filled with anticipation.

After greetings were shared and orders were placed, silence fell over the table.

"Well?" Sylvie asked after a minute.

"Well, what?" Lindsay asked.

"Don't give me that. Why did you need to change from dinner to lunch? What's going on that is so urgent it couldn't wait until later?"

Lindsay sighed. "I got a very unexpected call this morning. My boss wants me to come back to work."

"I thought he fired you!"

"So did I. He said it was just 'taking a break.' Apparently, the firm's big client is requesting me personally, and now he insists he can't live without me. I guess the person who was handling the account hasn't been doing a good enough job. He even offered me a raise."

"Oh, my," Sylvie replied, taking a sip of her water. "Are you going to go back to it?"

Lindsay looked over at the kids, who were busy on their phones. "I don't know. A week ago I probably would have said yes, just for the stability because the whole applying for jobs thing has completely overwhelmed me and I didn't have other decent options. But a few days ago I got a very interesting call from Zachary White, and that has had my brain going a million miles a minute with all the possibilities." Lindsay filled them in on the call and the offers Zachary had made.

"Oh my goodness," Sylvie said. Ed seemed equally dumbfounded. "I mean, I gave him your number after he came across your idea books. He seemed interested in your input. But I didn't know he was quite so taken."

"It was beyond unexpected," Lindsay replied. "But when it happened, I sat the kids down and asked them their opinion. At the time, they seemed okay with the possibility of moving. They knew I had lost my job, and they knew there would likely be changes as a result. But when I got the call this morning and discussed it with them, now they seem to think it's a given that we'll go back to the way things were."

"And you're not convinced."

Lindsay shook her head. Her eyes were damp. "Even before I lost my job, I had been thinking how much I no longer enjoyed what I was doing. Being in Pine Valley, working on ideas for the motel, sparked my creativity again, and I realized I wanted to do something more creative. The job – any of the jobs – with the motel would let me do that. And it's probably the only one I would get. All of the other ones I saw required experience and portfolios, and I don't have anything recent to show. But my old job has better pay, and more stability, and the kids would be happier."

"Would they?"

Lindsay shrugged. "It would be their choice."

Ed took one of Lindsay's hands in his. "Lindsay, this is your life, and your decision. I will never try to force you one way or the other. But from everything your mother said about how you were feeling this spring, and how you looked and acted when you first came back home, I find it hard to believe that going back to the way things were would make any of you happier."

"But Jeremy especially has had such a hard time adjusting to life here."

"Has he?" Ed asked. "Because from what I've seen, he had a rough start, and a really rough patch for a bit, but once he got over that hump, he's settled in just fine. I would even say he's been successful here, finally getting his nose out of his screen once in a while and doing other things."

Linsday fell silent. After a moment she continued, as if she just needed to think up other excuses. "But he's had trouble making friends. He had some really good friends back home. And I don't even know if I would like the job here. Would you guys even be okay with it? I mean, wouldn't that be weird: me working at the motel, but for someone else?"

Sylvie looked at Ed, and they both shrugged. "Just because that chapter of our lives is over, Lindsay, doesn't mean we have hard feelings about it." Sylvie patted Lindsay's hand, still clutching Ed's. "We never even considered that you would want to run the motel and never wanted to put that kind of pressure on you. But if it is something you would like to do, you most certainly have our blessing."

Lindsay closed her eyes and took a deep breath. A week ago she had been anxious and overwhelmed from not having any options. Now she was overwhelmed from having too many. She wished she knew which option would be best. Not just for her, but for all of them. Did she really want to uproot all of their lives for something she may not end up liking? But did she really want to go back to a job she didn't like just because it was comfortable? Which option would she regret more?

Maybe life in Pennsylvania would be better now, now that they had had a break and got to spend time together as a family. Maybe they would be able to take what they learned and apply it to their old life, have the best of both worlds. And if it didn't work out, there was no reason they couldn't move later on. Even if the job at the motel was no longer available, there would be others. And Pine Valley wasn't the only small town out there. Even if it was the one she had a connection with.

"I think," said Lindsay after a moment. "I think we need to go back. For closure, if nothing else. I need to see if things are different now. And, as superficial as it sounds, I need the money. I was already spending too much before I lost my job. Having the last few weeks without a paycheck has dwindled my already meager savings. With the pay raise, I can catch up and start putting more aside."

Sylvie and Ed shared another look. "If that's really what you want, Lindsay, we'll support you," Sylvie said. "You know that."

"It's not all about what I want. Sometimes I have to think logically. And between what the kids want and what will provide more security for us, I think I have to do it."

Silence fell again, until Jordan brought over their meals.

"Can I get you anything else?" he asked with a smile.

"No, I think we're all set," Sylvie replied with her own smile. "Thank you, Jordan."

They ate in silence for a few moments.

"But maybe," Lindsay said finally. "Maybe I'll see if Mr. White will still let me do the part-time consulting. You know, to keep my creativity alive and my options open."

Sylvie smiled as she cut into her open-faced sandwich, but she didn't say a word.

Chapter 53

Jeremy's community service hours were almost complete, though neither he nor Jake said anything about it. Jake signed the paperwork every week, and that was it. Jeremy seemed to be enjoying his work on the committee, so Jake was reluctant to bring it up, afraid Jeremy would take it as a sign he wasn't wanted or needed anymore, when the truth was, Jake wished he would be able to stay and see things through to the end.

Jake knew the family would be leaving town soon, and he was sad to see them go. He had grown rather fond of Jeremy, and his interactions with Lindsay had left him wishing they could get to know each other better, too.

The task for the week had been to search for sponsors. The committee would be breaking up into pairs and approaching different businesses in the area, both within Pine Valley and in neighboring towns, to solicit donations and prize contributions. Since some of the teen members were on the young side, they would be paired up with adults, and Jake and Jeremy became a team. The committee had made a list of businesses to approach and divided it amongst the teams to ensure businesses were not approached multiple times. Jake and Jeremy were starting with five businesses in the center of town.

They decided to start with the Pine Valley Diner. Knowing Maggie and Richard, they would be more than willing to contribute something, and Jake figured they could use an easy win to boost morale and get them started on the right foot.

Jordan was the greeter that morning, and he welcomed them both with a smile. "Good morning, gentlemen. Table for two?"

"No, thanks, Jordan, we were actually hoping to speak with Maggie or Richard. Is either one of them in?"

"Sure. Let me get Mr. Richard for you."

Richard was working in the kitchen, and he glanced up through the window when Jordan approached. He waved at Jake and Jeremy with a spatula. "Be with you in a minute," he called out.

"Now, I'm not sure if you've met Richard yet," Jake said to Jeremy, "but he's a really nice guy. I would be surprised if he's not willing to donate something to the event, so it should be an easy sell. Would you like to give it a try, warm up a bit?"

Jeremy seemed nervous and unsure, but Jake smiled reassuringly, and Jeremy eventually nodded. "Okay. I'll try."

"Great. Here he comes now."

Richard approached them with a broad smile and held out one hand to shake Jake's. "Good morning, Jake. What can I do for you?" He turned to Jeremy. "Hello, young man. I don't believe we've met."

"Good morning, Richard. This here is Jeremy. He's Ed and Sylvie's grandson."

"Ah! Well, welcome. It's nice to meet you. What brings you in today?"

Jake turned to Jeremy and nodded. Jeremy took a deep breath and stood up straighter, then looked Richard in the eye.

"We are putting together an event to take place this fall, and we were looking for sponsors to help with donations and prizes. Would the diner like to contribute something?" The words came out rather quickly, and Richard smiled again.

"I'm not quite sure I caught all that, but it sounded like you're planning an event? What kind of event?"

"It's going to be a kind of fair, with lots of activities for kids and teens."

"That sounds great. And you're looking for donations?"

Jeremy nodded. "Yeah. We need to raise money to pay for supplies and stuff, so we're looking for sponsors to help out. And we're going to have prizes for people who come, so we're looking for people to donate prizes, too."

Jake watched Jeremy and smiled. He was so proud of this kid. He had come such a long way.

"Well, Jeremy, I'm sure we can help out in some way. What do you think people might like as a prize?"

Jeremy looked around. "Well, personally, I'd like an ice cream sundae. But that might be a little tricky to have outside for a while."

Richard laughed. "This is true. Well, we could do something edible, like a pie or something, but what do you think about a gift certificate instead, so people can pick out their own treats?"

Jeremy nodded. "That would work."

"Now, were there different levels of sponsorship available, or is just whatever people are willing to give?"

Jake interrupted to handle the specifics. "We hadn't really set levels. We're kind of new at this, so if you'd like to donate, we would gladly accept anything you're willing to offer."

"Hmm. Gotcha. Okay. How about this: we'll give a hundred-dollar cash donation as a small sponsor, and a twenty-five-dollar gift certificate as a prize. Would that work?"

Jeremy grinned. "That would be great. Thanks!"

Richard returned the grin. "Great. Now when would you need them by? Do you want a check now?"

They worked out logistics and went on their way. Jake was really glad one of the committee members had suggested opening up a bank account for the event. It was a lot more professional for people to write a check out to an organization instead of an individual.

When Jake and Jeremy were back on the sidewalk, Jeremy turned to Jake and grinned. "That was easy."

Jake laughed. "They won't all be that easy, but I'm glad it went well. Let's see who's next on our list."

By the time they finished their list an hour later, they had acquired one more sponsor, one prize donation, and a couple of "let me think about it" responses.

Jake tucked the checks they had received, and the business cards and flyers to go with them, into the gift bag holding the physical prize donation. "I think this is a great start, though I just realized we hadn't established where the prizes were going to get stored, so I guess I'll just hold onto these things until the next committee meeting."

"Okay. Are we done for today?" Jeremy asked.

Jake nodded. "Yup. That was everyone on our list. And I'm going to have to head to work soon. I'm glad we were able to get to them all today."

"Me, too."

They walked to Jake's car so he could drive Jeremy back to the rental house.

"Okay. I, um, have my community service sheet, if you could sign it?" Jeremy dug out a folded piece of paper from his pocket and handed it to Jake.

"Yeah, of course." Jake found a pen in his center console and signed the paper, then handed it back. "Here you go."

They were sitting in the car now, though Jake hadn't started the engine yet.

"So, uh, I think that was my last hour. So I think I'm done with my community service?" Jeremy seemed awkward.

"Oh, okay. So I can actually take that paper and submit it at the station, get everything all official."

"Okay. Thanks."

"No problem."

Silence fell, and Jake could tell Jeremy wanted to say something else.

"Was there something else?"

"Yeah, uh. I think I'm not here for much longer, but could I still help with the event stuff? Even if I don't need any more hours?"

Jake smiled. "Of course. We'd be happy to have you. I have to be honest, I wish you were going to be here until the end. It's a shame you won't get to see the results of your hard work and ideas."

Jeremy shrugged. "Yeah. It sucks. But doing the other stuff has been fun, too. And I hope you get a good turnout."

"Me, too."

They drove off in silence then, and when they arrived at the rental house, Jeremy said "thanks" and got out of the car. Jake waved goodbye, made sure he got into the house, and left.

He was going to miss that kid.

Chapter 54

Despite the kids' desire to get home, everyone seemed a bit lethargic as they packed up everything that had accumulated or used over the summer. They still had a couple of days, but Lindsay wanted to get the bulk of it done early, so they could make sure they hadn't left anything behind. She had given Alyson her contact information, though, just in case something turned up after they had left.

Lindsay wasn't sure how to feel. A big part of her really wanted to stay in Pine Valley. It had been a crazy summer, but being here had brought her so much fulfillment. It was hard to let it go. But they had to go back. She couldn't pass up the stability of her job, and the kids were anxious to be with their friends again. And she had to see if what they had learned would transfer to real life. Because this summer had not been real life. It had been a vacation, a departure from reality, a dream. Or a nightmare, depending on how you looked at it. She definitely did not wish to relive Jeremy's arrest or her mother's heart attack.

She did worry about her mother. While Sylvie seemed to be doing fine health-wise – and had assured Lindsay that her checkups since the heart attack had gone well – Lindsay wouldn't forgive herself if something happened the moment they left. She hoped her parents would decide to move closer to them. Sylvie said they were waiting for Lindsay to get settled again. Why, Lindsay could only guess. It wasn't as if they were starting over somewhere new. They were going back home.

Lindsay had spent the last week working remotely, with the understanding that she would be back in person the Monday after they got back. She had already started feeling herself get dragged down, but she brushed it off, telling herself she was still in vacation mode. Once they got into their regular routines, things would get better. And if they didn't, she would figure out a way to deal with it. At least she had her side project to help her cope. That would be different. And it was already bringing her joy.

Though he had been disappointed she hadn't taken him up on one of the full-time positions, Zachary was happy to have her help with the motel renovation in a part-time capacity. Lindsay had met with him twice to go through her idea books and discuss the plans she had started to compile before her parents sold the motel. When she got back to Pennsylvania, she would be able to work remotely, helping to design the website and conferring about other plans, as well. Lindsay was enjoying the work and hoped it continued for a while. She didn't know how long the renovation would take, but she was already dreading when it ended and the position stopped. Maybe Zachary would be willing to let her consult on other projects he took on, too. She found herself craving the creative outlet. Plus, she reasoned, it would help her build a creative portfolio, too, so if going back to her old job didn't work out, she would have something to show as experience for new opportunities.

They decided to leave on Saturday, so they would have a day or so to settle in before having to return to work and school on Monday. The kids were not looking forward to school, but they were happy to see their friends, so they didn't complain too much. Lindsay realized with a groan that they would have to figure out school supplies when they got back, too. And with Jeremy starting high school, they really needed to get into the right headspace. Maybe they should have given themselves more time to settle in. But she had been so reluctant to leave.

On Friday, Lindsay and the kids made their rounds to say goodbye to everyone they had met in Pine Valley. Emma wanted to say goodbye to her new friends.

Lindsay wanted to extend her appreciation to Officer Jake. And they all wanted to say goodbye to the librarians and staff at the community center, the staff at The Art Spot, and Natalie at the cafe, who had helped keep Lindsay fueled with coffee. Walking along Main Street, Lindsay breathed in the fresh air and took in the sights and sounds. She would miss this.

Ed and Sylvie came to the rental house Friday night, carrying pizza, for a last hurrah. They had planned a night of pizza and board games, a little relaxation and fun before the drive back to reality.

Sylvie was sorry to see them go. She had seen Lindsay and the kids blossom over the last couple of months. Gone were the pale, drawn faces. In their place were smiling, content faces. Or there had been, before the packing and goodbyes had set in. Lindsay had said the kids wanted to go back, but Sylvie wasn't convinced. They all seemed pretty disappointed about leaving. But she knew Lindsay got nervous about change. Her failure of an ex-husband offered little to no support, so it was up to her to make sure the kids had what they needed, even if it meant sacrificing her own happiness. But they could have had it all here, if Lindsay had been willing to take a chance.

Or maybe it was just wishful thinking on Sylvie's part. Maybe it was her own feelings of not being able to let go that made her think Pine Valley would be perfect for her family. After all, she and Ed still needed to decide if they wanted to stay or leave. Even without the motel, it was hard to think about leaving the home they had known their whole lives. They knew these streets, these people. Good or bad, it was home. So maybe she was just projecting. Maybe she was just hoping Lindsay would stay so they would have a reason to stay, too. Maybe Lindsay felt that way about her home in Pennsylvania, even if she had grown up here.

Sylvie sighed but tried to cover it with a smile as she set up the pizza boxes on the dining table. They were going casual so no one would have to do dishes: paper plates or eating straight out of the boxes.

She felt strange hosting, in a sense, in someone else's house. She was so used to Lindsay and the kids coming to the motel apartment. It still felt strange living in someone else's house, even though Giuseppe and Maria had been gracious hosts. It hadn't felt right inviting people over. But this didn't feel right, either, especially with suitcases lined up against one wall and an air of sadness hanging over everything. She had to shake this melancholy.

Sylvie did her best to brush off the sadness, and they had a pleasant evening eating and playing games, chatting and laughing. She was going to miss this time together. Hopefully they would be able to see each other again soon.

As they drove back to their temporary residence, Sylvie turned to Ed.

"I'm going to miss them," she said.

"Me, too."

"Think they'll come back?"

Ed glanced at Sylvie. "I hope so. I think being here was good for them."

"Me, too. I wish that dumb old boss of Lindsay's hadn't called her. I think they might actually have considered staying if he hadn't."

"Maybe. But maybe they just needed a break. Maybe going back will be good for them now."

Sylvie harrumphed. "I hope not."

Ed chuckled. "You want them to be miserable?"

"I want them to stay here."

Ed sighed. "I know. But they have to live their own lives."

"What will we do if they don't come back?"

"I guess we'll have to decide where we want to live our own lives."

Sylvie watched the town pass through the side window. "I can't imagine living anywhere else."

Chapter 55

The house felt stuffy and stale. Lindsay had had a neighbor check on it periodically, but no one had stayed there for two months. It felt much longer.

They brought the suitcases and bags into the house and deposited them in the living room. Then Lindsay turned on the central air, turned on the water, and collapsed onto her bed. She felt both physically and emotionally exhausted. It was only mid-afternoon, but it felt like midnight. She could hear the kids moving around before settling in their own bedrooms, probably to touch base with friends or zone out to screens, even though they had spent most of the drive home on their devices.

At some point Lindsay would have to go grocery shopping and school supply shopping, dust and vacuum the house, and get herself and the kids organized for Monday morning. But she was pretty sure she had a box of pasta and a jar of sauce she could use for dinner. The rest could wait until tomorrow. For now, she just wanted to sleep.

Lindsay woke up two hours later. with the sun now shining in her eyes through her bedroom window. The kids were quiet. The entire house was quiet. She felt groggy but at least somewhat capable of functioning now. She went upstairs to check on the kids. Faces glued to screens, as anticipated.

"Hey, guys," she said, standing in the hallway between the kids' rooms, "I think we should probably take a screen break. I'm going to go make dinner now."

"Okay," they both said without moving.

Lindsay rolled her eyes. "Five minutes on screens, then I want you downstairs and doing something else."

They were tired, too, she reasoned. They needed the downtime, too. And if she was firm, set some ground rules, they wouldn't slip into their old habits of screens twenty-four seven.

Finding the pasta and sauce, Lindsay put together a quick meal. The kids had begrudgingly come downstairs when she had reminded them their time was up, but they hadn't moved past the living room, where they both sat reading in silence. At least that was an improvement.

"Time for dinner, guys."

They ate quietly, each in their own world. Even Lindsay wasn't up to making conversation. After they ate and put their bowls in the kitchen sink, the kids went off and did their own thing. They were probably on their devices again, but Lindsay didn't have the energy to argue with them about it, so she let it slide.

Tomorrow would be better. After a good night's sleep, they would be ready to get things done. She hoped.

Jake hadn't been expecting to hear from them, but at a quarter to four in the afternoon, he received a text from Jeremy.

> we're home

Simple, to the point, but still unexpected.

> I'm glad you made it back ok.

Should he keep the conversation going? Had Jeremy reached out because he needed someone to talk to, or was he just being polite? Then again, since when did fourteen-year-old boys do anything just to be polite?

> How does it feel to be back?

> weird

> Weird how?

> it's quiet here. well the house is quiet but outside is noisy

Jake laughed, but he knew what Jeremy meant.

> Probably because your house is bigger but there's more going on outside than there is in Pine Valley.

> i guess

When no additional message was forthcoming, Jake went about his day. He was just about to head to the gym when he got another text notification.

> can i still text you even if we dont live in pine valley anymore

Jake felt like his heart would burst.

> Of course. I'm here whenever you need to chat, or any-time.

> thx

Jake knew that Jeremy's dad wasn't really in the picture, that their parents had divorced and he only saw his dad once or twice a year now, if that. He was at a tough age, growing up but not quite there yet. If Jake could offer any kind of guidance or support, he would be honored. He wondered if there was something on Jeremy's mind now, or if he was just feeling anxious about being back home and starting high school soon. He would take Jeremy's lead and see what happened.

At about ten that night, when he figured Jeremy should already be in bed, Jake received another text notification.

i dont think we should have left pine valley

Chapter 56

It had been two days since Lindsay and the kids had left, and with them gone and the motel sold, Sylvie felt a bit lost. And, despite her statement to Ed about not wanting to live anywhere else, she was finding that Pine Valley just didn't feel the same.

Ed had started meeting up with some buddies at the senior center to play cards and chat about who knew what. She had started volunteering with any committee or organization that would take her: the library, the senior center, the food bank, the town's beautification committee, Officer Jake's event committee. Without a home to spread out in, she was just looking for ways to keep busy. She didn't want to wear out their welcome with Giuseppe and Maria, and she was still uncertain about what to do long-term. Should they try to rent an apartment in the meantime, until they came up with a plan? Should they accept that Lindsay had moved away again? And if so, should they follow her, or should they stay here?

Ed was no help. He said he would be fine wherever. But whenever he wasn't at the senior center, Sylvie saw him wandering a bit aimlessly, too. Without his million and one projects at the motel, he didn't seem to know how to fill his days.

"Why don't you see if anyone needs anything fixed?" Sylvie suggested one day, after watching Ed flip through television stations for fifteen minutes without settling on anything.

He looked up at her. "What?"

Sylvie sighed. "You obviously don't know what to do with yourself. And I know at the motel you would be wandering around finding something to fix. So why don't you ask around and see if anyone needs anything fixed? You could be a handyman."

Ed's eyes lit up. "Do you think?"

Sylvie laughed. "Oh, Ed. You can be so thick-headed sometimes. If that is something you would enjoy, then go for it. It will keep you busy and out of my hair, at least."

Ed grinned and got up with renewed energy. Sylvie laughed again. When he left the room, however, her smile faded. She didn't have any projects or tasks for the rest of the day, and she was feeling antsy. She wanted to touch base with Lindsay, but it was Monday, and she knew Lindsay would be back at work and the kids would be back at school. She wondered how they were all adjusting. Of course, the first day back would be a difficult adjustment for anyone, but after everything that had transpired over the last few months, Sylvie was sure they would all be feeling anxious.

With no specific goal in mind, Sylvie decided to take a walk. The one good thing that had come about after the motel sold was that she was no longer chained to one place. She could wander and waste time, go where she pleased. And they had taken a few day trips, and she had been working with her volunteering, but she felt like she needed something more. She hadn't been quite ready to retire, and if things had been different with the motel, she would have been fine staying there for at least a few more years.

Maybe she needed a part-time job or something. Hadn't she been thinking along those lines before, anyway? The money that they got for the motel wouldn't last forever, and they had hardly anything set aside for retirement. The motel had eaten up almost all of their savings. They had started collecting social security a year or so ago, so they weren't destitute, but she wanted a cushion. She wanted to do more than just get by. But what would she do?

With the idea in mind, Sylvie wandered around town, thinking of the possibilities. She could probably work as a receptionist somewhere; she certainly had enough office experience. But did she want that again? Maybe she needed something more active. Her doctor told her she needed more exercise to get her heart back in shape. But she and Ed had started taking walks after dinner. Maybe that would be enough. She supposed she would have to give it some thought.

By the time she had walked from the house to the center of town, up and down Main Street, and back to the house, Sylvie was tired. Though she hadn't hurried, it was a good few miles. But at least she wasn't feeling antsy anymore. And it was now late enough to call Lindsay. They would have to figure out dinner soon, but she had time.

Ed wasn't back yet, so Sylvie got comfortable on the chair in their room and took out her cell phone. Did she want Lindsay to have had a good day or a not good day? She was undecided. Obviously, she didn't want her daughter miserable, but if it gave her a nudge back to Pine Valley...

Lindsay heard her phone ring and sighed. It had been quite the day, and she was tempted to let it go to voicemail. But a glance at the screen told her it was her mother, and she couldn't take the chance if something was wrong.

"Hi, Mom." She knew she sounded tired and distracted, but she couldn't help it.

"Hello, Lindsay. Is now a bad time?"

Lindsay looked around, at where shoes and backpacks had been tossed by the back door, pans and assorted food items were scattered on the kitchen counter waiting to make dinner, and dishes were piled in the sink. But she could use a few minutes to decompress, so she pulled out a dining chair and sat down. "No, it's fine. I was just trying to figure out dinner."

"You sound tired. Was it a rough day back?"

"Just...an adjustment." Had her boss always been that demanding? Had the clients always been that whiny? She was probably exaggerating things. She just wasn't used to it anymore.

"How about the kids?"

The kids had been relatively quiet when she came home. They had said their day was fine. They didn't have homework yet. They hadn't heard about clubs or anything yet. But she had had to pry every answer out of them, and that was exhausting in and of itself. "They said their day was fine. Neither was all that enthusiastic. But I don't think any kid is excited to go back to school after summer break."

"I suppose. How are you settling back in at home?"

"Oh, just the typical stuff. Had to get us caught up, go grocery shopping, all that. I imagine it will be a little while before we get used to the new routines again."

Sylvie fell quiet.

"How are things on your end?"

"Oh, they're all right, I suppose. Trying to figure out our new routines, too. I'm not sure where you father went. He was at loose ends, so I suggested he go out and fix something, and I haven't seen him since. Hopefully he hasn't gotten himself into trouble."

Lindsay laughed, and it felt good. "I think you may have unleashed a monster. Before you know it, he'll have fixed any problem in Pine Valley."

"There are worse things."

"Yes, I suppose there are."

Silence fell again.

"Well, I know you're busy," Sylvie said after a moment. "I won't take up any more of your time. I just wanted to check in, see how you were doing. Let me know if you need anything."

"Okay. Thanks, Mom. I'll talk to you soon."

They disconnected the call, and Lindsay sat for a moment with her phone in her hand. She had known it would be hard coming back. The simple act of returning to work in person would be difficult, regardless of the job itself. It would be easier when she got back into the swing of things. And the kids would be better, too. Going back to school was never fun. She should probably make sure they had everything they needed, though, with new classes and schedules.

They could discuss it over dinner. Speaking of which, she had to get that going. With a deep breath, Lindsay stood up and began chopping vegetables.

Chapter 57

Jake hadn't pressed Jeremy for details about why he thought they shouldn't have left Pine Valley, but he was curious. Figuring it was most likely due to the difficult adjustment of going back home and starting school again, he made a mental note to check in periodically and make sure Jeremy was doing okay. Since school started on Monday, Jake sent a quick text to see how the day had gone.

> How was your first day back at school?

it sucked

> Because it's school? Or did something happen?

its school. plus, high school. the building is huge and i dont know most of the kids and we have 2 min to get to our classes

> Aren't your friends there?

i guess. theyre mad at me for ditching them this summer

> I thought you kept in touch with them.

for a while. after the thing which shall not be named it felt weird to talk to them

> I get that.

And he did. Friends could be fickle, especially if you didn't get to see them face to face. And if you were feeling guilty about something they wouldn't understand, that made it even harder.

> Maybe you'll make some new friends. More kids means more chances.

im just not feeling it

> I know. Give it time. It was the first day. Maybe things will get better.

Jake wanted to suggest talking to his mom, but he wasn't sure how that would go over. Besides, Lindsay probably had enough on her plate. She had to go back to work plus juggle two kids. No sense putting additional burden on her unless it was necessary. He would do his best to be there for Jeremy from a distance.

The first week back felt like a month. Lindsay hadn't realized how much of her job she did on autopilot while her brain wished it was doing something else. The client who had insisted she come back was demanding, her boss offered her next to no support, and Vivian, who had been handling the account in Lindsay's absence, had basically sent her the files and said it was her problem now.

On top of that, the kids had been moody, she had had hardly any time to work on her side gig, and she collapsed into bed every night exhausted. The free time she did have was spent zoning out to some movie on television because she didn't have the mental capacity for anything else.

It didn't take a genius to figure out that things were just as bad as they had been before. And, while the boosted paychecks were helping to pay the bills, Lindsay was thinking it wasn't worth it.

When the weekend finally came around, Lindsay called another family meeting.

"Okay, guys. I know this has been a rough week."

Emma rolled her eyes and crossed her arms, leaning back on the sofa. "You can say that again."

"What's going on, Em?"

Emma shrugged. "I don't know. School is boring."

"School is always boring," Lindsay countered. "But you don't usually mind it."

"It's okay, I guess. I just feel...I don't know."

Lindsay nodded. "Okay. How about you, Jeremy? I know you haven't been happy, too. Is it school?"

Jeremy shrugged. "High school sucks. And my friends ditched me. I'm trying to make new friends, like Officer Jake suggested, but everyone has their friend groups already."

Emma nodded in agreement, but Lindsay said, "Officer Jake? When did you talk to Officer Jake?"

Jeremy's ears got red. "We text sometimes."

Lindsay swallowed. Was this something to worry about? Or was Jake looking out for her son?

"Okay. What do you text about?"

"Just stuff. School. Life."

"Okay." She would have to tuck that away to unpack later. And maybe discuss with Officer Jake. "I'm sorry you've been having a tough time, too."

Jeremy shrugged again.

Lindsay took a deep breath. "Okay. Well, it's been a tough week, but we have the entire weekend ahead of us. What should we do? It doesn't sound like you've made any plans with friends."

Silence fell.

"I thought I might paint a little," Emma said after a moment. "I never got to finish the picture I was working on before we left Pine Valley."

"Okay. Jeremy?"

"I dunno. I'll probably just game and maybe do some coding."

"Okay. Did you guys want to go anywhere? Do anything together?"

"We could play a board game maybe later," Jeremy said. "Get pizza?"

Lindsay smiled. "We could do that."

The kids went off and did their own thing, so Lindsay took the opportunity to work on her motel consulting. According to Zach, the renovation was going well. The painting was completed, and the carpet was scheduled to be installed the following week. Lindsay wished she could see the fresh rooms. She had helped pick out the colors and the new bedding and artwork, intended to tie in the calming nature theme. Zach seemed to trust her judgement. They had also discussed plans for new partnerships with local businesses, to try and put together the packages Lindsay had come up with. Since she had time now, Lindsay figured she could send off some emails to business owners in town, try to get them on board. She figured if the motel could bring in new business, that would help everyone.

Her thoughts kept drifting back to the kids, though. Neither one seemed very happy to be home, and that worried her. They had wanted to come home, or at least they had said they did. Was it just going back to school that was getting them down? And what was that about texting Jake? Maybe Lindsay should call him, find out what that was all about.

Lindsay rubbed her eyes. She had known it would be tough to come back. But she had hoped the time away would let them all unwind and reconnect. They had – for a while. Now they were back to square one. Well, not quite, Lindsay thought, thinking back to Jeremy's request. They would be having pizza and board game time later. Maybe they could make that a regular thing. It was always easier to talk about things while you were doing something else, too. Maybe she would learn something that would ease her mind. Or at least help her figure out what was wrong.

In the meantime, though, she had to give Officer Jake a call.

Jake's phone rang just as he was getting in his car to drive home. He glanced at the screen. Lindsay. Was that a good thing or a bad thing?

"Hello?"

"Hi, Jake?"

"Yeah."

"It's Lindsay. Jeremy's mom."

"How's it going?"

He could hear Lindsay sigh. "Okay, I guess. I hear you've been texting my son."

"Yeah. Once in a while. I was surprised when he texted me the other day. He had my number from when we were working on the event committee together. It tends to be easier to connect with teens via text. But usually we just discussed meetings and all that." He knew he was babbling, but her tone had been accusatory, like he was doing something wrong by being there for Jeremy. Did she think something inappropriate was going on?

"He texted you first?"

"Yeah, last Saturday, to let me know you guys had gotten home okay."

Silence fell.

"Lindsay?"

"Yeah, I'm here. I'm just surprised."

"Threw me off, too."

"Is he okay?" Lindsay's voice had gotten quiet.

Jake took a deep breath. "Yeah, he's okay. Not really happy right now, but okay. If I had to guess, I think he just wanted someone to talk to. I'm not family, so I think that helped."

"Neither of the kids seems really happy right now. They said they wanted to come back, and I thought I was doing the right thing, but we're all miserable, and I don't know what to do." Her voice faded, and Jake heard a sniffle. Was she crying?

"Hey, it'll be okay. You're doing your best."

Lindsay sniffled again. "Well, my best doesn't seem to be good enough. Maybe we should have just stayed in Pine Valley."

"Do you think things would have been better if you had?"

"I don't know. That's the problem. I don't know how much of this is normal back-to-real-life-after-vacation stuff and how much of this is realizing that we were happier in Pine Valley. I mean, even if we had stayed, the kids would have to go to school, and I would be working full time again. So maybe we would be just as miserable."

"Look, I don't have kids, so I can't really offer advice there. But I would suggest trying to figure out what specifically makes you happy and unhappy. If it's just the fact that you would rather be staying home and doing fun stuff or whatever, then the location probably doesn't matter. But if there are specific things about your current situation making you unhappy, and those specific things would be different in Pine Valley, then maybe it's worth considering. It's not like the end of summer is the only possible time to make a life change."

"I'm sorry to unload all of this on you. And I'm sorry if Jeremy has been a nuisance."

"Jeremy is not a nuisance. There is zero reason to apologize here. I have loved getting to know Jeremy, and I am more than happy to help with whatever I can."

"Thanks." He could hear her take a deep breath. She seemed to be composing herself. "I'll let you go now. But..."

"Yeah?"

"If something happens with Jeremy. Like, something I should know. If he's getting lost or really struggling. Can you let me know?"

"Of course."

"Thanks."

"Any time."

Silence fell for a moment before they said their goodbyes and disconnected the call. Jake leaned back in his seat and stared out the windshield. He hoped he had helped.

Chapter 58

Lindsay got off the phone with Jake feeling emotional but determined. She knew what was wrong on her end: not liking her job, getting bogged down with chores and responsibilities, and feeling disconnected with her kids. But those weren't location specific. They wouldn't automatically get better if they moved. She could find a new job locally. In theory, at least. And if she got something with a better schedule, that would help with the other stuff, too. Connecting with her kids would require effort, but they could do that here, too. They had started connecting in Pine Valley, but they didn't have to be there to be connected.

Okay. So she would look for a new job. At least she wouldn't be in panic mode like she had been before. She could think more rationally about the job listings, and put together that portfolio she had thought about now that she had the work with Zach to share. She would just have to find a way to survive until something panned out.

Or she could take the job in Pine Valley. Assuming it was still available.

But she had to know what was going on with the kids before making any plans. She would see if she could get to the bottom of things tonight when they had their family time.

But it would be really helpful to know if the job was even still an option. If they moved and she was in the same boat she was in now, that wouldn't help anything, at least not on her end.

Lindsay took a deep breath. Okay. She would call Zach. She had a couple of things she could discuss with him, anyway, so it wouldn't be just about the job.

Twenty minutes later, Lindsay had learned the job was hers if she wanted it. Until renovations were close to being completed, Zach didn't plan on starting the search for staff. She would have maybe a month to decide.

Okay. A deadline was good. At least she had a possible timeline.

But if they moved, would they even have a place to live? What was the real estate market like in Pine Valley? They could do an apartment temporarily, but she had gotten the impression that apartments were hard to come by, especially since the building collapse of the previous year. All those people had had to go somewhere. And they would probably be happier in a house, anyway. But were houses even available? It wasn't like they could rent the in-law apartment again. It would definitely be too small for them long-term, even if it had brought them closer. Besides, wasn't Alyson thinking about selling? It wouldn't be available, anyway.

Unless they bought it. It could be the perfect solution: Lindsay and the kids could live in the main house, and her parents could live in the in-law apartment.

But selling it had been conditional. Alyson said they would only sell if they found something they liked to purchase. And, again, that brought them back to the real estate market.

Maybe she should call Alyson and see if there was any information. She could ask for general information, and then segue into the possibility. But that might be jumping the gun. She would hold off on that phone call. She knew how Pine Valley worked. The news would make it to her parents before she could even think about calling to let them know she was maybe thinking of it.

Okay. Talking to the kids had to be next. In the meantime, she would work on the motel project so that option didn't disappear. And through it all, butterflies would flutter in her belly as she thought about the possibilities.

By the time they had settled in with their pizza and board game, the flutters of anticipation had turned into flutters of anxiety. She had no idea what her kids were thinking or how they were feeling besides unhappy. For all she knew, math was just harder this year and that was bumming them out. She could be reading way too far into this. But she had to know.

She decided to wait until they were well into their game before attempting any conversation of substance. If they suspected she had an ulterior motive, they would clam up tighter than, well, a clam. Her kids were not exactly known for being forthcoming.

"So school sucks this year, huh?" she began.

Both kids shrugged.

"I guess," Emma replied, flipping a card and moving her piece. "It's not too bad. My teachers are okay and stuff. I miss my friends from Pine Valley though."

"Don't you have friends here, too?"

"Yeah, but we're not really into the same things anymore. They're all into makeup and boys and stuff." Emma made a face.

Lindsay restrained herself from smiling. "You know, you'll probably be into that stuff soon enough, too."

Emma shrugged again. "Maybe. But right now I'm more into art. I'd rather put paint on a canvas than my face."

"I will not argue with you on that one. Maybe things will get better once art club starts up again."

"Maybe. I know at least a couple of my friends who did it last year aren't joining this year, though."

"That's a shame."

"Yeah."

They each took another turn in the game.

"How about you, Jeremy? How are you holding up? What do you think of high school?"

"It's okay, I guess."

"Do you like your teachers?"

"They're okay."

"How's your friend situation?"

"I don't really see them. They're not in many of my classes."

"That's a shame."

"It's okay. I'm not really close to them anymore anyway."

Lindsay was at a loss. What was she supposed to make of this?

"Hey, guys, can I ask you a question?"

Both kids looked at her expectantly.

"When we were in Pine Valley, talking about the whole job thing and where to live, you were both pretty set on moving back here and picking up where we left off. But ever since we got home, you both seem miserable. What changed?"

The kids looked at each other, then back at Lindsay. After a moment, Emma leaned back on one arm and sighed.

"I don't know about Jeremy, but for me, I just figured this was home. It's where I grew up. I knew what to expect, and I had my friends. I didn't want to start all over if I didn't have to."

Jeremy nodded. "Yeah, me, too. I mean, all my stuff is here, and it seemed to make more sense. If it ain't broke, don't fix it."

"What if it is broken?" Lindsay asked.

They both gave her blank stares.

"What I mean is: just because we're used to something doesn't mean it's what works best for us. I went back to my job because it offered the stability I thought we needed, and it gave me good money. And I figured if this is what you guys want, I could make that be enough. But I don't like my job. And there is more to life than money. And now I find out that you guys aren't happy, either. So it sounds to me like things are broken. So the question is: how do we fix it? Do we try to turn things around here, or do we start over somewhere else?"

"Would you like that other job better?" Emma asked. "The one at the motel?"

Lindsay shrugged. "I can't say for sure. But I think so. And I think it could be a good fit for all of us. But it's not just about what I want."

"Could you find a job you like here?"

"Maybe. Jobs are available, but I may not get them. There are other people who are more qualified than I am."

"Do we have to decide now?" asked Jeremy.

"No, we don't. But I suspect the longer we wait the harder it will be. And there's no guarantee the motel job will be available anymore if we wait too long. Plus it would be harder for you guys to catch up in school."

Silence fell, and the kids looked deep in thought.

"How about this: think about it a bit, and we'll talk more tomorrow, okay? Nothing needs to be decided tonight."

The kids nodded, and the game continued without another word on the subject.

Chapter 59

i dont know what to do

About what?

i think mom wants to move back to pine valley

And what do you want?

i dont know

Jake was sitting at his kitchen table eating a bowl of cereal for dinner. He was tired from a full day at work followed by errands for the event committee. He wasn't sure he was in the right emotional shape to be offering advice right now. But he would try.

You said a week ago that you thought you should have stayed in Pine Valley. What's changed?

dunno. i guess i just realized that things wouldnt be any easier there. i would still need to figure out high school and make new friends. and we all know how well that worked out before.

You had a rough start here, but you started making friends on the committee. I know you and Ashley had gotten pretty close, and you seemed to get along with some of the others, too.

i guess

What does your sister think?

she doesnt seem very happy either. but i think she would be ok either way. she had friends in pine valley tho

Friends can make all the difference. But I think you can make friends anywhere.

my mom hates her job. i think thats part of the reason she wants to leave

Having the right job can be a big deal when you're a grownup. You spend a lot of time at work.

do you like being a cop

I do. But I'm actually going to be applying to be a detective. I liked working on the case this summer. BTW Jack is in jail and will be for a long time.

thats good. im glad you caught him

> Me, too. And we couldn't have done it without your help. You made a real difference here.

> hows the event coming

> Pretty good. The committee misses you, but it's coming together.

> maybe it would be good to go back

> Only you know what will be right for you. But I know whatever you decide, you will do just fine. You are tougher than you think you are.

> thx

When Jake didn't get another response, he got up and put his bowl in the sink. He would like them to come back, but it had to be their decision.

He thought back to the conversation. He had said he was applying to be detective, but the completed application was still sitting on his computer, awaiting submission. He hadn't made any decisions about his future, either. But it was about time he started. Pine Valley was his home. He didn't want to go anywhere else. Without another moment's thought, Jake turned on his computer, pulled up the application, and submitted it. Now it was out of his hands.

Lindsay woke up on Sunday with nervous butterflies in her stomach again. What had the kids decided?

The house was quiet, so Lindsay made coffee and stuck a bagel in the toaster. She looked out the window holding her coffee mug. The scene wasn't quite as peaceful as Pine Valley; she saw more houses than trees. But, she supposed, it could be worse.

She remembered when she and Kyle had bought this house, full of hope and promise. It would be where they would raise their family and grow old together. Well, at least part of that had happened. But it was the only home her kids had ever known. Was it fair for her to make them leave it?

If the kids didn't want to leave, she wouldn't force them. But she couldn't go on the way she had. Her life needed to change, and it had to start with her job. If they didn't go to Pine Valley, she would start applying like crazy to other jobs around here. Something was bound to pan out eventually.

The kids wandered into the kitchen just as Lindsay was finishing up her bagel.

"Good morning," she greeted them.

They gave half-hearted greetings back before grabbing their phones and heading into the living room. Obviously, they weren't ready to discuss things yet. She would give them time and space, even if she was slowly dying inside.

After placing her mug and plate into the dishwasher, Lindsay walked past the living room to head to her room. As she passed, she peeked in. Both kids seemed very focused on their phones – no surprise there – but were talking to each other at the same time. That was different. Usually, they did their own thing. She wondered what they were discussing so animatedly. But she was reluctant to disrupt the conversation, so she continued past to her room.

An hour later, she had just sat down at the kitchen table with her laptop, hoping to get some work done on the motel project, when the kids came in. Together.

Lindsay looked up. They were both staring at her expectantly. She almost laughed out loud. "Yes? Can I help you?"

"We would like to call a family meeting," Emma said in a serious voice.

"Okay. In here, or should we get comfy in the living room?"

"Definitely comfy," Jeremy replied. So they all retreated to the living room.

The kids sat on the sofa, and she sat on a nearby recliner. It felt almost like an interrogation. "So, what would you like to discuss?"

Emma looked at Jeremy, and he looked back at her. She gave him a little nod, and he took a deep breath and looked back at Lindsay.

"We have given it a lot of thought and discussed the situation with other people," he said.

"Okay..."

"And considering everything that's happened, and how we've all been feeling..."

Emma sighed exasperatedly. "What this bonehead is taking forever to say is that we decided we want to go back to Pine Valley."

Lindsay's breath caught. "Really?"

They both nodded.

"We know it was tough," Emma said. "Like, really tough. It was really boring in the beginning. But we liked having you around, and seeing Gran and Pops. And the people were all nice."

"Well, not all of them," Jeremy interrupted.

"Okay, not all of them, but most of them. And it felt like we mattered there. Like, here we just go to school, come home, talk to friends or whatever, but there we felt like people got to know us."

"And cared about what happened to us."

Lindsay felt like she was going to cry. "I hope you know that I have always cared about what happened to you. You guys are my everything."

Emma rolled her eyes. "We know, Mom. But you're our mom. It's different with other people."

"I know. And you're right, in Pine Valley, there is that sense of community, that people look out for each other."

"So we want to go back."

"And you're sure?"

They nodded.

"We can't just up and move and then change our minds in a couple of months and come back. It's not that simple."

"We know," Jeremy said. "We're sure."

"Okay, then." Lindsay took a deep breath and smiled. "I guess we're moving to Pine Valley."

Epilogue

The day of the fall festival dawned cool and crisp. Jeremy was up early to help set up tents and tables, and Lindsay and Emma joined him a bit later to see if they could help out, too. It looked like it would be the perfect day in terms of weather. They just hoped people would come.

By the time the festival had officially begun, crowds were gathering around the town green, chatting and buzzing with enthusiasm. The event was free, and each attendee would get a raffle ticket for prize drawings that would take place that afternoon. But it was the activities that had everyone excited. Arts and crafts tables courtesy of The Art Spot. A gaming truck courtesy of a business a couple of towns over. Carnival-style games supported by local organizations. Wood building kits provided by a local hardware store. And so much more. Booths covered the town green, and it seemed like there was something for everyone, even two different hay mazes for different challenge levels. It had all come together in magnificent fashion.

Sylvie and Ed wandered in with some of their friends and took it all in. Ed had helped with some of the preliminary setup the day before. Sylvie would be manning the library booth a little while later to help hand out free books. It seemed everyone in the community had had some part in putting this event together.

The motel had a booth, and Lindsay would be there for much of the day, promoting the grand reopening as part of her duties as its new general manager. They were running some specials to encourage new guests, even offering a "stay-cay vacay" package to encourage local residents to take a night off from reality and stay at the motel, eat at a local restaurant, and participate in some of the new activities they offered on the grounds.

Jake was thrilled with the turnout. As Cherise had predicted, once the school year started, teen volunteers came from every corner wanting to help out to get their hours in. Local businesses and organizations had all wanted to help, offering funding, prizes, volunteers, and their own activities at their sponsor tables. And the result was even better than he had imagined. But his favorite part had been when Jeremy said he would be there to help.

He found Jeremy in line for the gaming truck, and he patted him on the back. "We did good, kid."

Jeremy grinned. "Not too bad, huh?"

"Not bad at all. And I'm glad you were here for it."

"Me, too." Jeremy's grin turned sheepish. "Me, too."

Also by Vanessa E. Kelman

<u>*Pine Valley Series*</u>
Searching for Home
Between the Moments
A Simpler Life

<u>*Fate Trilogy*</u>
Chasing Fate
Accepting Fate
Tempting Fate

<u>*NonFiction*</u>
A Life You Want: Take Charge of Your Life!

www.ingramcontent.com/pod-product-compliance
Lightning Source LLC
Chambersburg PA
CBHW071249300726
48975CB00002B/605